FEMALE
TROUBLE

A Collection of Short Stories

Antonya Nelson

SCRIBNER

NEW YORK   LONDON
TORONTO   SYDNEY   SINGAPORE

SCRIBNER
1230 Avenue of the Americas
New York, NY 10020

SCRIBNER and design are registered trademarks of Macmillan Library Reference USA, Inc., used under license by Simon and Schuster, the publisher of this work. For information regarding special discounts for bulk purchases, please contact Simon & Schuster Special Sales at 1-800-456-6798 or business@simonandschuster.com

Design by Kyoko Watanabe
Set in Minion

Manufactured in the United States of America

1 3 5 7 9 10 8 6 4 2

Library of Congress Cataloging-in-Publication Data

Nelson, Antonya
Female trouble: a collection of short stories / Antonya Nelson
p.   cm.
1. Women—Fiction. I. Title.
PS3564.E428 F46 2002
813'.54—dc21   2001049669

ISBN 0-7432-1871-X

Some of these stories have been published, sometimes under different titles and in slightly altered forms, by the following magazines: "Ball Peen" (Harper's), "Female Trouble" (Epoch; Prize Stories: The O. Henry Awards, 2001), "Goodfellows" (American Short Fiction), "Happy Hour" (Redbook), "Incognito" (American Short Fiction), "Irony, Irony, Irony" (TriQuarterly), "The Lonely Doll" (Epoch), "Loose Cannon" (Prairie Schooner), "One Dog Is People" (Redbook), "The Other Daughter" (Columbia magazine), "Palisades" (Ploughshares), "Stitches" (The New Yorker), "The Unified Front" (The Midwesterner; Best American Short Stories, 1998).

For Robert

◎ Contents

The kiss originated when the first male reptile licked the first female reptile, implying in a subtle, complimentary way that she was as succulent as the small reptile he had for dinner the night before.

—F. SCOTT FITZGERALD

Every woman is a rebel, and usually in wild revolt against herself.

—OSCAR WILDE

FEMALE
TROUBLE

⇌ *Incognito*

You can live a second life under your first one, something functioning covertly like a subway beneath a city, a disease inside the flesh. I did once for several years. On top I went to school and remained in my parents' house, looking after my younger siblings—two brothers, two sisters—and working part-time at my father's store. His business was located in a toney neighborhood mall called Happiness Plaza; he sold tasteful home decorations. Perhaps tastefulness always augurs uselessness: large vases from which sprouted bountiful arrangements of parched grass. Brightly gilded cherubs to bear innocent witness to your dreams. An indoor fountain whose steady drip might help you forget the outdoor unbalance, the world.

It might have been inside my father's store that my second life took shape, some Saturday afternoon while the women—always and forever women—moved through the cluttered floor displays, touching things in this manicured hypnotic way they had, caressing the inessential. No doubt my friends—I had two—joined me; we often stood alongside one another at work, sentries. We had several jobs among us, each defined, now that I consider it, ideally by vigilant watchfulness. Amanda worked at the Y, lifeguarding; Kip hostessed at the Grape Arbor; and I oversaw curios at my father's store. Before our steady gazes the patrons moved: down the lap lanes, through the lounge into the restaurant, around the pampas and wind chimes and birdbaths.

In our crafty boredom we created a new friend, spun her out of air and desire. Her name was Dawn Wrigley. She ordered racy catalogs, she wrote to men in prison, she complained over the radio on behalf of Kansas adolescence. She was brash and outrageous, had a terrible temper and few scruples, she'd ingested every fathomable pharmaceutical, and she was our spokesman, our voice, our splash of brilliant graffiti on the high white wall erected between Us and Them.

Our secret energy impelled her, the buzz inside our hive.

Some nights she phoned the college dorms, the three-digit fixed prefix and the subsequent random numbers. Down a hall of boys she went, offering pleasures the three of us had never known. Kip was best at this; we never asked ourselves why. On the weekends we found the bar that would not question our birth dates—the Fraternal Order of Police—or FOP—Lounge, ironically, was one of the best, a barroom full of cops, wooing the underaged—and sat in a dark corner waiting for companionship, drove recklessly through the city in search of more, eventually dropped ourselves into the basement of my family's house around the telephone and summoned Dawn Wrigley. The evening was never over for Dawn.

"Baby?" Kip would say, gripping the receiver, sometimes tearfully, as if spurned, sometimes breathlessly, as if having run to the phone, but always as if it were the college boy who'd phoned her, and always hours later than he promised. "Baby, it's me, Dawn, where are you? Why aren't you here, you said you'd be here? It's pitch black here, and I'm so terrified. I can't talk, I'm just borrowing this phone, so listen—" and they always stopped trying to get her attention when she said this, they stopped trying to correct her misunderstanding, and they listened "—instead of picking me up at the park, I'm going to walk over to Douglas, over by Happiness Plaza. You know Happiness Plaza? Please come as soon as you can, come pl—" and now Kip would slam the two phone halves back together, receiver to cradle, as if the kindly neighbor who'd opened his door for her had taken it into his head to ravish her. I guess. We had about fifty percent success with any Dawn Wrigley ploy. Off to Happiness Plaza we would trek, the three of us still drunk, now warmed from the safety of my parents' house, from the bounty of their larder, back aglow in the cold world, protected by Dawn Wrigley's broad pseudonymous force. Why did it satisfy us to see the car—Nova, Malibu, Mustang—rumble into the parking lot of my father's business? To see it crawl slowly by, the two boys—they did not come alone, these boys—peering along the six closed shops, florist, travel agent, dry cleaners, pharmacy, real estate, and City Essentials, my father's store of the utterly nonessential? We used St. James's Episcopal Church as our cover. The doorway on its west side faced Happiness Plaza and provided sanctuary; we arrived first and waited, hidden by foliage and shadows. They drove their beaters through the parking lot, they cruised around the block, mufflers murmuring. Slowly. Two in the morning, no one else about, the city lit but silent, perhaps the fog of our breath the only motion besides their car. Where was that girl? Had the neighbor whose phone she used strangled her with its cord, left her for dead in some distant cistern? Or had they been duped, there was no girl, there'd never been a girl? Bewitched by Dawn Wrigley. Tomorrow she would be a story on their lips, her vitality boosted beyond our little trio's universe. Perhaps in their story the evening wore on, Dawn performing for them some further favor. Sometimes they drove the route between College Hill Park and Happiness Plaza, the three blocks that separated them, searching as if for a lost pet. Here, girl, come on. We had a back passage home, down pathways between church structures, between fences between yards, right up the steps and through the door to my parents' house, its solid middle-class deadbolt.

Our power had the force to push that car through the streets, to summon those boys from sleep or party, to play them for fools. I think we liked to imagine their confusion: was there a real girl, or a mere prank? We were making our contribution to the continuing dilemma we intuitively understood to propel the world: what did women want? Rescue, or amusement?

A third alternative had not really occurred to us until the night it resulted. The other thing that could happen was our getting caught. Undone. It wasn't Happiness Plaza, then, and it wasn't a phone call to the dorms that initiated the trouble. Dawn Wrigley was born in 1978, full-blown in our imaginations, capable only of expansion, not diminishment. She had a post office box where she regularly received credit card applications and sex toys; eventually, she had a lease on a downtown apartment. Kip signed; we pooled our money, the three of us, and rented by the month. We didn't need an apartment, as each of us was indulged nearly complete freedom anyway. Our parents had sufficient trust—mine trusted me, Amanda's trusted her, Kip's trusted nobody, so their lack didn't register—and we did what we were supposed to: maintained grades, saved money for college, did not get caught. None of them was a parent who had to look the other way, who had to strain for ignorance; we made it hard to find fault.

So why an apartment? Because it could be done, of course. With it we sailed over yet another hurdle on the way to adulthood. We worked, we took home paychecks, we had our weekends, and now we were tenants. We could with confidence swing open both a Murphy bed and the doors to a liquor cabinet. From the Fraternal Order of Police Lounge we brought our fops, young officers whose hair was too short, whose Boy Scout attitude was too tiresome to get them anywhere with their peers. We were sixteen years old; our buzzer read "Dawn Wrigley," and when it buzzed, she came to life in each of us. Her cockiness swelled manifest among us, and charmed the cops, three of them, three of us, benighted by Dawn Wrigley, her essence infusing the air like perfume. Together, there was no problem;

together, we *were* Dawn Wrigley, we could spring her, we could contain her.

Alone, we could not. The cop who came, one Sunday night when Kip agreed to meet him alone, nearly killed her. Close as we were—raw with one another, flagrant, pure—we did not tread beyond prescribed sexual limits with our dates, best described by what our worried high school counselors named Heavy Petting. Cops came, plural, to our apartment, and nothing happened beyond what could be witnessed, plural. Which I suppose Amanda and I both supposed was what we all three wanted. A shared concept, sort of sleazy, sort of virginal, certainly safe. Safe. We each had a set of keys, downstairs and up, and although we might visit the apartment over lunch during the school week, would definitely spend both Friday and Saturday nights there, Sunday was an airlock, the chamber wherein we dropped our secret toxic life in exchange for our other one, the clean one where we were children in our parents' homes.

So alone Kip met her rookie, alone she led him to our apartment, alone she took her punishment. It did not please him to discover her real age, her status as virgin, the ass he'd made of himself for her. He raped her, but only after they'd already made love. He struck her, but only after he'd had her permission to spank her. He bit her, but only after he'd been nibbling. Nibbling at Kip, while Dawn Wrigley was not about.

When school resumed on Monday without Kip, Amanda and I flew to the apartment, finding her there at our folding table, vodka bottles and orange juice cans before her like a science experiment, bloody sheets hanging akimbo from the shower rod, her eyes on their way to being black, the skin on her arms red from his twisting it, wringing her limbs like laundry. Because she was drunk, she told us everything, concentrating on the thin lines between what had been done with her permission and what had not.

"He has a sister our age," Kip said through loosened teeth. "Like that's relevant?"

Kip had white-blond hair, thick and blunt cut so even the tips felt like needles. Now her hair was stiff with blood, a section stuck to her forehead. The urge to flee from her struck me, warm and liquid, a shameful gag reflex. It had as much to do with her unself-consciousness as anything else. I felt I could no longer be with her, not in the way I had once been. Before, we had operated in the manner of the precocious, taking early what was already coming. Kip's drunken explanation, brave as it was, complicated and painful and enlightened, still made me blanch. To this day, I cannot drink screwdrivers, the tainted citrus flavor just that potent.

"He's named Buddy," Kip told us, "but that's not his name either. I was Dawn, he was Buddy, the incognito couple."

There were no reports to file, no charges to levy, no official death certificate bearing Dawn Wrigley's name to issue, but we bid farewell to our triumvirate, farewell to it and all it had produced. The End.

And then, meanwhile, it came to pass, years went by. Let's say ten, and then eight more. Kip splintered from us, went her own way, which was into the Wichita work force: hostess to bartender, bartender to manager, manager to marriage and then cosmetic surgery, divorce, AA, pyramid schemes. Amanda attended a Christian college in Dallas because her mother had a stroke, and bullied her from her sickbed to be a virtuous girl. I fled for California and first lived among the hedonists in the North, then among the capitalists in the South. I never found a group I could join, not the way I'd enlisted under the flag of Dawn Wrigley, having pledged something crucial and unspoken and singular. In San Francisco the club was too large; in L.A. too hard to find. I returned to Kansas, big empty plain, place where figures in the landscape could do no less nor more than stand alone. I brought my daughter, a girl nearing twelve years, and left her father to fend for himself among the savages.

Perhaps it was the divorce—not unlike leaving a limb behind, having chewed it off in order to escape—or perhaps the return home, or perhaps my daughter's sudden leap to puberty. In any case, my adolescence came back to me with a ghastly clarity, a sickening poignancy. It might have been as simple as the extraordinary difference between a Los Angeles city street and its Kansas counterpart. Drivers yielded, boys held doors, and nearly everyone sincerely wished you'd have a good day. And night? Well, in February, the streets were just as I remembered them, brittle with silence, wide and empty, our little orderly grid of urban sprawl surrounded by grain silos, intersected by railroads, fat Arkansas River twisting through like an eel. In Wichita, the muzziness in the air was not pollution; it was memory. Wherever I went in that city I saw myself as a young, unhappy girl.

My father had died of a heart attack by then, and my littlest brother, Eddie, ran City Essentials with my mother. They'd updated it, adding a cappuccino machine and a sandwich service. The clientele seemed unchanged, wealthy women, slimmer than in my youth, quicker, aerobicized. My mother the widow had revealed a boisterous yet needy personality, now that she was alone, and Eddie, least favorite sibling, oily since young, did nothing more superbly than prop her up. He'd been the consummately polite boy, the one who used *sir* and *ma'am* reflexively, like a parrot, like a soldier. In the intervening years, he'd gone to business school to hone his sycophancy, to ready himself to step into my father's shoes. Such as they were.

"You want a job?" Eddie asked suspiciously when I came home.

"Not for a million bucks."

He shrugged; he'd never gotten me, either. His wife and baby were guileless redheads, plump and freckled; they seemed afraid of me, unwilling to let my daughter baby-sit, although she offered to do so for free. She loved babies; it was what made me worry for her. Who knew what awaited a girl who loved babies?

A full year after my homecoming, not long after I turned an uneventful thirty-six, an ad appeared in the Wichita *Eagle Beacon* personals: *ISO Don Wrigley.* The newspaper is such that you read all of it, front page straight through to the used car ads, and all with an antsy hopefulness, as if something, someday, might be unveiled. In search of Don Wrigley, that and a box number. Not the same number we'd once possessed, but a larger one. I scanned the ad first, then studied it, then clipped it. In the telephone book there were no Dawn or Don Wrigleys. Surely Kip and Amanda and I had checked the book before, all those years ago, looked for our creature's name among the living.

Further, there was no one to tell. The last I'd known of Amanda, she had married another alum of her Christian college, found a job in Nebraska with the governor, left long ago under a name I could not hope to locate, confederated by an apparent political zeal I'd never have guessed. Her parents—mother now in a wheelchair—had moved to mild Florida. As for Kip, only rumor remained.

"Why'd you cut that out?" my daughter asked from the other side of the kitchen table. I was tempted to tell her; she would have enjoyed Dawn Wrigley's exploits in the way she has always enjoyed my past, my big novel family and its big cavernous house. She listened to her aunts and uncles recount our shared history with a soap opera fan's reverence for a complicated and endlessly contradictory plot. She's a good girl, my girl, soft where I was early hard, recipient of undiluted love, inclined in a placid optimistic direction that she inherited from neither me nor her father. Dawn Wrigley would have disappointed or scared her, marking as it did the end of one kind of antic and the beginning of another.

"It's just funny," I said of the ad, shrugging. She let it go at that, her head unturned by evasiveness.

So, later, alone, I worried the shred of paper in my hands, considering responses. It was late at night, in my old bedroom on the second floor. Clocks ticked and bonged throughout the house; my mother's feeble dog groaned downstairs on a couch. Tree limbs rubbed achingly against the gutters the way they always had, and dry snow snicked at my window. With my mother across the hall, and my daughter in the room that had once been my little sisters', I should have felt the connective power of the generations, my own, my predecessors', my progeny's. Instead, I had never felt so alone in my life—so alone I could not even summon my abiding conviction that an intruder would break in. My isolation was that profound: it defied burglary.

I wrote: *Don or Dawn?* I studied the box number once more looking for meaning. I sent the envelope without implicating myself with a return address. This was the method of Dawn Wrigley: she did not leave traces.

We were also thieves, in our old life, the underground one, that idling hum that vibrated inside as we sat through classes and meals and dates and lectures and movies and family vacations. Stealing was not necessary for any of us. Amanda's father was a surgeon, Kip's sold real estate, my parents ran a profitable business. There was enough money, plenty of clothes, every foolish object offered over the television we already owned. Still, we stole. The act seemed nearly instinctive, playful, practice—like toppling lion cubs, in training to hunt and kill. We stole quirkily. Mice from the pet store, smuggled one at a time inside our coat pockets, their scrambling feet and scared hearts. Sugar bowls from restaurants, silver and stemware. License plates. Bags of frozen vegetables from Safeway. A NO PARKING sign. Lawn ornaments. A television from Montgomery Ward, nestled inside a wicker basket, the most brazen of our booty, engineered by Kip, but surely the brainchild of Dawn Wrigley.

We checked car ignitions the way others check pay phone coin returns: looking for the overlooked. Outside the Century II convention center one winter night, we found a station wagon with its keys stashed beneath the seat. Away we went, leaving Kip's Datsun like collateral. For an hour we used up gas, aimless and in a hurry, then returned to the lot, parked the wagon three rows from where it had been, and drove away. What would that driver imagine? Car smelling faintly of Love's Baby Soft, of beer and bubble gum and Doritos, perhaps vaguely warm, tank empty, and resting elsewhere, as if it, too, had a life to lead. The car was like us: it would come back, it would be reliable, but it had some other needs, ones better met in sneaky circumstances.

We stole the predictable, as well, bathing suits and underwear, earrings, eight-track tapes, candy bars, and so on. I was confessing these thefts, the average and the outrageous alike, to a man I met at my daughter's school. He coached the handicapped, who arrived every morning on what Alane had named the Retarded Bus. Her unusual unkind mouth was what had brought me to her middle school, and it was a Mr. Schweda I had to meet with and appease. He tripped as he entered the room, and rather than cover it, or look back with irritated blame at the object that had leapt into his way, he made a spontaneous and elaborate stumble, knees liquid, feet slippery, hauling himself rumpled and slapstick to the desk where I waited. Who could not be attracted to such a man?

"The thing is," he said immediately, "your daughter was in the right." That very morning Alane had engaged in what her principal had named foul language as the handicapped children entered the building. I had driven over set to defend her: a girl deserved not to see a boy's penis if she didn't want to, even if that boy was mentally retarded and unaware of what he was doing. Even if the exposure were at the level of a wheelchair. Alane had been stubborn in asserting her rights: *Zip yourself up!* she'd yelled. *Asshole,* she'd unfortunately added. The boy had had his own arsenal of choice phrases, but the principal hadn't gone into those. Neither Schweda nor I had witnessed the event, and neither of us had a stake in pursuing it as a subject except to make the principal happy. When I asked, he told me he'd lived in Wichita since the day he was born. I wondered where his type had been when I was in high school.

"I stole things, too," he claimed at the bar where we went for lunch.

"But why did we steal?"

He shrugged affably, mouth crooked with perplexity.

I said, "In our family there were too many children, and I think I felt owed. Somebody, somewhere, owed me something. And I stole things to make up for it." He was the kind of man I could say that to without fearing the hundred wrong responses. He did not look appalled, nor superior, did not scoff, was not bored, did not care to analyze my overbearing mother or emotionally absent father.

He said, "We could walk out of here without paying for our lunch."

"But we won't. I never think of stealing anymore, even though for a couple of years that was how I did my Christmas shopping. Christmas lifting, my friends and I called it."

"I still think of doing it," he said. "First of all, I like to get away with things. And second, I like objects that fit into my pocket. Solid objects, like weights, for example, from those old-fashioned scales." He cupped his palm that wasn't holding a stein of beer to indicate the treasured heft of what he loved. It was as much his soft baggy eyelids—so like the loose skin of testicles, no?—as his gesture that made me feel that cool cylindrical density. "Maybe you just liked to keep secrets," he suggested. "Maybe having a rodent in your coat was thrilling."

"Why do you live here?" I asked. He did not question the transition, the logic that led from his observation to my question seemingly clear.

"Custody," he said. "And inertia, and nostalgia, and a fondness for ... " Here he looked out the bar window at the blocky limestone facade across the street, the two construction workers sitting on a bench in front of it watching us, the steely sky and thin clouds sliding along as if on a sheet of aluminum, the single tree someone had blasted through the concrete to accommodate, now bent sideways in the infernal Kansas wind. Bleakness incarnate, gray on gray on gray. One of the men lifted his blowtorch and shot a tongue of fire, holding it to the end of a cigarette in his mouth. Startled, the two of us laughed—and with that laughter, sealed ourselves away from everyone else at the bar.

I had not recognized the closet my loneliness had made around me until that chamber opened to let in Greg Schweda. The view beyond us became a landscape suddenly dear to me, but dear in a bare, frightening, somber fashion, the dearness of bitter truth, of responsibility accepted. I felt—perhaps it was the beer, the infatuation with a man after a long leave from infatuation, the rare gift of laughter—the way I had when I gave birth to Alane, that I had passed irrevocably into the next chapter.

"Schweda," I whispered, when I was alone. His name itself seemed a secret.

His daughter was four years older than Alane, a blonde girl with a slow eye. Also an injured brain, invisible damage, profound and mysterious. For several months of her eighth year, she had lain in a coma, coming out of it slowly, recovering most motor function except for the crimped turn of her left foot, and her wandering right eye. Standing before you, her body language sent a subtle message: the foot seemed shy, tucking itself away, while that one eye swam luxuriantly, casting about drunkenly as if for better company at a cocktail party. She'd been hit by a car while riding her bike. Greg's attachment to the Retarded Bus had to do with Sarah, whose short-term memory was practically nonexistent. My daughter, never a cruel child, was scared of Sarah's class, a rollicking group of the lame and imperfect. I told Greg I thought her fear illustrated a deeper sympathy than the smarmy patronization many of her peers exhibited toward the disabled children.

"She can better imagine it happening to her. She feels really bad, like a grown-up feels, like I would feel. It makes her feel angry, that it's unfair." I had no idea how my daughter felt; I was talking about myself.

He nodded, no doubt knowing this about me. We were in bed at his house. His house was close enough to my parents' for him to be an almost-neighbor. Far too fast we had fallen into intimacy, as if we'd been married to each other before, as if one of us had been somewhere for a while, but had come back, welcome home. I guessed that our marriages had been not unlike, although he did not remind me of my husband. But he was of the same tribe. The sex was bittersweet, each of us openly eager but with long histories of other partners, preferences, routines. Once, sex had been an activity of amalgamation, but these days it seemed like two people performing simultaneous monologues, each with a sense of what had to happen next.

It was his daughter's accident that had humbled Greg Schweda, derailed whatever anger and passion had created all his other interesting characteristics. He was an anomaly, something set to become one thing, then headed off at the pass. It was his utter command of priority that made me trust him, the way, when he rose in the morning, he knew precisely what had to be done.

On Saturdays, he and Sarah went to the mall. "Don't let her buy black loafers," he cautioned when we met them at the north entrance. "She has a half dozen pairs already."

"I must be . . . a shoe-buying fool," Sarah said slowly, smiling. She was sixteen years old, but those years seemed acquired in clumps: two eight year olds, one riding atop the other's shoulders, sturdy foundation and then tottering burden lodged precariously upstairs, straining to make adult conversation from the folds of her grown-up disguise. The first child was the intact third grader who'd gone bike riding one blameless day; the next grew dreamily, in slow motion and at warp speed, and was concealed, lacking operating instructions.

The four of us wandered the Valentine-laden circus. This was the mall I'd grown up with, revised only in superficial ways since those distant times. Our daughters did not know how to behave with us, and we were hardly better in their presence. Each girl, sensing I suppose the sexual content of her parent's attention, took her respective parent's hand, as if to keep that hand from seeking a new alliance. This interested me, touched me, my daughter who had not held my hand for a couple of years now. We strolled, Sarah in a halting gait that was so systematized as to appear graceful, like a foreign accent. At shoe stores, she would swerve toward the entrance in a kind of daze, something inviting her there. It was the one article of clothing that she could not purchase for herself in a common store, as her shy foot needed special fitting.

"She wants what she can't buy," my daughter said to me softly, raptly, as Greg semaphored vigorously for Sarah to keep right on moving, onto the next shop. Sarah smiled sheepishly, briefly recalling and enjoying her mind's joke on herself.

"I sure do . . . like shoes," she called back to us, just a little too loud, only slightly too slow.

The crowd and lights blurred as my eyes filled, then cleared once more. Alane bought herself a CD. We ate pizza and watched Wichitans flow by, me always expecting to see someone I knew from my eighteen year past, but never doing so. Sarah asked, every now and then, if she had already eaten, if we had cruised the shoes, and, smiling sweetly at me and Alane, extending her young girl's hand over the crusts and empty cups, have we met before? "You look fa . . . miliar," she said.

When we parted in the parking lot, Greg gave me an unexpected hug, opening his coat to include me in it for a moment, like someone beckoning beneath the covers, a little private huddle in a pocket of body heat. My eyes filled again, while our daughters looked away. "Schweda," I whispered. Love is sadness, I thought, tragedy, just as we'd always supposed when we were in high school.

For several weeks, the Dawn Wrigley ad in the newspaper continued to run exactly as I'd found it. Then, one Sunday, it altered. *ISO Dawn Wrigley, of course.* What did it mean, *of course*? With what tone had *of course* been added? Someone was speaking to me, across time and through the newspaper, the print of which smudged off on my fingers.

"Is Kip's mom still in town?" I asked my mother.

She looked steadily at me from inside her new bodily bulk; since my father's death she had gained nearly one hundred pounds. In her grief, she ate, as if to compensate, or to fortify herself. I thought of her as *inside,* armored with flesh. Over her thick cakey toast she looked out blankly at me, waiting for further prompts. "Katherine Pratt," I pressed. "Kip. Lived on Thirteenth."

"Oh, Kip," she said, daintily tamping a bite into her mouth, nodding as she chewed. "Yes, I remember Kip. She was a bad influence. One night her mother phoned here at three in the morning, asked me to go smell you girls' breath, you and Amanda and Katherine. I said certainly not and hung up on her."

"Really?" Her loyalty—and blind, blind naivete—touched me.

Now she frowned. "But her folks divorced way back when, and her mother died in a car accident. A single car accident," she added meaningfully. "What's Kip doing these days?"

I told her I had no notion, and she looked both sad and disgruntled. Like Greg Schweda, my mother has lived all her years in Wichita; it never failed to surprise her that not only had I forgotten the names of most major traffic thoroughfares and what they bisected, but that I had apparently lost track of my best friends. Her high school chums and college sorority sisters, after all, still convened. She felt sorry for my solitude, and, at the same time, probably thought I was a snob. Because she had five children, she tended to assign us roles: I was the one who had moved away and renounced my roots. It was easier that way, our characters cataloged just as our tastes were at Christmas time by well-meaning relatives—I was the one who drank tea, Jean loved earrings, Margot became the cat fanatic, Tim wore flannel shirts, and Eddie was supposed to want train memorabilia.

There were several K. Pratts in the phone book, but I wasn't really after Kip, and I flipped through the pages impassively. It wasn't Kip who interested me, although I would have been glad to hear about her; the wild squalid strain in her life had always had an appeal, had often permitted me the sanctimonious opportunity to take the other route. But for now it was Dawn Wrigley that had caught my eye. And the way of pursuing Dawn Wrigley was less direct than the phone book, less straightforward than dialing up Kip Pratt.

Our mythic creature's sudden reincarnation reminded me of Alane's talking in her sleep. Since she was a toddler, she had spoken aloud in the night, broken phrases, incensed exclamations—"No, Mama, no!"—or, most wonderful and strange, laughter. It was her nocturnal happiness that most rewarded me, proof that her pleasure was not something she put on in the morning, not something that had to be tricked out of her, but which emanated from a healthy deep-seated source, easily cheerful even in unconsciousness. You had to be ready to catch her amusement; you had to be awake and listening. So not unlike Dawn Wrigley, who also seemed elusive, half concoction, half hijacking. *Why ISO Dawn Wrigley?* I queried in my next note to the newspaper.

"There are two Davids," Greg Schweda told me as we toured his classroom.

"There are two everyones," I responded, trying on glibness in the special ed trailer.

"In that case, there are four Davids." One David was a five-year-old child no larger than an infant, lying curled in a beanbag chair. His limbs were covered with dark hair, his eyes hazy as a newborn's. He reminded me of a hatching bird, sticky and constricted. "You could lube him up," Greg suggested, indicating the baby oil. I was his volunteer today, wearing a postcoital force field here amidst the strange, something tangibly warm to ward off nausea. "Or you could read to Mary. Good morning, Mary."

The girl was utterly rigid in her walker, as if frozen, or under the influence of electric voltage. When she spoke back, her lips seemed not to move. "Who is she?"

Friend and helper, according to Greg, but I felt ill-intentioned, voyeuristic. Twelve children came here every day, this trailer parked between Annesley Elementary and Truman Middle School. I could not imagine how David of the beanbag chair was transported, but I could envision his mother's relief to leave him for a while. A few members of the class, including Sarah Schweda, made daily forays into normal classrooms. Sarah took fifth grade reading and spelling at Annesley, freshman math and home economics at Truman, art and physical therapy back here at the trailer.

"And this is the other David," Greg informed me. This David was enormous, the boy in the wheelchair who'd exposed himself to Alane. He had limited control of his neck muscles, so his large head lolled, jerked forward to take a glimpse of things, then swung back— like someone trying not to nod off. One of his hands lay ever ready on his penis; he was only thirteen but was as overdeveloped as little David was under. Half a dozen times that morning, he managed to work his zipper down and liberate his erection; his attempts at jacking off seemed to involve me, as he tried to keep his eyes on me as he used his hand. This hand worked as if sharpening a knife. It was terrifying, fascinating. The children who could, responded by wearily reminding him to put away his willy.

For three hours that morning I worked with little David, at first merely massaging baby oil into the places made abnormally dry by his fetal position, inside the elbows and behind the knees, around the neck, between his shriveled toes, trying hard not to let him remind me of poultry beneath my hands. Eventually I began to talk as I worked, muttering softly, self-consciously, watching his eyelids for confirmation of his hearing: "Good boy," I told him. "How does that feel? Don't you like the warm sunshine on your face? Can you bend that leg, sweetheart? Does that hurt?" He flinched, ever so slightly, a tremor across his furry feral cheek, there and gone in an instant, no one but me the wiser. I unfolded the leg a second time, just to see this faint sign of pain reappear. When it did, I apologized, and was sincerely sorry, but what made me need proof that I could hurt him?

"You're patient," Greg Schweda told me.

"No, I'm not. I just want you to think I'm patient."

"Then I'm flattered," he said. "Hardly anybody likes me well enough to pretend to be something she isn't."

For the remainder of the day I could feel little David's winglike arms between my fingers. I lay on my mother's kitchen floor that evening to stare up at the light, trying to feature the world from the limited perspective of a beanbag chair, the looming balloonlike faces and unanticipated noises, what I hoped was the soothing sensation of warm oil.

"Are you okay?" Alane asked, stepping around me to open the refrigerator.

"When I was a little older than you, I had an alter ego," I told her.

She poured milk, tall and telescopic, shoes beside my face smelling faintly of dog shit.

"What does that mean," she asked.

"I think I needed to be bad sometimes," I told her, "so I had this alter ego, a made-up friend, named Dawn Wrigley, who did bad things."

"Acting out," she informed me. "I heard all about it from Uncle Eddie."

"What did he tell you?"

"He told me you were really wild in high school, that Grandma was thinking of sending you to reform school."

"Reform school? What does he know about it? He was seven years old when I was in high school."

Alane returned the milk carton to the fridge shelf. "You couldn't have been that bad, Mom." I resisted the temptation to correct her; let her have faith in a better me, why not? Soon enough she would find me overwhelmingly lacking, frumpy and monstrous and insufferable. "Besides," she added, "an imaginary friend is not really, like, evil."

"I'm not sure," I said from the floor, ready to defend my evil honor. "Open that newspaper and I'll show you something."

She sat at the table and located the personals, found Dawn Wrigley in the place where Dawn Wrigley now lived. "Eerie," she proclaimed it.

"Kind of." I did not mention that I had responded to the ad; no one really wants evidence of her mother's immaturity. I'd grown accustomed to looking for Dawn in the paper, waiting for my own message to register, for the ante to up. We were taking turns; I was patient, curiously comforted by our exchange.

Alane put her elbows on her knees, rested her chin on her knuckles, and gave me a hard look. "Are you going to stay down there much longer?"

"Don't know." Had I been sitting in a chair when she entered the kitchen, she might never have learned about Dawn Wrigley. I peered up into the light fixture and, when I closed my eyes, five pulsing bulbs burned like stars inside my brain.

My friends and I had convened at school, at our apartment, at our jobs, and, oddly, quite often at my house. I reviewed this fact, living there again. Why did so much of our bad behavior seem to have been hatched in these rooms? Was it because my parents were lenient? Because there was no television to arrange ourselves around? We once made marijuana brownies in my parents' kitchen while they went to a party. The glass canister holding flour shattered; we were undoubtedly drunk when we began cooking. We cleaned up the shards as best we could, but throwing out the batter was not an option: our ingredients were far too expensive. Biting into the warm brownies, later, we all felt the glass between our teeth, sparkling grit on the tongue. Out the door the brownies went, crumbled into bite-size portions on the frozen yard. We laughed to picture the stoned rodents, the testy little squirrels finally mellowed out.

But almost simultaneous with our having thrown the pan's contents, we envisioned those creatures' bleeding mouths, punctured intestines. Before the scattered mess had time to cool on the ground, Kip and Amanda and I were out there on our hands and knees, gathering what we could find in the dark.

In the morning our fingers were crosshatched with tiny cuts, bedsheets speckled with blood.

Baking a chocolate cake for Alane's thirteenth birthday, I remembered those brownies, the three of us laboriously rescuing the hapless animals, scavenging there the wasted and uproarious end of our cracked evening, laughing until we leaked—tears and urine, wrung with fierce pleasure.

For her birthday, Alane had chosen a family party. The group sat around the large dining room table where we'd always gathered for celebration, cousins and aunts and uncles, my newest sister-in-law Bambi, Tim's second wife. Greg Schweda and Sarah were there, and my family worked hard not to stare at the girl, who beamed as if it were *her* birthday, *her* stack of gifts, *her* indulgent crowd of friendly relations. My family took to Greg only because Sarah made such short work of P.R. in his favor. Otherwise they would have found him as they had my husband: moody, quiet, negative. Plus, he kept filling his champagne glass.

"I drink too much," he'd told me after our first night together, when we were listing our drawbacks. "I drink too much," he repeated. "Just a fact."

"Okay," I said. My days of drinking too much had been in high school; that's when I'd needed to do so, to go to that fuzzy place inside myself. His days were now. It seemed an acceptable habit, given that he spent a great deal of his time answering the same questions over and over again, that he had to constantly narrate for his daughter the simple daily things that would not adhere in her mind.

"Who's the birthday girl?" Sarah asked.

"Me," Alane told her patiently; everyone else had responded at least once to this pleasant query.

"Mazel tov!" Sarah crowed for the tenth time, raising her curled empty hand as if lifting a glass. Alane followed suit. After the party, Greg and I took a walk around the neighborhood, both of us tipsy, the wind arctic. We stopped to admire Happiness Plaza, the opulent displays in the large windows of City Essentials, my family's fatuous contribution to our town. Just looking at the twittering fountains made me feel colder. I turned us into the wind and directed our way to the park, where we circled its borders. The trees had gotten more massive since my childhood, the open space compressed. We met not one other person on that walk, and when he took my hand I realized that I had begun to love Greg Schweda. I told him so, between the park and home.

I didn't care if he returned the compliment; for the first time, it meant more to extend it than receive it. Besides that, he didn't have a chance: outside my house sat an ambulance, and we sprinted toward it each praying selfishly to be spared.

Her doctor named my mother lucky: to be so surrounded by help when her stroke came on. She could have been alone, she might have fallen down a flight of stairs instead of merely forward, into the remains of cake and ice cream, empty bowl waiting there as if to cradle her plump cheek. She was home within two days, seeming mostly herself although a bewildered and stunned version, perpetually as if she'd just wakened. She misspoke our names although she did not confuse our identities; what her mind provided her tongue with were names of the generation before: I was her sister Betty whom she called Beetle; Alane became my sister Margot. She did not forget our real positions, just how to refer to us.

Sitting with her was not unlike sitting with beanbag David; only by an enforced patience did I have some brief access to her point of view. For instance, it occurred to me that the decor of her house bore no resemblance whatsoever to the decor City Essentials seemed to advocate. Here at home were very few knickknacks, little ornamentation, heavy objects with functional uses. My mother's taste had prevailed at our house, while my father's had made the store successful. Also, I recalled as I sat in her bedroom, the funny tradition of our childhood, the Sunday nap, a ritual as honored as churchgoing in other families. My parents abandoned us then, Sunday afternoons, closed their bedroom door against their five children, and purportedly rested. We went to great lengths, once, to catch them at sex; it had to have been my idea, as I was the oldest. A trellis was involved, a neighbor, some startled pigeons, some crushed flowers. All our nonsense just so we could uncover their secret intimate assembly and find them, sure enough, asleep. They must have had sex on a few of those sacred Sunday times; they both worked long hours at the store; their evenings surely would have been shared in exhaustion, homework, housekeeping, billpaying, normal domestic maintenance. That they preserved a window of unproductivity, of ease, of lazy sexuality, blatant and of the body, sort of impressed me. Sort of repulsed me.

"Honey?" my mother would plead now, suddenly swept in by a stray vain impulse. "Please pluck my chin." Her whiskers were soft, simple enough to remove. Doing it, I recognized how impossible it had been for my old friend Amanda, all those years ago, to resist *her* mother's stroke-reduced voice, imploring her to attend SMU, to turn her back on the party girl life she'd indulged in high school with her ne'er-do-well bad girl friends, me and Kip Pratt. My mother lay beneath my fingers in her bed, her youthful self hidden, her pristine sensibility overridden by malfunction, misfired synaptical attraction. She was in there—plum pit hidden inside the dumb red sponge of its flesh—and she was also gone.

Alane now looked for the Dawn Wrigley message in the personals. The ad became a daily touchstone, part of our new routine, which involved my taking my mother's place at the store while she recovered.

"Who keeps paying for this ad?" my daughter demanded. Her grandmother's stroke had caught her off-balance; she wanted to lodge a complaint. "It's just stupid, like a twisted game." The response to my last move had been as cryptic as the rest: *Dawn Wrigley, I have news.* "What is the point of looking for somebody who does not exist?" One afternoon, at Happiness Plaza, I found out.

She had so thoroughly disappeared from my memory that I

physically startled when I saw her again, coming through the doors of City Essentials. Then I recalled her fully, like the plot of a movie, like a dream. She was as tall as a man, big and imperious, full-bosomed and fast-walking, with long thick brown hair wavy as if just taken from braids, and intense little eyes set off by round glass lenses. She wore a dress far out of fashion, apricot and yellow cotton floral cinched with a cloth belt that matched, even its buckle sheathed in daisies and mums. As she approached the writing desk from which my mother conducted business, I was tempted to fear her—at the very least, I could worry for the tiny fragile objects she threatened to knock off their pedestals. From her shoulders she dropped the peach cardigan that served as her wrap, revealing the capped short sleeves of her strange dress, the pale freckled length of her bare arms and extremely large hands. She put her palms on my mother's desk and leaned toward me. Despite her intensity and seeming anger, it was the dress that most alarmed.

"You don't remember me," she accused, squinting at me.

"Jilly Houston," I said instantly, her name on my lips as her image had been in my mind, waiting to be of use. In high school, Jilly Houston had been our fan, our audience, paying us the great compliment of wanting to join my little group of friends. We included her once, maybe more; I could remember eating lunch with her at the worn old bar that reminded me of an animal burrow, situated not far from East High, where we bought ham sandwiches and thick dill pickles and pitchers of beer, nestled in booths listening to soothing country music. We all got stoned driving back to school, and Jilly surprised us by being so good at being stoned, she who had seemed merely weird, huge, and bizarre, and reportedly brilliant, her steady gaze, her deadpan delivery, that hair. She would not let us initiate her slowly into our group, although we might have, as she added an interesting spin. But she proceeded too blatantly, took too pronounced a lead, phoning up or just stopping by a locker to demand to know what was on the evening's agenda.

Had she come to our apartment? I could still see that place as it

had been rather than as it now stood, its seediness even then seductive, the view of downtown, of the empty pay parking lot across the
street, the slight odor of dentist office in the halls, the too-hot radia-
tor that clanged nonstop as if someone were downstairs hammering
its pipes with a small wrench. Could I put Jilly Houston in those
warm bare rooms? Seat her on the Murphy bed, place her beaky pro-
file against the single window? Outside, the gray sky and the brown
river, never varying, despite the season. Us in our tall brick building,
alone on its block, brick the color and texture of tree bark, pebbled
with something like lichen . . .

Leaning toward me now, she seemed unsoftened by the years,
aggrieved still by our rejection. "How're you?" she asked abruptly,
removing her hands from the desk to pull her flaring hair into a stat-
icky bundle, knotting it with crackling efficiency around one fist. "I
heard you were back in town," she went on, "and I thought you
would know where Kip Pratt might be."

I shook my head. "I haven't seen Kip in years, not since Christmas
of '86." Alane had been a toddler and we were making one of our
infrequent visits to Wichita. Kip brought over a large Santa Claus tin
of homemade candies. At first, I'd been tempted to turn it into a
joke, ready to find a small bag of marijuana inside, or coiled snakes.
A gift as straightforward as candy at Christmas was a gesture we
would have ridiculed as teenagers, but it seemed she was sincere,
she'd whipped up fudge and peanut brittle and some other odd
rock-hard white confection sprinkled with what looked to me like
ground glass. I don't think I would have been surprised to have that
glittery texture in my mouth once more. She'd had surgery on her
face by then, her nose and eyes altered somehow. At my parents'
kitchen table she talked exclusively about the way our neighborhood
was falling apart, ignoring my sulky brother and bored husband and
charming child, forgetting to inquire as to the whereabouts of my
father (dead only a month at that time), and when she left, nobody
would eat any of the candy. Her reputation as a hell-raiser still had
currency in my family; one visit with a suspicious gift wouldn't cure

it. I told Jilly Houston the whole of that strange Christmas because she would not shift from my face her beady stare.

"I've seen her since *then*," she said flatly, disappointed by my uselessness, or maybe bragging. "She was racing horses in Oklahoma just a few years ago."

"Really?"

"Yeah." She then took stock of her surroundings, shocked herself by realizing how many mirrors reflected her image. I had never seen a woman more out of place. It was a slow day at the store; every now and then the phone would ring, my brother calling from his car to confirm my incompetence as shopkeeper. After school, Alane would join me the way I had joined my father when I was a teenager. "My husband's a cop," said Jilly Houston, apropos of nothing, fixing her gaze once more on me. "I have seven children."

"Good lord," I said, just the way my mother would have. This news—and the way it was delivered—struck me as the wildest thing yet. Already I was constructing the anecdote for Greg or Alane or possibly my mother, to whom I often had too little to say.

"Listen," she said, this mother of seven, this wife of a cop, getting down to business. "I was trying to find Kip, I wanted to tell her some news about a guy she used to know."

I shrugged; I'd already revealed all that I planned to about Kip Pratt.

"This guy's in prison, Kip would want to know. He's in prison on sexual assault." Jilly waited for me to be impressed by this, then repeated the information that her husband was a cop. "We met at the Fraternal Order of Police bar."

"We used to go there, too. I didn't know you—"

"Kip and I went there after debate practice. All the time," she added, smug; the revelation was meant to sting me. "I wanted to get ahold of Kip to tell her what happened to this guy. When we went out, we always used a made-up name, our alibi, we would call this guy and tell him we were—"

"Dawn Wrigley." I wanted to say it before she did, wanting to stake prior claim in that creature's life. My secret life now appeared to have an addendum, a hidden clause in the form of Jilly Houston. How peculiar to feel betrayed by this, the past, and so mild a betrayal, given what Kip had been through, but still I felt it: she had lied to me. She had lied to both me and Amanda, trading us for someone as grotesque and unthinkable as Jilly Houston. "You ran an ad," I said.

Jilly nodded without surprise. "It's you who answered," she said, deflated, annoyed. This was our mutual disappointment, our dud blind date. She now plunged her large fists and arms back into the pale peach sweater. "See ya," she said, and strode right out of City Essentials, opening the door for Alane, who was entering, the two of them brushing against each other in passing.

Later, I imagined a conversation they might have had, Jilly Houston and my daughter; their intersection would feature me as its hub. "Your mother thought she was Kip Pratt's best friend," Jilly could say, "but it was really me." Which very well may have been true. I was ready to cede that likelihood. My old friend had been a complicated piece of work, and I hadn't been prepared, then or probably now, to be of use to her. I had been too busy starring in the drama of my teenage life. Jilly Houston, bossy and frank, audience and critic, future mother of seven, could be counted upon. I wished her well, in her quest for Dawn Wrigley; clearly, my rights to that character had long ago dissolved. "Your mother thinks she made up Dawn Wrigley," Jilly Houston might have told Alane, "but I'm the one who really did."

"It's gone," Alane noted, of the personal ad.

"Let's see," I said, as if needing proof.

You can embark on a new life, a second or third one, parts A and B, appendix IV, but it won't be like stepping aboard a ship amidst fanfare and confetti. It will be more like wandering the local mall some windswept Saturday, accompanied by those people who've gathered themselves in the same foxhole with you: your evolving daughter and her invalid grandmother, your fatigued boyfriend and his unflappable brain-damaged child. A version of yourself will be left behind with every step, tracks that nobody will ever bother to pick up. Introductions will be required all around, and often.

"Who are you?" someone will say. "You look fa . . . miliar."

☞ *Stitches*

*M*ama?" she said. The word cut through every layer: the dark house, the late hour, the deep sleep, the gin still polluting her blood, the dream still spinning whimsically. All of it sliced away as if with a scalpel by her daughter's voice on the telephone.

"Baby." Ellen emerged from the murk: naked, conscious, attuned. "Baby?"

"I'm okay, Mama, but something happened, something happened here." *Here* was in her college town, two hours away from her parents' home, this her first semester. Ellen felt her heart beating.

"But you're okay?"

"I'm okay."

"Not hurt?"

"I'm okay. I'm scared."

Skeered, the children used to say, Tracy and Lonnie, Ellen's girl and boy. "Scared of what?" Ellen's house was lit only by the moon and a streetlamp, 3:30 in the morning, the worst of the witching hours. Without thinking she had brought the telephone from the hall to her son's room, where he slept, safe. Ellen had been dreaming about her ex-lover, whom she had been missing now for longer than the relationship itself had endured; this longing now felt normal, a facet of who she was. On the telephone her daughter was almost crying, as if to punish Ellen for her unfaithful dream: look what can happen if you aren't paying attention, if your affections go wandering. "Scared of what?"

"What's she scared of?" asked Ellen's husband, his breath bitter with sleep and age, his presence here at her elbow similar to his presence beside her in bed: she wanted to push him away, she wanted to pull him close. Sometimes she sunk her teeth into his shoulder and pretended it was erotic. He loved his daughter without hesitation, the way he loved his wife, his son. It was cloying, reassuring, inescapable, horrifying. Secure: like a safety belt or a prison sentence.

"Mama, I was *raped*." Now Tracy began to cry sincerely.

"What?" Ellen's husband shouted. They went back to their own bedroom and he was dressing, muttering, lights were igniting, drawers were slammed as Ellen clutched the phone with both hands as though it might leap through the air.

"Where *are* you?" she asked. "Where are you, darling?"

"In my . . . dorm," said her daughter, and that building erected itself, proud and institutional, enclosing the girl on its fourth floor, in her room full of posters and stuffed bears and empty beer cans.

"Police?" her husband asked, as he tried to extricate the phone.

"Not the police!" came Tracy's voice over the line, "it was someone I *know*." Now Ellen's husband was working pants over boxer shorts, the material bunching at his waist, storming from room to room in search of wallet and keys and eyeglasses and jacket, shirt flapping open like a flag.

"It was someone she knows," Ellen repeated for him.

"I heard," he said grimly. "I'm on my way," he added, tucking his shorts into his fly and zipping sharply. His decision had been made just as automatically as pulling a zipper; or, rather, his thinking had cleared a path through the fog of the night: blinding, exact, preemp-

tory. Ahead of himself he saw only his daughter. Ellen had to marvel.
"You stay on the phone," he told her. His hair was wild, his shoelaces
trailing him as he slammed the door.

"Don't let him come here," her daughter had been saying, repeatedly. "*Please* don't let him come here." As if he could have been
stopped.

"I'm going to talk to you, honey," said Ellen to her seventeen year
old. A young college student, she was a girl who'd always been ahead
of her years in some ways and behind them in others. Smart yet sentimental, maternal yet childlike, she was rounded and soft, dark,
vaguely furred on her upper lip and forearms, the nape of her neck.
She bore an uncanny resemblance to her maternal grandmother.
Ellen would never escape that particular blend of bossiness and
naivete. They book-ended her, her mother and her daughter, dark
stocky peasants. Practical, conscientious, good: they exerted force
from either side, like a flower press. Like a vise.

"Oh, why does he have to come here?" Tracy wailed rhetorically.
And Ellen could easily envision her daughter's olive skin, wet with
tears, as she wandered back into her son's room. His skin was exactly
the opposite—fair, nearly hairless—and it covered a very different,
knobby body. In his face you could see the child he'd been and the
man he would become, lean and frail, charming and awkward. "Of
course your father's coming, and we'll just talk until he gets there."
The hundred miles between them appeared in Ellen's mind, the
desert, the bright moon, and the animals as they blindly scurried out
of his trajectory. His trip would be a clear shot, simple as a bullet
from a gun. He had raised the garage door with enough force to
make the lights in the house flicker.

But Lonnie hadn't woken up, twelve years old, skinny, innocent,
eyelids almost translucent; he was sleeping the passionate sleep of an
early teenager.

"Is he mad?" Tracy asked.

"Frightened," Ellen said. "Men get angry when they're frightened.
He's mad at whoever raped you."

"Mama?" she sucked wetly in. "It wasn't exactly rape?"

"Tracy." Ellen pulled her bathrobe closer around her; the heater came on and the cat wandered to the floor vent beside Lonnie's guitar stand. When had she draped herself in her bathrobe? What had she been thinking, a few minutes ago, standing naked in her son's bedroom? She and her husband had had sex before going to sleep, she recalled now, which explained both her nudity and her dream of her ex-lover. "Trace. What do you mean, it wasn't exactly rape?" She was used to her daughter's amendments: the extremity, and then the backpedaling.

"I mean, I knew him, I know him, and he invited me to his house, and I went there, and I knew we were going to have sex. Don't keep saying my name," she added, stepping out of her tragedy for a moment to be irritated.

"There can still be rape—"

"I don't think it was rape. I agreed, I wanted it. I mean, I wanted some of it. He's my professor."

Ellen's heart hammered in a new kind of anger, the anger that comes after the fear, the anger that begins to refine itself, take shape in more intricate ways, like lace, like coral, around any extenuating circumstance. The worst thing, well, that wasn't what had happened to Tracy. It wasn't simple violence of the sort Ellen had envisioned. The man hadn't been a stranger in an alley, or a burglar in the dorm. He hadn't been a frat boy at a party, or one of a gang of drunks in a bar. Instead, it was a middle-aged man in a bed with a headboard, piles of books on the table beside it, floral sheets, prescription meds in the night table drawer, a room not unlike the room Ellen shared with her husband, filled with the familiar objects of comfort and respectable living, complication and texture, history. Instantly that house formed in Ellen's mind, growing swiftly from one fruitful word, *professor,* the divorced professor, the separated professor, the lecherous professor whose wife was out of town or teaching her own seminar, and Tracy there in that house, seduced by the older man's flattering attention to her. "Tell me," Ellen said to her daughter. "Tell me what happened."

"He's my movement teacher," she began, and what followed was not surprising, not to Ellen, who'd also been to college, who'd also developed crushes on professors, who knew all about the liberal arts. What was surprising, what had always surprised Ellen about this daughter of hers, was how she never failed to bring her female business to her mother. Breasts, boys, menstruation, makeup, cat fights, betrayal. It was unnerving to be this girl's mother. She was so *forthcoming*. So frankly healthy and unfucked-up. How had she gotten this way? Ellen felt somehow excluded from the process; she wasn't so healthy herself, still vaguely anorexic, still drinking too much and smoking occasionally, lying to her husband about her affections. She kept secrets—not in drawers or closets or diaries, but in her heart, behind her eyes, on her lips. Tracy's admirable openness seemed not to have been inherited from Ellen, so it must have come from her father.

"How old is this professor?" Ellen asked suddenly. Something Tracy had said made the image of the man shift. The bed, it was a *waterbed*.

"He's not actually a professor, per se," Tracy said. "He's more like the TA."

"Per se."

"What?"

"How old is the TA?"

"I dunno. Twenty-five?"

Ellen sighed. Not so much younger than her ex-lover. Now the professor's stately bedroom was devolving into her ex-lover's ratty apartment. Mattress on the floor, stolen silverware, chairs festooned with duct tape, disposable razors, wine in a box.

"He raped you? Or you had sex when you didn't want to? Or what?"

"Mama?"

"What, babe? What, Trace?"

"You know the most awful thing? The awfullest-seeming thing, the thing that's just really *really* hard to handle?"

"What, doll?" Ellen played with the phone's telescoping antenna, up and then down, patience a tone of voice she put on like a hat.

"A man crying," Tracy said. "I don't know why, but I can't take it."

Ellen thought of her husband's crying. When he had believed that their life together was over, he had wept. Tracy was right. It was an *awful* thing, it left her full of awe. Frightening, pathetic, to be patted on the head, to be avoided, shunned, locked out of the house. There was no good reaction to a man's crying, not one that would work. Men didn't know how to do it, how to modulate, how to breathe or minister to their own sudden emissions. Ellen thought that men would be inept at childbirth, as well: they were so ugly in pain, so bad at giving in to a force larger than themselves. She was remembering her ex-lover's contorted face, he'd been tearful a time or two, as well. "Baby," she said.

"It can just about kill you, watching a boy cry."

"Why was he crying? Why?"

"Because he hurt me."

Once more Ellen felt anger rise in her. Anger and empathy: these accompanied the guilt and the love she felt toward her daughter and always would. She paced the house's flowchart of a floor plan, hallway-kitchen-dining room-living room-hall, a smooth oval that her children used to chase around as if at a racetrack. The cat, the same age as Tracy, watched her, blinking sagely and calmly. This man in distant Albuquerque kept shifting character in Ellen's mind, elastic as a superhero. She focused instead on the image of her husband, driving steadfastly through the desert, the bright moon beaming uncomplicatedly down upon him, both of his hands on the wheel. *He* was not a shape-changer. "*How* did he hurt you? What did he do?"

"Oh, it's embarrassing."

Ellen heard a near giggle in the girl's voice. Tracy always had frivolity just beneath the surface. She was a ticklish person, a jolly girl who liked to find things funny, who more than once had started laughing in the middle of a harsh scolding from her parents, so confident was she of their indulgence. Ellen could recall slapping her—

how dare she mock her punishment?—and being glad to see that smirk disappear.

"Embarrassing how?" she asked, skeptical suddenly of the phone call, the tears. *Drama overdrive,* her son would have said. That was Tracy's M.O. She had a long history as a theater major. Even before she'd been in college she was majoring in it, back when no one had majors, just tendencies. She wanted her family members to prove their love; she wanted to sound an alarm in the middle of the night and see them jump. She depended on their willingness to play along.

"Like sex," Tracy said. "You know."

"I *don't* know. Tell me." The cat rolled onto its back on the dining room floor, splayed fat and relaxed, like a smiling drunk. Tracy was talking about her flirtation with her TA. His name was Henry Fielding.

"It is not," Ellen declared.

"It is so."

"Henry *Field*ing?"

"You've heard of him?"

"Tracy," she began, then thought better of it. Had she herself heard of Henry Fielding when she was seventeen? What had she been doing at seventeen? Why was her daughter supposed to be doing something nobler?

"Everyone else calls him Hank, but I like Henry. Is Daddy really coming here?"

"Of course he is. You call, he comes."

Tracy laughed, and it turned into tears. Ellen left the cat and found a chair at the kitchen table, where the two halves of a squeezed lime lay in a puddle of melted ice. She leaned over the telephone, creating a pocket in which her ear and her daughter's mouth made contact. "Sweetie," she said, "what happened?"

"Sometimes it's called 'deliveries in rear.' Coming in the back door." She paused. "In my bottom?"

"Darling." Ellen shivered. She could not help imagining her daughter's naked body, there before her as if in time-lapse photography, the grinning chubby baby, the naked little girl splashing in the bathtub, the adolescent who ran on tiptoe from shower to bedroom with a towel clutched under her arms.

Tracy said, "So that wasn't actually rape, was it?"

"No?"

"No. It was more like . . ."

"Consensual?"

"Not exactly. More like a car wreck. Just. Out of control."

"Okay, honey. Out of control." Ellen fell into the echoing habit of the shrink. She could be grateful for that simple trick, if nothing else, from all of her tedious expensive sessions in therapy, all her attempts to be cured of that ex-lover of hers, that obsession like a virus, like a new life-form present in her body.

"And he said his waterbed might have had a leak."

"Waterbeds," Ellen recalled. "I thought those days were gone."

"It sloshed. Like being in a boat."

Ellen asked for the whole story. She had only one policy with this girl: frankness. "I'll be the most angry if you lie." It had seemed obvious to Ellen: the truth. But many people in fact did not want to know it. Her husband didn't. He did not want to know that Ellen loved someone else. He put his money on the wedding ring, on the indisputable evidence that every night he climbed into bed with Ellen, and she with him.

Tracy heaved a monumental sigh, backing up to the beginning of her evening. "First I went to a bar, with some friends. We had to cheer Tiffany up."

Ellen breathed evenly, trying to match her mood to the cat's. Beebee had survived, years and years, just by roaming calmly from room to room, meal to meal, allowing Tracy to come and go, love her and then forget her.

"So when I got to Hank's, I was kinda drunk. I had some beer."

"How did you get to his house?"

"I didn't drive, Mama, I walked. I walked there. It's a guest house behind a real house." Ellen's ex-lover's apartment now transformed into a tiny lighted cottage, and the revision was not unpleasant. What bothered her was her daughter drunk on Albuquerque's Central Avenue, wandering toward that cottage through the traffic and the whores and the roaming wolfish men.

When she got there, Tracy went on, Henry was listening to music.

"What kind?" her mother asked, thinking that this would define him, this movement class TA, his taste in music. But what kind would save him in her eyes? Classical? Jazz? Polka?

"I have no idea, some stuff, you know, like *guitars*. Henry's allergic to smoke, and I stank like the bar," Tracy went on. "You know how you stink after a bar?" As if she and her mother were now confidantes at the dorm, hanging their smelly clothing out the windows to air, hoping their underpants wouldn't wind up on the lawn below. Shouldn't a mother reprimand a girl who was four years too young to be at a bar? But where could she begin, with this reprimand? She herself had been to bars underage, to the homes of professors and married men, to the apartment of her ex-lover, and not so long ago. Ellen tossed the soggy limes into the sink and wiped her hand over the puddle, as if to erase her own evening of drink. "So I took off my clothes and showered." They'd been flirting with each other in class, she reported. He was shy, awkward, far from home, which was that famous daunting place, "Back East," a recent theater major himself, and he wanted to be an actor. An actor! And she wanted to sing. Like that maternal grandmother of hers, Tracy had an astonishingly strong voice, rising from her ample chest, which housed her extraordinary heart. How could Henry Fielding be worthy of that heart, Ellen wondered? Only her husband was worthy, only Tracy's father. Again she featured him, behind the wheel, completely untutored on the complexity of this so-called rape. He was acquiring rage as he drove.

"Henry lended me one of his shirts. He wears these great old button shirts . . ." *Lended?* What had happened to the SAT champ they'd sent to college a semester early? "And then," Tracy continued, "then we started to kiss." She would have smelled like his Ivory soap, her mother imagined. Boys often had Ivory soap, unperfumed, familiar. His shower would be so ill-equipped that Tracy would have had to use the soap on her hair, that thick wavy Italian hair inherited from her grandmother. Ellen knew exactly how that hair looked, damp. The tips of it saturated and dripping, like paint from a brush, steady trails of water sliding down her cheek. She had beautiful plump purple lips, a gorgeous soprano singing voice, a quirky sense of humor. She turned her eyes toward the people she loved, as guileless and faithful as a puppy. She was a solid slow-moving girl, heavy and sexy, her body utterly different from her mother's, her nature sweeter, her keel evener, that sly funny girl. Yet innocent. Would Henry Fielding have recognized her innocence, despite her acting skill, her mature voice, her cleverness?

"He cooks," Tracy said, as if just to keep the line from going silent for too long. "He likes to cook, a lot, he says. Like Dad. Remember when Lonnie said Dad's cooking all tasted like underarm sweat?"

"Yes," Ellen said. She swelled at the memory. She loved her son more purely than the others she loved. He'd told his father the food tasted like underarm sweat, it was true, but it hadn't been an insult, just an observation. That was only one of the million things Ellen loved about Lonnie.

"I liked most of the sex," Tracy said as if reviewing a meal or movie. "It didn't hurt as much as I thought it would, the regular part."

"This was the first time?"

"Duh." Ellen, of course, would have been informed if it were otherwise.

"He *knew* it was the first time?"

"No. I lied." Now Tracy was crying again, the hiccuping variety of crying that would leave her eyes plumlike. Dark as she was, the underside of Tracy's eyes were nearly black, like her grandmother's. These shadows made her look older, wiser, than she was. She could fool bartenders and TAs with the bruisy rings beneath her eyes.

"I lied the other way, when I first had sex," Ellen said speculatively.

"Really?" Tracy snuffled. "You were nineteen, right? And the first time Daddy had sex he was fourteen."

"I'd forgotten that." She wasn't sure she'd ever known it.

"But I wonder, did anyone ever . . . does everyone have to . . . "

"Anal sex?" Ellen stalled while waiting for an answer to occur to her. What was the answer? *All men want it.* "I don't know a single woman who enjoys it," she said.

"I can see why," Tracy said, and then burst out afresh. Ellen let her. All those years ago, when she herself had been in college, calling home, her mother would never have let the line go unoccupied this way, silence and tears, dead air. In those days, with that generation, one was always aware of the ticking long-distance meter, the phone bill, the expense, the simple unease of intimate discussion, over the phone—or even in person. Her own mother absolutely refused to accept the human traits that weren't virtuous. She did not allow them in her loved ones. Ellen listened to her daughter cry with a kind of pride; she would let her cry for hours, if need be, hundreds of dollars' worth of tears.

"He didn't mean to put his penis there!" Tracy exclaimed. "It slipped, I think. He was confused," she sobbed. Oh, the confused penis, the slippage, the proximity of those two apertures, the slick bodies in the dark, the heated excitement of love, or its possible beginning. They were at sea in a leaky waterbed, it was a storm, an emergency, he'd made a mistake. Or not. If not, he was rough, unkind, piratical, dangerous. If not, then he did not care for Tracy, neither her pain nor her pleasure. Ellen didn't want to think of her daughter having sex at all, let alone painful sex, ambiguous sex. That body had been under Ellen's purview for a few years; she had been an exemplary steward. Who was this boy to use it so?

"It hurt, Mama, it hurt so bad."

Ellen involuntarily squeezed the muscles of her own buttocks. *Sphincter,* she thought. She had no idea what to advise for her daughter's pain; whatever the damage, something as straightforward as stitches was not the answer. Ellen could see the dorm room, its view of a nearby smokestack, the wheat fields, the little city at night. Except that had been her own dorm room, from twenty years ago, in winter, in Kansas. Freshman loneliness: it struck her with the force of a blow to the stomach. Loneliness never stopped stunning her; it was a lesson to learn again and again. "Baby, what can I do? I wish I could . . . " She wished she could take her pain, drain it from Tracy and absorb it herself. That was how her children's suffering always wounded her, her inability to suffer it for them.

"It's more psychological than . . . whatever," Tracy responded, "you know, else."

Ellen's head hurt. She had a hangover, she realized. Her daughter's phone call had distracted her from it, but now it claimed her suddenly in a wash of dizzy nausea. Her own past evening was coming back: drinks, sex, passing out. Water, she thought, she needed water and a white slice of soft bread and some ibuprofen and a hot wet washcloth on her forehead. "Baby, did you bleed?" she asked, as she went in search of the components of her cure.

"A little," Tracy said.

"And do you still hurt, now?"

"Yeah. Two different kinds of hurts. I'm lying on my stomach, on my bed." She paused. "He used condoms," she added.

"Good," Ellen said, woozy at the use of the plural.

"Condoms *are* good," Tracy agreed. She was a girl who'd been educated early about their virtues, carrying one in her backpack since tenth grade, just in case.

Tipping the phone away from her mouth, swallowing water, Ellen thought, Hangover is crapulence. She thought of that word often on Sunday mornings, which this morning was. Sunday. *Crapulence.* It was the perfect word.

"I feel yucky," Tracy said. "I feel all wrong."

"Turn on the television," Ellen recommended. "TV is familiar." She headed now to the living room, to the enormous screen on which the family had watched movies the way their ancestors had sat in the glow of a hearth fire, communing. "Turn on Jack Hanna, honey." Wouldn't his golly-gee voice be a kind of comfort? Everything amazed and excited him: he was perpetually pleasantly surprised, like a kid. And *shouldn't* surprises be pleasant? Poor Tracy, with her bad date and awful surprise. "Liquor in the front, poker in the rear," Ellen recalled, a once-funny pun. "Jack Hanna's talking to elks," she said, watching the animals swing through the woods, knocking into trees with their heavy racks of antlers. A hangover felt like that, she thought, like a rack of antlers.

"I don't have cable," Tracy said flatly, "and Jack Hanna is dumb."

"Many men are dumb," her mother said. "But he's harmless, which a lot of men are not."

"Henry Fielding didn't even know how to get blood out of sheets," Tracy said. "That's how dumb he was. He was going to use hot water."

Ellen tried not to envision her daughter's blood on some boy's sheets. Ellen had spent a summer changing sheets, cleaning hotel rooms, in high school. People abandoned everything in hotel rooms: shame. Decency. Vomit. Pubic hairs. Leftover drugs, drink, food, clothing. She'd once pulled open a set of drapes over a large plate glass patio window to reveal a huge shattered piece of glass, cracked and distorted, appalling in its shocking violent intactness. But, mostly, at that hotel were the beds with bodily fluids on them, urine, semen, saliva, blood. The blood had never been enough to signal a murder. Just enough to suggest pain. A humiliation of some degree. The virginal. The menstrual. The reluctant anus. Ellen had wrapped them all into bundles, stuffed them deep into a trolley she would deposit downstairs, where the Mexican illegals would apply bleach. Onto those beds Ellen spread clean sheets, crisp and creased, tucked at the corners the way her mother had taught her, a neat fold like a sealed white envelope waiting to be undone.

"What will I tell Daddy?" Tracy said. "I don't want to tell Daddy about all this."

"Your father loves you," Ellen said, which was supposed to mean that Tracy could tell him anything.

"He'll think I'm a slut," Tracy cried.

"No, honey. No." But Ellen knew, as Tracy did, that her father would not be able to bear the details. "Just tell him it was the first time you had sex. He'll understand that. You don't have to lie about feeling upset. You are upset."

"I don't want to lie at all!"

"It's not lying to not tell him everything." That was Ellen's gift to her husband; she had saved him with it before. Listening to Tracy sniffle, Ellen was tempted to tell her daughter that her father loved her more than he loved anyone else. Was Tracy ready for that piece of parental honesty? To hear also that Ellen loved Lonnie that same way, *more*? Better? At what point was this blunt information fair game for her daughter? Her husband would never admit that he loved Tracy best. How could he admit something he didn't even know?

Ellen knew it for him.

"You and Daddy met in college," Tracy pleaded. "He was *your* TA."

"That's true."

"I want to meet someone, I wanted to, I thought . . . "

"You will." Would she? Ellen wondered. "You probably will, someone like Daddy. Someone who loves you."

"I know he loves me," Tracy said, "but I don't want him to know what happened."

"I understand," Ellen said. She walked once more to her son's room. There he lay, sprawled, wearing boxer shorts and a T-shirt in bed, just the way his father did. In the fly lay his boy's penis. He had one, his father had one, Henry Fielding had one. They got hard and wanted to fit somewhere. They had the power to harm. They stood out like vulnerable targets. A woman had cut her husband's off, thrown it in the street. There it must have lain, rootless and forsaken as a toadstool.

"Hear Lonnie snoring?" Ellen whispered.

"You know what, Mama?" Tracy whispered back. "Henry Fielding reminds me a little bit of Lonnie."

How could her heart not soften at that news? Her lover had reminded her of Lonnie, too.

"Yeah," Tracy went on dreamily, "you know, he has these clumsy big feet."

Ellen sighed. Her son was the one who had kept her from abandoning everything a few years earlier. He was a funny boy, prickly, eccentric, tearful one minute, punch-drunk the next. It didn't surprise Ellen to hear that Tracy had been attracted to a boy like her brother. Her son could someday make a mistake, put his penis someplace wrong, end up crying. Ellen's eyes filled. For Lonnie, for Tracy, for herself and her husband, for that lost lover, even for Henry Fielding, no doubt.

Ellen considered fixing herself a drink. The clock read 5:03. Never had she had a drink at this hour of the day. She'd had them at 4 A.M., and she'd had them at 9:00 A.M., but never at five in the morning. It was both too late and too early. Why not? she thought. This was what her bartender Paco said instead of "yes." "Why not?" in a bright exclamatory. Ellen adored her bartender. She visited him every evening, just the way her father had *his* bartender, when she was young. She and her father needed escape from the innocence that was their spouse—her mother, her husband, the placating good-hearted. Only a smoky bar would do, some days. If it were 5:00 P.M., that's where she would be headed.

"Mama," Tracy said now. It had been her first word, way back when. The next had been "Daddy."

"Baby."

Ellen returned to her bedroom. She had switched off the lights and muted Jack Hanna, and now settled her sore head on her pillow, daughter beside her. The cat jumped onto her feet and walked up her blanketed thighs.

"Now it'll be all weird in class," Tracy said forlornly. "It's not fair." She sounded weary, depleted, capable of falling into an exhausted sleep.

"No, it's not fair." This was what college would teach Tracy. It was, after all, the only lesson, and some people never learned it.

"I'm sorry, Mama."

"You don't have to be sorry, darling. You just have to convince your father that you're okay."

"I know. I figured that out. You think I'm okay?"

"I think you are." She did, actually. Ellen listened sleepily to the lack of static. Did she need to say that this was only the beginning of Tracy's difficult education? That no love would be pure, no gesture uncomplicated, for a long long time? Over the phone line there was silence, as if they would now slip into sleep, into the same dream.

"I'm a good actor," Tracy said faintly, as if trying to rally. "I can make my eyes water in a New York minute."

"Useful," Ellen said. Then she heard her husband's knock on Tracy's dorm door and was startled lucid once more. From a hundred miles she recognized the confident force of his fist. There was no mistaking it.

"Shhh! There's someone at the door," Tracy said, fear in her voice.

"It's your father. He made record time." Ellen sat up and checked her bedside clock: an hour and a half. The cat had stopped purring, ears perked, eye whiskers lifted.

"Let him in," she told Tracy as the cat jumped briskly to the floor.

"He'll know!" Tracy wailed. "I've *never* been able to fool him!"

"He won't," her mother assured her. "You have." When Tracy dropped the receiver, Ellen had the sensation of being let go, left behind. Now she was just a plastic instrument lying on the dorm table while a lock was turned and a door was opened. *He won't,* Ellen heard, and would hear for a long time, reverberating, *you have.*

Far away her daughter said her next word. "Daddy," she said, and Ellen hung up.

The Lonely Doll

I owned one for a while," she told him. "I found it, you won't believe this, in my grandfather's bedside table, in a drawer. There were three, in fact, like the bears, big, medium, baby. Maybe I was innocent at age eleven, I can't really say. It's true I was snooping, but it was *naive* snooping. That's the thing about being eleven: you feel so stupid, so duped, like the grown-ups are still holding out. I expected to find maybe a cigar or a hip flask, you know, Peepaw's *public* foul habits. Instead I found a plastic penis. Three of them, each the weight of, like, a flashlight.

"My first instinct was to slam the drawer, as if they might hup-to and start acting like billy clubs. *Whap whap whap!* But when I looked again, there they were, lying innocent. Alongside a tub of Vaseline. They were always there, week after week. The Vaseline seemed fairly wiggy, don't ask me why. Finally, I stole one. I stayed the night at my grandparents' on Friday nights forever. I slept with my grandma, while Peepaw had his own bedroom. He snored. Sometimes his snoring would wake me up. He'd spend the evening in his La-Z-Boy confusing the mystery shows. He loved to watch them, but he was always drinking. He'd pass out during *Mannix* and suddenly get all startled in the middle of *Barnaby Jones*, shaking his glass of melty ice cubes and bourbon. 'Who's that fellow? What happened to the fisherman with the gun?' He didn't *seem* like the kind of guy who'd keep battery-operated penises.

"So I took one, the baby one, like maybe he wouldn't notice. I used it all the time. It made me come so fast I thought I'd turn into a freak, like I'd use up all my fun before I was twelve. Or maybe I thought boys would somehow know I'd been practicing. *Some*thing. Something made me really nervous about using it, even though I couldn't stop using it."

Her guest made no encouraging murmur, no indication that he wanted to hear the rest. Abruptly, Edith cut herself off. "So. Enough about me and my sordid past. What about you? And yours?"

He was silent but not sleeping. Oh, she'd blundered, she thought as she blushed uselessly. She sensed the stranger's wakefulness as she had sensed it throughout her narrative, an attuned curious listening. It had substance in her bedroom like the dark: consummate yet fleeting. While she was talking, his company beside her had been inclusive, she and he equaled the universe, but in the aftermath, in its lengthening silence, he seemed to have been sucked away, now tiny as a man through the peephole in a closed door. That was the thing about the dark and talking in it. Conversation after sex was complicated. It was much much much more complicated than fucking.

"You're a talker," he eventually said, not unkindly. "Chatty Cathy."

"My name is Edith."

"As if I would forget your name."

Because he sounded wounded, Edith went on, "I never owned a Chatty Cathy, but I did have a book about a doll named Edith. She and her naughty friend the teddy bear." The book was disturbing; instead of regular illustrations, it featured black-and-white photographs of the doll and her small stuffed bear friend and a fat live pigeon. They were posed around town in stilted ways, making mischief, committing the crimes of toys, punished eventually by an even bigger plaything named Mr. Bear, who bent the doll and little bear over his knee and spanked them with his paw. "I don't always talk a lot," she added, which was true, but which he wouldn't have any reason to believe; she'd been talking incessantly since they'd met. She couldn't help herself, happiness loosened her tongue. A man in bed with her, listening, seemed to her the most blissful state of affairs imaginable. The bed held them, the night surrounded them, the phone wouldn't ring, there was no appointment to keep, no place but here to be. The beauty of three or four in the morning was its aimlessness, its stolen quality. What was it good for, except this? The sun was busy on the other side of the world; exhaustion settled like pixie dust with the compliant darkness and all the people slept, in the building, on the block, throughout the far-flung city and country. This hour was for the lonely—the sole stalker, the brooding face waiting at the window, the empty cab—or, more rarely, for the fully living, the couples in love in bed in laughter. They were giddy, they were children, they had found each other against some big damn odds, as in a blindfolded game.

"I've never told anyone about that dildo," Edith lied. She had more than once used this childhood anecdote as a kind of talismanic virginity, something to trot out as proof of fondness, a display of trust.

"Why not?"

Why would she not have? she asked herself. "I don't know." She lay wondering at her hypothetical and uncharacteristic withholding.

But he seemed to understand that it was his turn. He said, "I don't have any interesting secrets."

"There's no such thing as a dull secret."

"A talker *and* a thinker."

"Are you being mean?"

"No. I just don't want to bore you."

In fact Edith wouldn't have found him interesting if she hadn't seen him trying to steal a CD. Brattiness drew her eye. She had met

Marco roughly twelve hours earlier, at a yard sale. The CD only cost a dollar; why steal? She'd grinned conspiringly when she caught him, delighted. He lived in her building on the tenth floor in a studio apartment whose layout and view, he claimed, were identical to hers, but four stories higher.

Entering an apartment as small as Edith's—and Marco's, she assumed—was like entering a hotel room: bed right there when you opened the door. A slower romance might have happened had she been able to afford a living room, a hall, or proper secluded separate space in which to sleep. Instead, they'd sat and then lain on the bed. That famous One Thing had led to this, more tricky, Other.

From the closet came the scratching of Edith's cat. She had had to banish him there when he jumped on the bed and made Marco scream in alarm. It had been a humiliatingly high-pitched scream, but the cat did weigh nearly twenty pounds. His tail was a half-inch stub, the end of which had no hair on it at all, as if the creature had a human fingertip poking out his rear end.

"What the *fuck!*" Marco had screeched, hurling the poor cat to the floor. Edith had been afraid she would have to hate her guest, then. That she would have to send him away and that he might not want to go. Then, when he'd recovered, he'd apologized, even going so far as to kneel, naked, and try to make friends with the cat. "Kitty, kitty, kitty?" he said in a feeble falsetto, and Edith had gallantly and gladly exiled her ancient pet to the closet. Every few minutes the cat reminded her he was still there, seething with his lack of an opposable thumb.

Marco raised up on his elbow and looked down at Edith. His eyebrows almost met over his large nose. He could kiss her, he could bite her, he could burst into song: she hardly knew him or what he'd do. Every passing day, the likelihood of love transpiring between people seemed more and more remote to Edith, disappearing like other quaint traditions: honorable politicians, anonymous philanthropy, love of culture. Culture reminded her of something. "Do you ever hear the opera singer?" she asked, "from up there in your apartment?"

"Opera?"

"So-called. The cat doesn't like her. He lays his ears down when she starts up." The opera singer had to practice her high warbling notes, repeatedly, a person in a formal rictus of pain.

"She's a figment of your imagination," he declared. In Edith's imagination, the woman threw back her head and opened her throat as if to swallow swords.

"You smell good," she told Marco, since he was still staring down at her. She made a point of breathing deep of his mixture of odors, which were in balance, the natural and the chemical. He was old enough to recognize the need for toothpaste and deodorant and shampoo, yet young enough for those to still have their desired effects. "Aren't you going to tell me a story of your youthful pranks?" she asked, rutting into his rib cage. "Please? I don't care if it's a secret or not."

"Hmm." He dropped his head back to the pillow and smiled at the ceiling. Already she saw that smiling was not about happiness, for him. It was pensiveness.

"Like, what were you like at eleven?"

"If I think about being eleven," he said slowly, "I mostly remember this silo."

"Grain?"

"Are there other kinds? Well, missile," he answered his own question. "This silo was empty, on the property of an abandoned farm in Kansas. Kansan, that's what I am."

Edith's imagination sailed out the window and over the city of Chicago, the twinkling grid of lights, the blue-black expanse of lake at her back, and southwest into the vast flatland of his childhood. She had seen that place from the air, from the road, from behind a gas pump one hot late summer. She found not only a silo, but the seesawing sound of cicadas, distant cauliflowerlike clouds.

"There was an abandoned farmhouse out there, along with the silo. My family used to go camping on the property, at the stream that ran through."

In Edith's mind the scene lit up like Andrew Wyeth, windswept and golden and lonely. For some reason her silo was tilted, like a little leaning tower, nostalgic and portentous. His voice was deep and when he spoke his words—transported, she supposed, by the bedsprings—hummed in her sternum, a pleasant resonance that felt like the beginning of love. "Camping?" she coached, unable to keep her hands from him: his chest, his arms, his earlobes. He was warm all over, the radiant heat that results from lying naked for a long while with another person in bed.

"My parents were hippies," he said. "They took us camping on this stream on an old farm. We went every weekend for a few years, them and their pothead friends and their friends' kids. 'Go *play* with them,' my mother was always saying, all annoyed if I didn't like her friends' kids." He reached for Edith's busy hands; she could have been blind, for all the eagerness of her fingers. They touched at the knuckles and the knees. She liked his hair, the stubble on his face, and the soft pelt on his head, which was slightly greasy with the product he thought would help him look more attractive. She liked his attention to looking more attractive, or trying anyway. He was a gawky guy who wore a smirk on his face, a mask put on to hide his maladroitness.

"Although I *did* like them, it turned out," he said glumly, of the kids he was forced to camp with. "There was this girl."

Edith listened more closely. She was going to learn the type of girl who would torment him for the rest of his life. Why else remember her? She was listening to hear if she were that kind of girl herself. *He* was *her* kind of torment, the shy sullenness, the bad posture, the flash of cruelty and ready heart-wrenching remorse. She and Marco had met at the Permanent Yard Sale that took place in the dumpy lawn beside their apartment building. Lately the owners of the bungalow weren't even hauling in their tables at night. They chained an evil dog to bark at hapless pedestrians and would-be thieves. Every morning there'd be different stuff on sale. Boom boxes, dusty clock radios, sticky Teflon pans, TVs, jewelry or running shoes, packages of food, half-burned votive candles. Edith had passed the yard for months before it finally dawned on her that this project was not only the household's sole livelihood but that the items for sale were probably stolen goods.

Yesterday—just yesterday!—she and Marco had been strangers, pawing through the CDs, snatching up plastic jewel cases as if gathering nuts for the long winter. Marco's music taste turned out to be hers, too, the whining nihilistic sort. When he sneaked the CD in his shirt, Edith addressed him. "I have their first album." His theft made her feel no longer in competition so much as collusion.

He'd glared until she motioned toward his chunky breast pocket. "Not *Mysterioso?*"

She nodded eagerly. "And all the live juvenalia, bootleg."

"Wow." He sighed appreciatively, hand over his heart and the purloined disc. "I would love to hear those." When they then found themselves walking into the same building, checking the same bank of mailboxes, and summoning the same elevator, it seemed to Edith nearly rude not to invite him to get off on her floor.

"I don't have speakers," she apologized. He'd slipped on the headphones, closed his eyes, and gone quickly rapturous. In silence Edith followed his pleasure by memory, vaguely embarrassed by his tongue trembling between his lips like an excited child's. Now she thought she'd offer Marco all of the scuffed CDs she'd bought, those and any others he desired. Affection made her want to give and give and give. Her once-upon-a-time therapist had told her she had "boundary issues," and long before that, her mother had warned her that she should be more protective with what was hers. "If you give too much," she had said in her bright direct way, "what will you have left for yourself?" Edith could appreciate her mother's concern, her therapist's longsightedness, but she considered generosity a virtue. It demonstrated trust; it resembled confidence; it was optimistic. Some nights, for example, she refused to lock her apartment door.

Marco said, "I was always going to that silo and climbing inside. I liked to be alone. And the sound in there was indescribable. I don't suppose you ever sat in an empty silo?"

"'I am a city child.'" It was a quote, one children's text having reminded Edith of another.

He described the sound of a silo. Noise echoed some but it also *didn't* echo, if she could feature such a thing. It muffled your voice but then you also could hear your voice going up to the sky, like smoke from a chimney, or maybe more like smoke rings, every word in its own ring, taking a ride up.

"Well, anyways," he said, "once when I was twelve I got an infected penis."

Edith laughed only because, when she was nervous, certain words operated as punch lines; *penis* was one of those. Marco grabbed her fingers and squeezed so fiercely that Edith thought he probably didn't get the chance to touch people very often. Again she pictured her dear old cat being launched off the bed, and was briefly frightened. "I'm sure you're laughing *with* me," he said, and Edith laughed harder, pulling her bare legs up in reflex. Every now and then she suffered laughing fits that would not stop, hysterical in nature, and she hoped this wasn't going to turn into one of those. Laughter like that seemed both potentially embarrassing and essentially selfish, masturbatory. "Okay," Marco warned, plopping his head wearily on the pillow, "but you're going to be sorry in a minute, sorry for mocking me, when I tell you what happens next."

From the closet came the sudden scrabbling of claws; Edith's cat was digging into the wood of the door. She could hear the low growl in his furious feline throat.

Marco paused. "That thing's a fucking *lynx*, what with the weird tail and all. Are cats allowed in this building? I was told just non-mammals."

"Meaning?"

"Birds. Fish."

"Alligators," Edith speculated. "Snakes."

"I have fish."

"Fish!" She wanted to clap: pets! Having them proved something.

"Betas. Beauteous, but they have to live in separate mayonnaise jars on top of my piano. Together in the same jar, they'd kill each other. That's their nature." Now he had not only fish but a piano; he listened to music, he played music. Edith imagined him a player of classical music, then revised to the more intriguing composer of tuneless modern pieces. Perhaps that was why he'd never heard the opera singer: he was making his own sad racket.

"To continue," he said, "I had to be circumcised when I was twelve years old." He informed her that twelve was very old for circumcision, which, he said, she'd have no reason to know, since she wasn't a boy or the mom of a boy, but it was old. And it was embarrassing, of course, and his parents, who hadn't believed in circumcision—they hadn't believed in it much earlier than other parents who didn't believe in it—failed to have it done when he was a baby, and then, because they were hippies, he was probably a filthy little runt with bad personal hygiene, which no doubt led to the infection. "Which was *gross.*" Here he placed her hand, with his over it, on top of the penis under discussion. His bundle of flesh was warm, skin the delicately pimpled surface that testicles shared with that of plucked chicken. The hair was wiry, tightly curled, totally unlike the hair on his head. "*Pus,*" he said with a sibilant hiss, and Edith laughed again, though she was no longer likely to go into hysterics.

His palm covering hers reminded Edith of how they'd shook hands out at the yard sale, sideways, his right hand in her left because she held the stack of CDs she'd bought in her right hand while he was still gripping his disc inside his shirt with his left. Greeting somebody sideways always made you more immediately intimate, as if you were holding rather than shaking hands.

"Excuse me," he said, kissing her on the forehead and then lightly slipping from bed to the bathroom. He did not strut, as some men might, but dashed. The bright unshaded light seemed an assault. It took a moment, but then she heard his urine hit the water. The bathroom door would never completely close, and she could see, if she looked, as he stood braced at the toilet. She remembered high school then, though not of sneaking glances at penises but of a boy she loved then, who used to stand at his locker in his low-slung jeans undoing his combination lock. He would cup it at his belt buckle, his expert thumb busy rotating the dial. It was sexy, his confident locker ritual, and Marco's stance at her toilet—now he spit just before flushing—made her heart leap in fresh attraction.

Then he held the door shut, still inside. What was he doing? Investigating the medicine cabinet? That's what Edith would have done, in his place. She liked to know the lay of the land. It was how she'd ended up with a dildo, all those years ago, snooping. What would he think of her drugs and unguents? Antidepressants and perfume, her two best bets. Nothing scarifying, no antifungals or hair dye or laxatives. Also nothing very fun, pharmaceutically speaking. She'd given those up, handed out her last Valium at a Halloween party.

Soon the door opened and the light went out. "Good toilets in this building," Marco noted as he slid back into bed, his feet chilly from the tile. "Industrial quality. I've never had to call the super about mine."

"Me, either. I only call the super about the opera singer."

"Her I never knew about."

"Sometimes I call the super, and sometimes I just let her make me mopey."

The cat hummed evilly from the closet.

"So," Marco said, returning them to Kansas, "I was operated on." It hurt like hell, having your foreskin sliced off, he notified her. Edith grimaced sympathetically. And then they, his enlightened party animal parents, insisted on going camping anyway because the weather was good. Naturally, all the other hippie parents came with, there was marijuana around the campfire, charades, singalongs, shenanigans involving other people's spouses, et cetera. The wholesome seventies, he said sourly, his parents the Midwest radicals. All the kids always went *swimming*—he removed his hands from beneath the covers to make bunny ears around the word—"Wading, if you will, wallowing in swampy muck." He returned his hands to Edith's and clutched them.

"I like you," she said impulsively, because she did, him and his dry-witted self-pitying, angry, ludicrous story.

"You wouldn't have liked me then," he said. "I was a punk, ready to become a skinhead just to piss my parents off. I had to spend the whole camping weekend mortified somebody was gonna knock me in the nuts and pretending I didn't feel like swimming, because I couldn't get my dick wet."

Edith frowned, then said, "What *is* it with that word?"

"Women hate it. They also hate the words for their own genitalia, but what are you going to do? Cunt," he said, and Edith felt herself recoil. She could imagine for a moment being his hippie mother, watching him slink off to his grain silo and being glad to be rid of him. He would have been sulky and hunched then, too, scowling and unpopular. He would have been her darling baby one moment, sunny and cheerful and cute, then a horrifying insolent boy bent on criticizing her lifestyle the next.

"What happened in that silo?" she asked, wanting to return to his point of view, to be inside the silo rather than out.

"I cried," he said simply, and Edith filled with love for him once more. Crying she understood. Crying she could love.

But there was more. The girl, the fantastical girl, another of the hippies' children, three years older than Marco, a full-blown untouchable fifteen: she discovered him weeping in the silo and crawled through the opening to come to his side. Edith wished to see herself as this girl, the one who would follow and know. She was a beautiful girl, in his memory, blonde hair so long its pale ends had grown dry and wispy. She wore tight jeans, a halter top, her plump skin sunburned pink, which made her seem both on fire and terribly vulnerable. She squatted on the ground beside him where he sat sobbing on a block of concrete. She smelled of a perfume all teenage girls wore, big, green apple-flavored babies. Her face was round, her teeth were straight, her eyes were glistening turquoise beneath turquoise shadow. Her name was Goldberry.

"It was not!" Edith said.

"Yah huh," he said, braying like a donkey.

Goldberry, named for a hobbit, Marco speculated. Because of her patience, by virtue of the odd location of their meeting, due to her usual teenager's utter lack of interest in him, she managed to elicit from him, that day, the difficult details of his trouble. Before she arrived, he couldn't have imagined saying what he was saying, telling anyone, especially her, what plagued him. His desire to confide in her had everything to do with the way the silo had made a hallowed space in the middle of a former wheat field, with the way one's voice, inside that space, was converted. The ground was soft, dirt turned to powder, which they sifted through their fingers as they spoke confidentially in the confines of that tall emptiness with its ceiling of blue. She flattered him by naming him brave; she lulled him by telling him she, too, had had embarrassing surgery. She'd found a lump in her breast, she said, just a few years earlier, when she was twelve, and believed she would die. For mortal hours she'd cried in her bedroom, wondering whether to tell her parents, composing her obituary and envisioning her funeral, the sorry visages of her seventh grade peers and her pesky brother as they bent over her casket. There'd been an awful doctor involved, a lech who took some pleasure in squeezing the young breast, then later excising the benign cyst, leaving a set of wicked black stitches just below her pink nipple. Goldberry, like Marco, had been too ashamed to tell her friends. Like Marco she'd not been able to go swimming, nor offer an explanation. She'd found herself tending her breast as it healed, treating it not like a body part but a new pet, protecting her injury the way Marco had been protecting his.

"Like me," Marco said to Edith. "I liked that she said she was like me. I trusted her, we shared secrets."

This bed was similar to the silo, Edith thought dreamily. Two people in a private space, speaking in a vacuum together, watching their words float above in unfamiliar pleasing circles. She saw young Marco and sweet Goldberry touching each other tenderly where they'd been wounded, first love, damaged goods . . .

"Then she blabbed to everybody," Marco said flatly. Goldberry spread the news of his penis and its humiliating problems, his weeping. The hippie parents idled through the camping trip with typical orgiastic ignorance, but Marco suffered. Suffered the taunts of the small children, the lewd jokes of the older, everyone covering their genitals in imitation of his guarding gesture. And all because he'd trusted the wily Goldberry. "I concluded," he said, "that girls were evil. And boys dumb," he added, acknowledging his own part in the mix.

"I'm not evil," Edith swore. Now she no longer wanted to play the role of Goldberry, although she also understood that this girl loomed large in his unique history. She ran her thumb pad over the circumcised head of his penis, newly conscious of its shape, its open eye still vaguely sticky. How could she be evil, she wanted to point out, when she hadn't even insisted on a condom? "I'm *bossy*," she conceded, "but not evil. Occasionally I cry just to get my way, but I don't think that's evil. Is it?"

"You can be the exception," he said, but it sounded sarcastic.

"I'm so nice I have an IUD."

"But maybe that just means you're a slut?"

The word stung her; Edith willed the pain away. "Was Goldberry's benign cyst a true story?" she asked.

"Don't know, don't care. Old Goldberry went on to kill herself, later. And I'll tell you what, when I heard—this was high school, maybe first year of college—I wasn't all that unhappy. My mom acted like I'd be crushed, but I wasn't. Sad, but true: it didn't bother me that Goldberry was dead."

"How'd she kill herself?"

Now it was his turn to laugh too long. "You're funny," he said.

"Curious."

"Pills. The girls' way."

"And what's the boys' way?"

"Gun."

"Oh." She nodded. Once more she imagined herself his mother,

bearing the shocking news of the suicide, watching his cool, antiso-
cial reaction. He had felt, she thought, avenged. Even now he wasn't
ashamed of being unmoved. Had he not really grown up, since then?
Was he still holding a grudge against a dead girl named Goldberry?

"At least, that's how *I* tried to kill myself," he went on, "when I
tried. Gun." He took her hand from the warmth of inside the blan-
kets to the chill of the back of his head. Behind his ear he found the
place, a deep indentation in the skull, the path of a bullet that had
mostly missed.

"Baby," she said. Impossible not to keep falling for him. Edith
sensed the dangerous downward plunge. Perfectly the indentation
accommodated her finger. People fit together like missing puzzle
pieces, she thought, like plugs in drains, like ammo in weapons.

"Yeah. Boo hoo hoo." He cleared his throat. Edith put her face to
his and kissed him, not on the mouth but around it, the way you
might kiss an envelope containing a letter to your beloved, with
hope, faith. Yesterday she'd wakened in this bed, at this hour, with
only the cat for company, him and his odd tail and his surliness.

"Why?" she asked Marco softly.

"Why not?" He turned on his side suddenly, analytical, philo-
sophical. His hipbone stuck out in the aching way men's hips did, the
hollow socket below a thing of beauty. Their legs were hard, their
stomachs soft, they had dented heads and queerball parents, ironic
distance and sudden churlishness. These were the men she chose.
And the more she loved them, the more they thought her a chump,
until they finally had to break her heart. Which, she was starting to
see, must also be her choice. It was broken, and then, miraculously,
reassembled. Like a china sugar bowl, fraught with hairline frac-
tures. Or maybe more like a heavy lump of clay, dropped so often on
the floor and pushed so frequently back into shape that its identity
seems merely proximate, recognizable but peculiar. She had, she
guessed, an odd heart. Her mother had certainly seemed to think so,
warning her not to be too nice. Nice, but not too nice.

Marco was retracting. Edith felt distance opening between them like a sinkhole. She pressed her mouth against his to close the gap. He bit her, then rolled on top of her, hard and heavy and hot, and Edith felt tears form at the pleasure of his weight, at being pinned, at the knowledge of its merely temporary giftlike fact. She did not want to fuck, but it seemed the only way to keep him. Edith missed the moments following sex more than the sex itself. Intimacy, unlike orgasm, needed company. Her grandfather's dildo had taught her that, long ago.

"You're not feeling sorry for me, are you?" Marco asked, dabbing at her wet face.

"No," she said. "No, no. I was thinking about my Peepaw. Maybe I thought I was going to find a gun when I was rummaging around in his drawers?"

"You probably would have, if you hadn't gotten sidetracked by the wienies."

The cat mewed piteously now at Edith's closet door, weary and worn out, the prisoner in his cell, crying tiredly because hope, in the absence of his fiercer traits, he could fall back on. Edith pictured Marco's fish four flights up, circling their lonely jars.

"Why do we tell each other these childhood stories, anyway?" Marco asked. "I show you how I was a mess, you show me how you were a mess, we go tit for tat, like some weird competition to see who's the most fucked up. I say I sucked my thumb until eighth grade, and you say you sucked your *brother's* thumb—no, his *toe!*— and it went on till you were in *college,* the two of us telling just what total freaks we are, outdoing each other with our . . . what*ever*ness. Then what?"

"Then I know you?"

"Then you know how I'm *weak,*" he corrected.

"I don't even *have* a brother. To suck the toe of." Edith sighed, waiting for inspiration. It was exhausting to have to keep revising the way she felt about him; her stomach was tense with the effort. She eventually said, "Did you want to let me know how you're *not* weak?"

Marco rose above her, a warm wave of his body's odors rising with him, and—while she looked into his eyes—he fanned his hands before her face, thumb to thumb. Was this to be his demonstration? The bigger animal's brute ability to overtake the smaller, strangle life from her? He had large thick-fingered hands that he had used all night as if they were mittened, like paws, stroking Edith repeatedly. It was behind one of these big hands he'd hidden the CD, *yoink*, right into his shirt. Now he placed them at his own throat, like a ruff, and Edith's fantasy—spun swiftly and with brilliant vividness, in which her mother was notified that Edith had been murdered in her bed, unknown sperm still swimming blithely inside her—dissolved. He peered sincerely into her eyes with his own bugging ones, bloating his cheeks as if to wring his own neck, squeezing with fierce and fearsome passion. Edith swallowed with difficulty, as if those thumbs were bruising her throat.

He abruptly loosened the grip and dropped his forehead to hers. He was damp with sweat. "That was me, being a beta," he said. "Sometimes I jam their jars together and they see each other. Then they flare their necks and crash at the glass. They'd kill themselves, if I let them."

"You have a strange M.O.," Edith said.

He laughed. "*I* have a strange M.O.? You afraid?"

"Not of you," she said. And she wasn't. She was afraid of herself. She was afraid of tomorrow, of later, of forever.

"*Owww!*" said the cat. He repeated himself, and held the note like the hated opera singer, a lonesome creature swallowing a sword. It sounded like dying. Edith could not *not* go and release him; he shot through her legs and across the room, as if he might plow headlong into the oven, which waited at the end of his run. He seemed angry enough that he might never come near Edith again.

When she turned to the man in her bed, he was rising to leave, as well. "Have you seen my shirt?" he asked, ready to hide himself inside it, ready to steal himself from her.

When she first was in his presence, she had not noticed him until he stole the CD. That gesture had broken his camouflage, set him apart from the others. She herself had stolen a lot of things—she had a sense of deserving them, of needing them, earrings and knick-knacks and money and mementos—including her grandfather's dildo. It required two C batteries. It was seamless white plastic. Its switch made it vibrate and emit a buzz; it was not unlike holding an electric knife. She had fitted it where she knew it belonged and scared herself. Currency sizzled like lightning. Could she be electrocuted by a battery-powered device? That's how it felt—twitch, sneeze, forgetfulness, whimper—and it took her a little while to understand that the sensation was one of pleasure.

An uncanny pleasure, overwhelming, singular, frightening, addictive. Edith understood, at age eleven, that nothing good could come of it. Like the device's batteries, her body might wear out, might stop offering up the surge and immersion. And what if that feeling became the only one she wanted? So, after a few weeks, she threw away her scary toy, wrapped it up in a bag and rode her bike to the nearest Yellow Hen and stuffed it deep inside the Dumpster. Was that what it had taught her, that pleasure was illicit? That it would have to be renounced?

Was that why she made no move, no sound, to stop Marco from stepping through her front door and disappearing?

☞ *Irony, Irony, Irony*

*L*ionel took off Elaine's underwear in the yard. She'd spread a tatty blanket over the grass and fallen onto it; the summer sky above her was jam-packed with unknown constellations.

"If my parents open their curtains, they can see us," she whispered. Lionel hesitated in undressing her; it was freezing in the mountains, even in June, and goose bumps had risen on her stomach and chest. They'd been drinking rum and smoking marijuana: sticky, sweet—like youth. They laughed about Elaine's parents, whose bedroom window went dark a few minutes later. Their sex was heedless and exciting, as if between strangers. Afterward, they ran to the house wearing various garments, wrapped clumsily in the damp leafy blanket, leaving Elaine's panties in the yard, where her father found them in the morning.

They were a bright white; he thought he'd located one of his hankies.

Besides handkerchiefs, Elaine's father carried other mementos of bygone times: a signature ring, a pocket watch, a money clip. He belonged to the generation on its way out, one unable to wholly recover from the Depression or the Second World War, one that understood itself lucky simply to survive, a generation baffled by the whining one that followed it.

Some of his habits, which came with the territory, annoyed his offspring. He was cautious with money and took finances unnecessarily seriously. He did not believe gender irrelevant. Feminists made him defensive, homosexuals made him queasy, the Japanese made him nervous, addicts made him impatient, although blacks, as a rule, he felt an obligation to pity, still influenced as he was by the stretch of the 1960s and civil rights. Explosive displays within (and without) the family embarrassed him. He thought children should be seen rather than heard.

Other traits of his pleased Elaine and her siblings. For example, he had a gentleman's chivalry and would not tolerate rudeness toward Elaine's mother, to whom he'd been steadily married for forty-three years. He wished to protect his daughters. He did not want to know the inner workings of their lives, but he could not rest without assuming the general outer shape of them safe and intact. He honored the cocktail hour, and when they arrived at this house, he had waiting their favorite drinks, a margarita for Mary, dry red wine for Elaine, pink champagne for Dini. His son, with whom he had troubles, would drink whatever there was the most of.

This was the summer home, the frame house in the Rockies, the place where Elaine's family collected to remind themselves how badly they got along. Because the house stood empty for nine months of the year, the primary activity of the summer was mending its damage: screens, plumbing, painting. The side yard had seen the weddings of three of the four siblings; the fourth, Jonathan, seemed to be homosexual (the sisters were still debating; their father would have been appalled to learn what they thought). The original family had fit easily in the house—plenty of bedrooms, adequate bath—but now had grown too large: three husbands, six grandchildren, a new baby on the way. The small children slept like dogs: on the couch, on the porch, on the floor.

Elaine and her husband and children always came first, spending the whole summer in Telluride, while the others wandered in and out. Her parents established what they called "base" here, RV in the drive, extension cord attaching them to the house, and then they made side trips in the little Toyota they towed around behind their monstrous camper. Elaine's younger sister, Dini, appeared on the Fourth of July with her husband the misanthrope and her large belly, morosely pregnant. No one thought her ready for it. And Elaine, fearing her own unwanted, indiscreet pregnancy, sighed heavily. Had she consulted her mother, she would have been told, not for the first time, that her two sisters had been accidents. "Accidents," her mother would say, "but not mistakes." The oldest and the youngest, the first and the last, the unintended parentheses around Elaine and Jonathan. Her mother would have advised having the baby; she would have extolled—overextolled—the virtues of unplanned children.

Elaine, who already now had a boy and a girl of her own (both planned), indulged the fantasy of another baby, another pregnancy, knowing she would not follow through. She and her husband Lionel didn't have the requisite vigor for another child; it would exhaust them, the way her mother's last child, baby Dini, had exhausted her, leaving her dazed and depleted, emotionally anemic. Perhaps Elaine's mother had realized earlier, after Jonathan came along, that the household teams were no longer evenly matched, that the parents, outnumbered, would surely lose.

Elaine's youngest siblings were the closest of the grown children, separated from Elaine and her big sister, Mary, by their dependence on their parents, whom they resented because they were still financially beholden. This, despite Jonathan's being thirty years old and owner of his own business; this, despite Dini's marriage. It did not appear that her parents lorded the situation over Dini and Jonathan, though Elaine supposed they must, unwittingly.

Jonathan and Dini liked to complain about their mother and father, and Elaine and Mary would feel obliged to act as ambassadors for parenthood, their mission to explain why their mom and dad did what they did. Without Jonathan, Dini might surrender, but with Jonathan on her side, she would not relent: her parents were hideous, controlling, insufferable.

Mary, the oldest and most sentimental, had the shiny gloss of tears in her eyes; she couldn't bear their rancor, it broke her saintly heart.

"Why do you keep coming back to see them?" Elaine asked them, sincerely curious. Neither had an answer, although Elaine thought she understood their vain hope: that some day their parents would grasp who they truly were, and love them anyway.

When he wasn't egging on Dini in her tirades, Jonathan spent most of the reunion week underneath his motorcycle, either genuinely repairing it or pretending to, appearing for meals with oil on his clothing, black beneath his fingernails, an odor of machinery in his hair. Every morning, his shower lasted until the hot water turned tepid. Wearing only a towel around his waist, he stood on the sunny front porch and blew his nose over the railing. Elaine's five-year-old son was taking lessons, using his finger to close one nostril, leaning over and honking into the grass.

"Doesn't that destroy brain cells?" Dini asked, watching from the kitchen. Her clothes, because she refused to wear maternity outfits, strained against her body, leaving gaps, revealing her popped navel like a button.

Elaine said, "Women never do things like that, have you noticed?"

He was good with children, but Jonathan said he didn't want his own. Their father frowned, declaring—in the same peremptory tone he'd once used to advise a military stint—that of course Jonathan would change his mind when the right woman came along. The sisters exchanged glances while Jonathan turned red. They liked the idea of having a gay brother. It was novel and exotic; getting him out of the closet was their current chore, worrying about mortal disease would come later.

Jonathan had used to have a gang of friends here in Colorado, he'd been the popular one. A photograph of them had hung above the refrigerator forever, dimming, accumulating dust, the five boys all perched shirtless in their jeans, smoking their cigarettes, languishing on the hood of a sky blue Mustang that had, over time, faded a radiant white. This summer Jonathan took down the photo and blew it off, then left it lying on top of the refrigerator instead of hanging on its proper nail. "They're all dead but me," he told Dini.

"How can that be?" Elaine asked later, bewildered by the news, staring at the same photo while Dini angrily threw together dinner; it was her turn.

"They were stooges," Dini told her. "Wack jobs, losers. I slept with three of them," she added, and Elaine wouldn't give her the satisfaction of asking which three. Though she was only twenty-four years old, Dini had managed a lot of sleeping around.

There were Carl and Dward and Lenny and Dave, her brothers' friends, the small-town prodigal sons, lecherous and dull, their boyish grins shining up at Elaine from overexposed 1979. On nights when she couldn't find her own fun, Elaine used to condescend to ride around with them, listening to their eight-track tapes, drinking their Coors. The catalog of their deaths could not surprise—drunken drowning, high-speed car crash, overdose, elk hunting fiasco—but the fatal freakish statistic of Jonathan's survival made Elaine feel swung into another era, like his mother, his protector.

"Tough shit if people don't like mushrooms," Dini declared, dropping into her burbling pasta sauce handfuls of the spongy fungus.

"I hate mushrooms," Elaine's son said later, at dinner.

"So do I," said Elaine's father.

"Me, too," admitted Mary and all four of her children.

Dini grinned, eating her own mushrooms as well as her nephew's and father's, watching the pushed aside piles grow on the other plates.

"Maybe you'll give birth to a toadstool," Elaine said to her.

"Or maybe a toad," said Jonathan.

*   *   *

At night, they walked around town, a family parade, the children in front, the grandparents bringing up the rear. They made the same comments they made every summer, pointed out the same landmarks, disparaged the same developments, disputed the same history, misremembered the same memory. They ambled through the art galleries and they bypassed the seductive beery entryways of bars. Inside the picture window of a tavern called Total Liquidation sat a placid mountain lion wearing a collar and leash.

"That's different," said Elaine's mother.

"*I* want a lion," the children whined, hands pressed to the glass.

"*I* want a drink," whined Dini, *her* hand pressed to her tummy. The mountain lion blinked lazily, its tongue curling out of its mouth for an instant, making the children jump back.

Longtime locals called hello; the eight o'clock curfew siren wailed. The air went suddenly cold and the stars popped on. At home there was the bustle of baths and toothbrushing, evening wheedling and tears and the *shush* of pajama feet on linoleum. The dining table became the bridge table, lighted like a campfire in the center of the settling, whispering dark.

"When are you leaving?" asked Mary as she dealt cards. She had few talents beside caretaking. She liked to know itineraries and plans; she had a flair for cooking huge quantities of bland food and keeping her patience long past the point when others had lost theirs. They called her Sister Mary because she was too angelic for her own good.

"Miss Manners advises the following phrasing," Jonathan corrected his sister: "'How long will you be able to stay?'" He was methodically scooping up bites of cold cereal, using a soup spoon and a mixing bowl instead of their ordinary counterparts. Elaine, who'd purchased the last batch of groceries, resented her brother's voracious appetite. He seemed to be loading up at her expense, storing away fuel for the long winter.

"I'm out of here day after tomorrow," he continued. "Head over to Tahoe, check out the clubs."

"We're not leaving until school starts," Elaine said. She and her sister Dini were the only ones still on academic schedules, the only ones to have the whole summer free for Telluride. Their mother and father had retired from teaching and now liked to travel around during the summers; grown accustomed to hotels, to their humming recreational vehicle in the driveway, the shabby house was no longer comfortable to them; they only stayed in town for a few days before zipping away, off to Yellowstone, Glacier, Mesa Verde, now back for the annual reunion, due to leave soon for San Diego. Sister Mary was a dietitian in Dallas and took her annual vacation to come oversee her family; Jonathan owned a bar in New Orleans and came and went as he pleased on his big dangerous Harley; and Dini was simply broke, looking for the cheapest place on the planet she and her husband could crash.

Mary's husband and Dini's husband had the same first name, Bill, which Jonathan found endlessly amusing, as the two men couldn't have been more different. Mary's Bill delivered mail and had a knack for narrating the obvious—"Well, here we are eating," he would cheerfully note, or, "Guess I'll get myself a Kleenex now"; Dini's Bill never said anything. He hung around in the attic bedroom with his shirt off, listening to headphones and reading library books. Thirty years old, he was a perennial graduate student, holder of three master's degrees—art history, French literature, creative writing— and no career. Elaine supposed that in a clan of teachers—her parents, herself, her husband—someone like Dini's Bill had every right to expect tolerance, even encouragement, but nobody had much patience for him. All three sons-in-law, even Lionel, passed into eclipse in the presence of the larger family. Elaine could hardly recall her husband's full personality; he seemed lusterless and incomplete.

"We'll leave with Mom and Dad on the thirteenth," Mary let them know for the third or fourth time. All week long, the family recited the same lines, as if in rehearsal for the real performance.

The thirteenth was the same day that Elaine and Lionel had set aside for a trip to Montrose, the nearest city with a clinic. They'd asked Dini to watch their children. They would wait until everyone was gone so that they wouldn't have to explain their excursion: Elaine had scheduled an abortion, Lionel a vasectomy. It seemed wise to have both procedures done concurrently, a separate but equal ritual, a solemn ceremony of finality. And they wanted to do it before their wedding anniversary, which was a few days later. They'd been careless on the lawn, seven weeks ago, in June, but they approached the problem reasonably, maturely, Lionel finally submitting to a vasectomy after his squeamish objections of the last few years. Elaine had thought she might finish her fertile life without having to have an abortion, a luxury almost none of her friends had enjoyed, but if she had to get one, she supposed now was better than other times in her past.

"We have our children," Lionel had reminded her, patting her on the back. "We're financially solvent, our marriage is good." But Elaine resented that paternal pat. She hadn't even wanted to purchase an early pregnancy kit, since the only other times she'd bought them were when her children had been conceived, intentionally. She'd only had good associations with the process, the urinating in the little cup, the wait for a pink dipstick. Instead, she'd insisted on going to the Telluride OB-Gyn, who only came around every Thursday, like the bookmobile, and who had told her congratulations, she was expecting.

"Jonathan!" the children called now from their dark makeshift beds. They preferred him, his tastes resembled their own. "Jonathan, tell us about Tommy Torso!" Elaine, who was dummy, leaned away from the bridge table to listen. Outside the earshot of the other adults, Jonathan conjured up Tommy Torso, the loathsome boy with no arms or legs, who propelled his skateboard with his big calloused nose, a boy so gloriously ugly and unkind even his own mother didn't love him.

"We love him," the children swore. "We love Tommy Torso."

*   *   *

"Who will drive home?" Lionel asked on the evening of the twelfth. They were whispering in bed after many games of cribbage and bridge and charades. The children had stayed up late; popcorn had been popped, toddies poured, old record albums resurrected and played on the ancient player, Sam Hinton, Buffy Sainte-Marie, Glenn Miller.

"Afterward, neither of us will be able to drive," Lionel said. They began laughing, covering their faces with pillows so that the others wouldn't hear. It was hopelessly hysterical. Elaine had drunk more toddies than anyone else, just to keep her mood up. She didn't want to think about tomorrow. She didn't want to feel the way she felt: wrong, as usual.

"Dini will have to come with us," Lionel said.

"With the children? There won't be anyone here to watch the children if Dini drives."

"Except Bill."

"Right. Bill." They laughed more, until Elaine threatened to hyperventilate, to burst into tears. Her emotional state was an explosive cocktail churning inside: hormones, guilt, liquor, fear.

"Bill could drive and Dini could stay here," Lionel suggested.

"I don't want Bill to drive. I think Bill is philosophically opposed to the automobile." Elaine noticed that she was having difficulty with *philosophically* so she repeated it—"philosophically, philosophically"—until she didn't stumble.

"We'll have to all go together," Lionel said, pulling her close and folding her in, damping down her restlessness. "An outing."

In the morning Elaine had a terrible headache even though she hadn't mixed alcohols, had stayed within a single family—the scotch one—the way she'd heard to do to avoid hangover. She felt betrayed. Downstairs, her mother was busy making beds, delegating duties to the grandchildren, opening cupboards and directing what went where, occasionally calling for one of her daughters to stir the oatmeal or check on the biscuits. This was the traditional farewell breakfast, gluey and filling.

"Do you know what Jonathan told me?" Elaine's mother said to her as they pulled plates from the cabinet, knives and spoons from the drawer.

Elaine's head throbbed and her stomach roiled; her eyes felt like rubber balls. "What did Jonathan tell you?"

"He said he'd never have children because he couldn't stand what happened to them." Her mother held the napkins in her barely quaking hands; there was a time, not so long ago, when Elaine would have delighted in her mother's distress, would have felt victorious. "Do you understand that, Elaine?"

"No, Mom, I don't." Elaine understood it perfectly; she'd successfully squelched a similar feeling when she'd decided in favor of having her own children. "Don't think about it."

"Well, of course I will. He'd be such a good daddy, your brother." Her mother stepped away from the real issue so dexterously Elaine was tempted to tell her the things her mother refused to know.

"I always wanted a slightly different kind of mom," Dini had told Elaine the day before. "I wanted the mom who let her kids smoke and curse in front of her."

"I wanted the mom who liked to go shopping," Sister Mary had confessed. "The one who sewed clothes and dressed her kids up like dolls."

Elaine had hesitated; her sisters each wanted the kind of mother they themselves were or would be. What sort of mother was she, Elaine wondered? But the truth was that her mother wasn't the only family member whose casting she would have altered. There would have been a more lax father, one less invested in the outmoded past and, as a consequence, less injured by the present, a wilder older sister who might warn her about the dark slutty side of a girl's life, a jock brother who could protect her in the arenas her father had no access to, and an adoring younger sibling, male or female, it didn't matter which, who liked to follow orders. But her real sisters were waiting to hear about the mother she secretly desired. "I wanted to live on a horse farm," she finally said. "I wanted a couple of stable hand parents."

"Judy Garland," said Sister Mary. "Mickey Rooney."

"The suicide and the midget," Dini had said. "Perfect."

"Or maybe I wanted some glamorous academics," Elaine speculated. "Sort of *Who's Afraid of Virginia Woolf*-ish." Her parents' academia was not Ivy League but of a commuter college variety.

"Good-bye, good-bye," Elaine's children called to the family as the cars pulled away, caravan style, Jonathan's roaring motorcycle in the lead, his bandanna a receding flash of red.

"*I* want a motorcycle," Elaine's son said, bursting into tears. "You wouldn't let me get even one ride!" he accused Elaine.

"I miss my grandma," said the three year old, also beginning to sob.

Everyone felt tragic; disbanding made them think of death, Elaine supposed, its chilly guarantee falling now like a vapor.

"Who wants to go on a trip?" Lionel finally asked, clapping his hands together to dispel the fog, to inspire levity.

In the car, the little girl began her babble. "Snapper snapper, get me out of here! Thank you, sir, here's your bumbershoot." To everything, she responded with this stuff.

"Is she normal?" Dini asked.

"Of course," said Lionel. "They all do this."

"Dad called her a whippersnapper, I think," Elaine told Dini, who was driving in order to get a feel for the big strange family vehicle Elaine and Lionel owned. They kept lurching; Dini kept blaming the car.

"Grandpa said I had a big head," the boy put in.

Dini jumped at this, accelerating around a curve and sending everyone leaning left. "Here Dad goes, insulting the next generation.

No wonder we all have inferiority complexes; he bagged on us constantly."

Elaine was tired of defending her parents; in her opinion they all had *superiority* complexes, anyway. She had nothing to say; neither did her husband, who was thinking about surgery on his testicles. Finally Elaine said to her son, "Honey, you *do* have a big head. And I should know, since I gave birth to you."

Dini groaned at the thought of giving birth.

"This whole pregnancy thing *sucks*," she said.

"They hate it when you say 'suck'," Elaine told her. "Watch Mom's face next time. She kind of cringes."

"You think I don't *know* that?" Dini asked. "You think I don't know every little thing that pisses them off?"

After a while, the boy said, "I'm *car*sick."

"Close your eyes."

"Open the window."

"Give him water."

"Bumbershoot, bumbershoot," said the girl. "Toochi, toochi, I have a tail."

"Jonathan would think our trip was funny," Dini told them. "Irony, irony, irony." Outside, Ralph Lauren's ranch went by; a moment later, there *he* was, jogging on the highway, surprisingly short. "Jonathan calls him 'the wee haberdasher'," Dini said. "He's got a ranch the size of Idaho and he jogs on the highway. What a dope."

"Haberdasher," said the girl. "Haberdasher."

"What's irony?" the boy asked.

"For the clothes," said the girl. "With a board and the iron." She slid her pudgy palm along the front of her car seat to illustrate. "I want Jonathan," she said sadly. "Where is Jonathan?"

"Mama and Daddy are going to the doctor," Elaine told her children at the hospital parking lot. "You guys get to see *Seven Dwarfs* with Aunt Dini."

"*Seven* Dwarfs, *Seven Dwarfs!*" shouted the girl. "You hear that, Sammy? Seven Dwarfs."

"I don't want to go with Dini," the boy said in a voice Elaine recognized as provocative, probing. "I already saw *Snow White.*" He needed his parents' attention; something was going on and he knew it and he wanted someone to say so.

"You can wait in the waiting room," Elaine said. "But it's deadly dull, and little Beanhead here will be a pest. She'll eat cigarette butts and bother people."

Lionel, slow to recognize Elaine's strategy, pleaded, "Just go with Dini, Sam. Do what we ask, please." Lionel had been an only child; in Elaine's opinion, he had no idea how a real family worked.

"I don't want to," Sam declared.

"So he stays here," Elaine said, opening her car door and hopping out. Her nausea stirred up again like a flashback, like nostalgia. "Just don't complain later when you missed the movie and the Skittles and the popcorn and the Coke. Then it'll be too late." She wished her sister would step in and make a bid for Sam, cheerlead for her own funness, but Dini clearly felt her feelings had been hurt and was sulking.

"I'll go," Sam finally said, twisting his face from his mother's kiss.

Dini drove off with them, squealing around the corner. Elaine watched the backs of her children's heads disappear.

She said, "She's not taking them to see dwarfs; she's taking them to something rated R." Anger swelled in her like a balloon.

"She wouldn't do that," Lionel said.

"Of course she would." But Elaine laughed; there was satisfaction in knowing something so surely.

"Later, alligator," Lionel told her at admissions, pinching her soft bottom. She didn't want to be touched right now, especially on the bottom. "Don't be scared," he added.

"Yeah yeah yeah," she said.

*   *   *

"Nobody who performs vasectomies should be named Dr. Dick," Lionel said on the way home.

Dini said, "My OB-Gyn always tells the same joke: 'At your cervix.'"

"You're sitting in the wahwah seat," said the boy to his sister.

"Am not!"

"The wahwah seat."

It was a customary car argument.

Though he claimed not to be tired, Lionel fell asleep first on the trip back, his hands cupped chastely on his lap, protecting the remainder of his tender bunch of genitalia. Then the girl closed her eyes, and then Elaine dropped off, drugged, dreaming of R-rated chase scenes and her brother's dead friends. Having foreseen general sleepiness, she had arranged Sam in the front bench seat beside Dini, to keep her company. But even reliable, vigilant Sam could not resist shutting his eyes, and soon lay his sweaty head on Dini's shoulder so that steering was difficult.

While Elaine's little brood slept, Dini drove eighty miles an hour atop the dangerous cliffs.

At the dark summer house, she braked before pulling into the driveway just to stare at the familiar face the door and windows made, the porch slats like a broad wicked smile in the cold street-light. Bats flew crazily, as if someone were throwing them around. Her Bill seemed to have gone out, not bothering to leave on a lamp for their homecoming.

In that second Dini let herself feel utterly sorry for herself, let self-pity collapse around her like a smelly tent. Her life wasn't going to be anything like her parents'; it wasn't even going to be like her sisters'. It was going to be a lot harder. She allowed a tear or two to leak down her face; she prodded her own belly until her baby woke up and rolled over. Then she recovered and turned off the engine, opening her door to fill the car with bright light and a harassing metronomic beeping.

"Home," she told her passengers.

On the answering machine were messages from Mary and their mother: everyone had arrived safely from their day on the road. "It was a heck of a trip," Sister Mary's cheery voice admitted, "but we made it, of course."

"Hah," Elaine scoffed, "they think *they* had a trip," trudging toward the bathroom with a hand on her abdomen, a damp pad between her legs. "Who's going to carry in the kids?" she demanded of her pale husband and her irritable sister.

"*I* feel like a goat kicked me in the gonads," Lionel said. "How about you?"

"Ditto," said Elaine. "That hungover hell, that postpartum wooze."

"Prepartum, here," said Dini.

"We're hopeless," Lionel declared.

"Yes, but who's the most hopeless?" Dini asked, squatting over a footstool, her skirt blooming around her like a flower. "Just leave them there," she said, about the children.

"No," Elaine told her peevishly, already planning to wake them in a few minutes and make them walk. "No, I'm not going to just leave them there." Dini had a lot to learn about parenthood, she thought; Elaine sort of envied her her innocence while also being exasperated by it.

"Snapper snapper, get me out of here, you beanhead," said the three year old in her sleep. She clung to Elaine's knees until Elaine lifted her, feeling a rush of warmth between her legs as she did so. But she knew carrying her daughter wouldn't hurt her. Her baby needed to be held, and she felt nothing but good, warm with sleep, affectionate, easy. She was, after all, Elaine's last baby. In front of her, Lionel faltered as he lifted Sam.

"Did you see dwarfs?" he asked the boy.

"I told you, I already *saw* dwarfs." Sam dropped his head on his father's shoulder.

Before they went inside, Lionel asked Elaine if he should go look for Dini's Bill.

"What would you do if you found him?"

He shrugged.

"Then I see no point in looking."

Later, the three grown-ups turned on lights and made toddies, dealt out cards, and tuned in a distant gospel radio station. "Brothers and sisters," a woman sang, "welcome me in."

"She's a big fatso," Dini guessed. "A big black fatty." She and Elaine cracked sunflower seeds and made a soggy husk pile between them the way they always did, as if that might help them feel normal. From where the children slept, on the couch and the easy chair, came heavy, faithful breathing.

Still, the house seemed empty without the others, as if a wind had blown through, stealing all familiar smells. The place lacked people—ones who had just been there that morning, and ones who had been there many years past; those who might be there in the future, and those who would simply never be.

⁀ *Palisades*

I am a good confidante, and I'll tell you the secret: never offer advice, merely listen. You may repeat, ratify, sympathize, query, even divulge a tidbit or two, whip up the objective correlative, but you must *never* give an opinion about what your friend should do next. Never, never, never.

The summer of my separation from my husband I became the confidante of two different people, Sarah Siebert and Joel Metcalf. I met them at a Spanish-language performance of *Much Ado About Nothing,* the translation of which was *A Lot of Noise for No Reason*; the two of them zoomed in on me as if my skepticism were emitting sonar signals. Sarah was a psychologist at the tiny local clinic where Joel was the general practitioner. In fact, they were the clinic's sole employees: owners, receptionists, physicians, bill collectors. Except for emergencies, it was only open in the mornings. The two of them covered every ailment in little Palisades, New Mexico, knew nearly all the secret maladies. They came at me from opposite sides of the park, sniffing through the crowd until I'd been found. I was accustomed, those early days there that summer, to being observed. The town would have to learn how to befriend tourists, I thought, how to lure rather than frighten. Palisades was like someone desperate for a date, that hardly veiled hunger and awkward leer in its face.

I suppose the town had not changed much since I'd first seen it, twenty years ago, with my parents. I'd come back because I held the memory like a beloved locket, inside of which was preserved a tiny distorted image of happiness. For five years, at the height of my parents' best time together, we had summered in Palisades. There was a bar called Fool's Paradise, still in operation, where they'd posed for a legendary family picture, my father squashing my mother in his arms like a duffel, as if to throw her onto the back of a truck, her shirt rucked up, sandal flying from her foot, breasts hoisted under his chin where my father showed his smirking teeth as if just about to take a bite out of that plump flesh. My parents look slapdash, negligent, debauched, certainly not like parents. Where was I, their little girl, while they were out drinking and yukking it up? Roaming the woods, I thought, a habit I hadn't yet forsaken.

"This is awful," said the wiry woman who'd approached on my left. But she seemed pleased by the performance's awfulness, as I was. Sometimes bad art made me laugh, other times it made me want to throw a tantrum, as if it implicated me, as if I, too, were bad art.

"Terrible," I agreed enthusiastically. On my chest I wore my six-week-old daughter, whose dusk fussiness had sent me walking the dirt roads of Palisades. We were joined by another cheerfully irritated presence. My first impression of Joel Metcalf and Sarah Siebert was that they were longtime rivals, competing for something, like siblings for a parent's love. But it turned out they were married to each other, a good fifteen years older than I—the age of my husband, more or less. Their marriage, like all marriages longer lived than my own, seduced me with its caginess. They sniped, they baited, they did not flinch. Their humor was bitter. They seemed worn-out and stringy like the old animals at the zoo, the mangy lion, the weary wolf. Many avoid the zoo lifers; you might prefer the young animals, the ones who don't yet know precisely what they're in for and keep bounding to the fence. But I was attracted to jadedness, preferring to think of it as wisdom. Precocious, I had always looked to my elders for instruction.

They were overly glad about my Ph.D.—Palisades was a town about to explode into a fancy resort, full of real-estate agents and skiers, developers and bimbos, everyone with what Sarah called well-defined "thigh meat." Joel made a circle with his finger near his ear to indicate general dingbattiness, widespread unworth. *A Lot of Noise for No Reason* was put on, he told me, as a nod to the Mexican construction workers who, during the day, laid brick and blew up tree stumps, while at night had nothing to do but drink and graffiti the alley Dumpsters. But nobody I noticed at the performance was speaking Spanish except the actors themselves.

"We're from New York," Sarah informed me.

"L.A.," I responded. The two snotty coasts, represented here in an alpine paradise, a dearth of intellect. That was okay by me; I was tired of talking to people intelligently. My husband had sent me away for the summer. "I *have* to be alone," he'd pleaded. He forgot to eat, often did not sleep, could most frequently be found staring at his own painful thoughts. Or he cried, which made me helpless with fear. He flexed his thick hands and boxed his own ears, a convincing piece of anguish. Other times, he was simply indifferent, living in the same house like an intolerant tenant, besieged by rather than bonded to his baby. So I took the motherhood leave my office offered and returned to the site of my finest childhood memories. My feelings were hurt; I claimed my daughter's hurt feelings along with my own since she was too small to suffer them. How could he bear to do without her, I wondered as I stroked the hot moist lump of her on my chest. It was not to be understood.

"I walk," I told Joel and Sarah when they asked what I did with myself all day. "I walk everywhere." As a child, I had followed on my parents' expeditions in search of butterflies in the Palisades mountains. My parents adopted hobbies together, and it was in this spirit that I'd suggested to my husband that he come with us, me and his new daughter, to collect flowers or observe birds, camp even. He'd looked at me scornfully, pitying my Pollyanna tactics. He sneered at the photo of my parents, the sexy way my father strong-armed my mother aloft, the nearly palpable swearword between my father's teeth, just above those succulent breasts. It was true that having a baby had made me soft; I was not the cynic he'd married, not the cigarette-smoking anorexic anymore, my frenetic prettiness lost along the way to a slack healthiness my husband had encouraged by being older, by adoring me, by broadcasting his good luck. His sudden estrangement was like a slap; I appraised my lapsed beauty in mirrors with a fastidiousness I thought I had safely put aside after marriage. My husband had grown both restless and bored, trapped by the very domesticity he'd once claimed to have sought. I counted on him to know what we were doing, and now he was at sea, floundering, sending me on a summer holiday as if to spare me the details. I rented my cabin by the week, set up Lily's portable crib beside my single bunk, and waited to be summoned home. When I lay awake at night, I listened to a silence so profound I could detect my own idling blood.

By day I walked. Hence began my intimacies with Sarah Siebert and Joel Metcalf, avid walkers themselves. The nervous energy of New York was no match for placid Palisades; they had navigated every trail, taken in every waterfall, stood on every precipice, crawled into every cave—in short, knew everything there was to know. Each had a preferred route, and I alternated days in their company, Monday, Thursday, Saturday with Joel, Tuesday, Friday, Sunday with Sarah, Wednesday alone because that was when they took their practices on the road.

On Wednesday they also met their lovers.

Sarah drove to Durango, Colorado, thirty-five miles northwest of Palisades, to visit the battered women at the Indian clinic. Her lover was a degenerate girl named Beth, a pierced, tattooed, methamphetamine-making felon who had a master key to the Fort Lewis College dorms and lived like a scavenging animal pest on the campus. Beth the Rat, I thought of her. They coupled on the bare mattresses of dorm rooms, snacked from candy machines, eluded security. "I haven't been so thrilled since seventh grade shoplifting," Sarah told me giddily. "There's not one redeeming part to it. She's the baddest bad girl I ever met." I felt sure the rat was taking money from Sarah, but Sarah's pleasure in the shabbiness prevented me from feeling sorry for her. She seemed to have erected a force field around her heart, made herself bulletproof by a tough stance, by an attitude of doomed expectation. She knew it could not end well, this tryst, but she seemed to look forward to the fallout. She was in it purely for the sex, and it was purely nasty sex.

"Look at this," she instructed one day, lifting her shirt to show me a puckered red scratch the length of her rib cage.

"Good God! What is she, a pirate?"

"Bed spring," Sarah answered proudly, appreciating her wound. "There was blood all over the mattress."

You wanted to spread news like this; I wanted to use it to illustrate to my husband that I was still interesting, having found the most outrageous characters in all of Palisades to hang around with. We could have a baby, these stories would indicate, and still be in the vicinity of the cutting edge. But my husband never answered the phone. He'd changed our outgoing message on the machine, giving my New Mexico number to anyone looking to find me.

Sarah Siebert was endearingly neurotic, compulsive, fearful, paranoid. She was terrified of all sorts of STDs and had insisted that the girl in Durango go in for tests. "But I'm such an *idiot*," she wailed as we trudged through the beautiful aspens, whose trunks watched us with their black-lined blind eyes, whose shaking leaves sounded like maracas. "I made her get tested *after* we'd already hooked up."

"'Hooked up'?" I said. "Is that a euphemism? I feel very out of touch."

"Fucked," she clarified. "But what kind of moron waits until *after*?"

"Most morons," I assured her.

"Fortunately, she was clean—well, she *says* she's clean—but what if she hadn't been? I just can't get over how insistent passion is, how irresponsible it makes you. I mean, I'm not a careless person. You've seen me—I double tie my laces so I won't trip. I've got a house full of safety devices because I can imagine every conceivable disaster, you can't believe my imagination, smoke alarm, radon detector, lead monitor, a cellular phone in the car, vitamin pills, I've been told I'm a hypochondriac, I get to the airport two hours before all of my flights, and yet I was willing to just forget all of that, completely go against character, for a moment of passion."

"It defies explanation," I said. It did, really. It was spectacularly desperate.

She was shaking her head at herself, but I suspected she was a little proud of her indiscretion. Didn't it prove she was spontaneous? Brave? Unpredictable? Capable of surprising herself? Maybe the ability to surprise oneself was the most necessary of tools as time marched on. I posited this to Sarah, who nodded thoughtfully. Every now and then I said something that made her glad I was her companion, her confidante.

"She's so quiet," she said of Lily, offering a rare acknowledgment of my ever-present burden.

"She doesn't need much," I said, kissing the fuzz of her scalp.

"Ha," said my skeptical friend, she of the wretched, degrading needs.

Unlike his wife, Joel was a romantic. His lover lived in Palisades, was married herself, an alleged friend of the family, and had had a miscarriage not so long ago. "April fifteenth," Joel said, "just after we'd made love."

"That's Lily's birthday," I commented. My husband had been waiting in line at the post office when she was born, our taxes in his hands, while I had been stoically turning down painkillers, pushing Lily through a ridiculously inadequate aperture into the world. Here in Palisades, Joel had been frantically driving through a spring blizzard, his lover breathing heavily in the seat beside him, on their way to his own health clinic, her praying, him inventing a story to tell Sarah, whom he'd have to summon for help.

"It was absurd," he said as we walked together in the July sun, "me giving her just the simplest plotline. 'You were hiking, and you suddenly had abdominal pain, and then, by coincidence, I came along and helped you down the mountain.' It was absurd and shameful, at the same time, me worried about getting caught, about losing her because of exposure. It was only after the firemen drove her up to Durango in the ambulance that I realized she might die. It's funny how the mind gets so sidetracked. I'm the one who told her husband," he added a moment later. "He's handsome, but only has one leg. They haven't had sex in years."

"Years?"

"Well, maybe now and then they sleep together, like on their anniversary. I guess she must have let him think he got her pregnant. But it was my baby."

Once upon a time, facts like this would have appalled me; but by then I'd been married four years, and although we made love eighty-two times our first year together, for the last six months my husband had not touched me. I asked Joel, "Why do they stay married?"

"Why do most people? They have kids, it's comfortable, they make a good partnership."

A partnership. Comfort. This was why Joel and Sarah stayed together, I thought. They had their clinic to run; they liked each other's company. Joel needed Sarah's biting intelligence; Sarah needed Joel's conventional presentability. Where would either be without the other? That night I sort of admired my husband's reluctance to acquiesce to a business arrangement, to get too terribly comfortable, to worry about presentability. He'd claimed he wanted to continue choosing our relationship. "I don't want to just love you," he'd said. "I want to be *in* love with you." Still, he baffled me. I loved Lily to distraction, and I mean that literally. Every week my new friends and their lovers spun into their different alliances—

hiked into the woods, sped to the dorm—while I wandered the quiet dirt roads with my baby. I loved that baby. I loved the clarity of our relationship. I loved the single-mindedness of my thinking that summer. Her father would either come back to us or not; his decision was out of my hands. The only thing *in* my hands was this baby, whose desires were clear, pure, essential. Tabula rasa. Loving her was a pleasure. It was a verb I could do all day long.

When she slept, I slept; when she woke, I attended. On the rare occasions when she slept and I sat restlessly waiting for her to wake and need me, when my exhaustion had been sated, when there were no dishes nor clothes to wash, no phone call to make, no book to read, no television to watch, well, then I looked up at the beautiful mountain out my window and let myself be the baby, cry and cry.

They knew nothing of each other's lover. They shared a kind of disdainful blindness to, and lack of respect for, the other, and could believe no one else would find their spouse attractive enough to bother seducing. "I wish Sarah would just admit she's a dyke," Joel said one day after a particularly toxic fight they'd had the night before. "She told me I was getting lazy and overprescribing antidepressants, all because I couldn't get it up in bed. Like insults are sexy."

"That's what makes you think she's a lesbian?"

"Oh, that, and other stuff." His vagueness let me know that he didn't seriously believe she was homosexual. My omniscience was tantalizing, limited as it was to this couple and their sexual peccadilloes. I had only scant knowledge of their other facets—and, it seemed to me, less information on my own sexual urges. Those had been back burnered by my husband's weepy renunciation, by the fact of Lily—her inception, development, birth, and now our sequestered summer in the mountains. Sometimes when she nursed I felt an erotic current zip briefly through my solar plexus, there and gone, tiny electric shock, not enough to hurt, just enough to scare.

Sarah was never quite as blunt about Joel to me—perhaps she

understood that my real allegiance was with him, one heterosexual romantic to another. And he liked my baby, it might have made him think of the one his lover had lost.

Sarah preferred the dramatic hike and Joel favored the steady one. I was in it mainly for the gainful use of time, and alternated trails willingly. With Sarah I climbed steep Wainwright Trail that went upward, upward, upward, both of us breathing so hard we could not really talk until we topped it, forty minutes later, and then descended through the aspen grove, over the quaint wooden bridge, through the fairy-tale forest, and down the more gently sloping path of the other side. Sarah's hike was a loop; you did not have to retrace your steps. Her hike took exactly eighty-five minutes and was a perfect aerobic workout.

Joel's hike was into the Sheep Creek Preserve, a former mine road now closed to motorized vehicles. It rose the identical number of feet as Sarah's hike—twelve hundred—yet you completed the climb much more casually, walking as if on a vaguely inclined treadmill until you reached the top, where you would find a stunning waterfall, straight off the Coors beer can. Joel and I would sit then, soak our feet in the shockingly cold runoff, and eat a snack. Sarah did not hike with food; she didn't even carry water, just a pack of cigarettes, Zippo lighter, and chewing gum. She smoked at the summit of our loop—another of her guilty bad habits that Joel was not to know about—then quickly came down. But Joel liked to bring along treats, brownies or biscotti, cheese and apples, a Thermos of coffee or a sport bottle of wine. He was a sensualist, often standing absolutely still beneath the rippling tree leaves, eyes closed, fingers pinching the air like castanets, smiling serenely. Our hikes were more languid than mine with Sarah; I bared my chest and nursed Lily with my feet in the stream, sunshine illuminating the fine blonde down on her skull, faithful pulse of her fontanel. We identified birds, revealed our childhoods, passed back and forth food and drink and disclosure. The baby, whom he loved to cradle in his arms. Joel, I felt on those days, was my true friend, and Sarah a curiosity, a lost strange soul I might aid. Joel had a better sense of humor, listened more attentively, and although he was engaged in a most torrid love affair, took time to inquire after my problems now and then.

"He's depressed," he diagnosed my husband. "Midlife crisis stuff."

It was polite of him. I liked that he wanted to reciprocate, to at least feign an interest in my life.

Sarah, on the other hand, probably had no idea what was going on in my marriage. If she did, it was because Joel told her. It occurred to me more than once that summer that I would have been a natural subject of conversation between them, perhaps a safe and salving one. They could have convinced themselves that I was their project, the odd young woman who, although abidingly intimate with the landscape, had not one friend in town other than them to call upon. What if I needed a ride to the real hospital, thirty-five miles away, some dreadful night or other? What if the baby became ill? They were looking after me, in my version of their version of our mutual entanglement. I was their good deed.

One day when I was walking home from the market I noticed a commotion at the entrance of the Wainwright Trail. Two police vehicles were parked there, the four officers all standing against one of the jeeps staring up, passing among themselves a pair of binoculars trained on something. I looked where they were looking. The sky was cloudy yet bright; it was nearing dusk and the air was cool. Lily slept on my chest and a plastic sack of groceries hung from my hand. Up on the cliffs stood a man. I had to blink, so bright was the glare, so small the figure. What was he doing? Why were the police watching him do it? And did I have time to go retrieve my own binoculars, set down the groceries, get back and watch?

I stood there waiting, like the others. Soon another car pulled up, this one occupied by a young man and woman. The man was out the door and running toward the police before the car had properly stopped. Friend of the jumper, I thought. He spoke to the cops, then ran back to his car. "Radio," I heard him say to his companion, who hadn't left her seat. Off they sped. Other traffic passed slowly, people glancing up because I was, because the police were. Up high on the cliff, the man wandered into the dark spruce trees behind the red rocks, then out, onto the cliff, then away from it. This activity might have been nervous, or it might have been meditative. It was hard to tell. At one point, he pulled off his shirt. That made my heart thump; it seemed preparatory to action, and I wanted action. The baby was hot and damp against me, like the package of internal organs she was, and the straps of my grocery bag were cutting into my palm— the weight of milk and juice and water, fluids.

When the man removed his shirt, a second figure stepped into view, someone who'd been in the trees, perhaps accounting for the constant motion between the spruce and cliff of the first figure. What were they doing? Both now stood at cliff's edge, beside each other. Were they holding hands? They were gesturing in some way, not frantically, not randomly, either. Down on the ground the tension was extremely high; a third police vehicle had arrived, and one of the first two had driven off, as if for some sort of rescue device, but what? To get to those two people would require the same long hike they'd made—and, since I'd been many times on the trail just under their cliff, I knew that they'd had to do some dramatic scrambling to arrive where they had. Their perch was not on the beaten path. A helicopter could have reached them, I supposed, one with a rope ladder. Nothing less. Nobody appeared to be dashing up the trail, and the sky, aside from the bright clouds, was free of interruption. Now the two figures retreated once more to the trees behind them and the tension on the ground lessened. I found myself impatient, checking my watch. Come on, I thought, get on with it. Jump. You found yourself saying that sometimes, didn't you? *Jump already.* You had other things to do, your eyes were watering terribly from looking into the glare of the sky, your baby was heavy, your favorite show was going to start soon on TV, and it was cocktail hour and despite the hot load on your chest, the air was growing a bit nippy out here without a jacket . . . but you couldn't look away, either. We observers were not together, below; we were separate witnesses to the mysterious drama above. I wondered what the others were thinking, if they, too, had admitted their desire for the couple to jump. Or maybe they honestly didn't share my desire. I reminded myself that there weren't many people to whom you could just say exactly what you thought, anyway, never mind that what you thought was not what most people thought or admitted to thinking, besides. I could have spoken to Joel this way, but it was my husband I missed suddenly. The emptiness seemed abrupt, as if he'd been abducted just now from my side, against both our wills. "Come on," I murmured angrily, "jump."

Were they praying up there? Practicing tai chi? In the throes of a mushroom trip? Were they aware of their audience, the cops and rubberneckers? Was the second figure a woman? A young boy? Was it a suicide pact? A marriage ceremony?

I never found out. You couldn't stand all evening craning your neck. Lily woke, the police drove away, I walked home.

On my next hike with Sarah, I told her about the figures on the cliff. We were passing just beneath where they'd been. Of course there was no sign of trouble. Nature rarely betrays our skirmishes on its surface. Sarah had heard nothing of this event, which meant, I supposed, that nothing definite had come of it. No wedding, no death, no EMTs at the clinic. She listened in a gratifying silence; she was a conversational snob generally, and you had to say something interesting or she would interrupt you with a wholly nonsequitous observation, as if she'd quit attending to your dull insight long ago, had gone wandering down her own thought path, and now had this to say. I didn't find it rude, although others might have. Rather her style seemed to suggest that she would do you the favor of preventing your becoming tiresome. She would rescue the chat, should you have gone astray.

"Another man?" she asked, predictably. She was intrigued at the notion of a gay couple on the cliff.

"Possibly. I couldn't see. The one had his shirt off, the other seemed smaller, either a woman or a boy."

"Hmm," she said. Then, unable to contain her news, she rushed on, "I was so late coming home last Wednesday, I had to tell Joel I'd dropped acid. I told him I couldn't drive home right away. I had to wait for it to wear off!"

"That is quite a lie," I said, impressed with its idiosyncratic precision, its airtightness.

"He couldn't complain, of course."

"Of course."

"I thought it was brilliant."

Joel's most recent transgression was also stunning. He'd left Sarah in their bed at three in the morning, climbed onto his bicycle, and ridden to Melanie's, where they'd made love in the garage, in her Volvo.

"What if Sarah woke up and found you missing? What if the husband came to the garage?"

"I don't know. I wasn't thinking. I just needed Melanie. And she was awake when I got there, sitting in her kitchen with the lights off, thinking of me, she said. I can't tell you how amazing it was to look through her kitchen window in the middle of the night and see her looking right back at me, so sad, so in love."

Not long after, I met Melanie. I wished I hadn't, because she was an uninspiring love interest, much better left to the imagination. Older than Sarah, she was also unattractive, running to fat, and wore a constant insipid smile. She seemed a fool; the rest I might have forgiven. It was hard to feature Joel distraught over her mortality, dashing to her in the middle of the night, loving her as much as he claimed he did.

We ran into her and her husband on Main Street, the limping cowboy with his hand tucked into the crook of her elbow. He was handsome and rugged, deferential, and when he released his wife's arm long enough to gently touch the sleeping infant on my chest, I was struck with guilt. Was it fair that I not only knew that his wife deceived him but that he had sex just once a year? And smug Joel, grinning and fulsome, couldn't I wipe that smile off his face? I had the fleeting urge to clear the air, which was also maybe to brandish my arsenal of information, say something to the husband, his wife, her lover, watch three expressions distort and crumple as if gunshot.

"Purty baby," Melanie's husband said in the old-fashioned accent of the West.

"Pleasure," Melanie said of our meeting, curtsying slightly.

"Corny, isn't she?" Joel said excitedly as we made our way up Sheep Creek. "And he's such a hayseed!"

On Wednesday he and Melanie hiked this same trail—except that at a crucial juncture, "up ahead, beyond that rock that looks like a sleeping cow," they swerved off the road, waded across the stream, and journeyed into the trees on the opposite side. "We have a blanket there," he said, "tied up in a waterproof stuff sack, hung from a branch."

"Very romantic," I said. "I'm impressed."

"Melanie *is* very romantic," he confessed, pleased that I thought so, too. "She's the most unsarcastic woman I've ever met. It's refreshing—you know *Sarah,* you know what I mean, she's such an absolute *bitch.* But Melanie's innocent as a lamb. Do you know what else? She prays. I don't know anyone who actually prays, seriously prays to a serious God, but Melanie does."

"Church on Sunday?"

"Yes, that, too. See? Here's the turn." He pulled aside a small mountain ash to show me the way he and his lover went every Wednesday. We paused, as if to observe a moment of silence, then proceeded, his step slightly quicker, as if the glimpse into his love nest had inspired him. I'm sure it had. I nuzzled Lily's head with my lips, to keep from . . . what? Judgment? Or jealousy? The naive devoted husband—lame, he was—troubled me. "She's terribly Catholic," Joel said chirpily. "It will probably be our downfall, her guilt."

"You always think you can circumnavigate deep character traits, don't you?" I said speculatively.

"Oh, definitely. I pooh-pooh her religion and next thing I know she'll be crying over the telephone, breaking up with me out of guilt, ready to confess everything to her husband and my wife. Confession is such a Catholic cornerstone." But he didn't sound concerned, not really. He actually believed he could derail her faith, that their love was larger than her Catholicism. Love was beautiful, I thought, the way it made you dumb.

My employer phoned me in August to see how motherhood leave was going. He was awfully delicate about my situation, not asking about my husband, not even broaching a question that would indicate I'd ever had a husband, let alone left him in Los Angeles. I was a legal secretary, and good at my job. The office missed me, as I knew it would, and Frank, the partner now on the line, missed me especially. At home, I was his confidante, in a formal, executive way. He used me to test his own instincts, nodding when his opinion and my own matched up, validated. Although traditional in his demeanor, Frank didn't particularly play by the rules of hierarchy at the firm. Every now and then we had lunch together. For Christmas bonus, he gave me pieces of art instead of additional money. I liked that. And I liked the art, which proved that we were friends—either we shared the same taste, or he knew me well enough to make intelligent guesses about mine.

"You'll be back on the first of September," he reminded me after we'd caught up on business.

"That's right. At the latest."

"And you'll bring Lily in to visit us."

"I will." I was touched that he knew her name, that he could say it so naturally. My husband called her *the baby* when he called her anything.

"Okay then," Frank said. This was his signature phrase, said with a sigh. Okay then.

" 'Bye, Frank," I said, abruptly nostalgic for his good manners, my job in his lovely office, my old life, the city of noisy angels he was standing in as he spoke to me. "Thanks so much for calling," I added, a burst of sentiment that would make him awkward but I didn't care. I was going to cry, I thought, I was *not* "okay then," and I needed somewhere to discharge a piece of emotion.

It was after a whole summer of listening to Joel and Sarah discuss their infidelities that I finally figured out my husband's. It would have been obvious to somebody who wanted to see it. I was walking with Sarah, who was despondent after having taken incredible pains to meet Beth in Santa Fe for a night only to have Beth cancel.

"I'm afraid I'll never see her again," she said, unable to rise wryly above the scene, incapable of attributing her fear to paranoia, inept at seeing the humor. She was scared, and all whimsy and sarcasm had left her as she realized the extent of her affection, the depths to which her worst-case scenario could reduce her.

Sometimes insight hits you like a hailstone: icy *ping* to the skull. I recognized in Sarah's state a familiar despondency, and knew suddenly that my husband had had an affair himself, contrary to his claims. Furthermore, it was the woman, whoever she was, who had called it off. I could almost mark the day, if someone had given me a calendar, not long after I'd become pregnant. That was when she kissed him good-bye.

"Are you in love with someone else?" I'd demanded eventually of his moroseness and tears.

"No," he'd sighed, "but I understand the desire to be in love with someone else." He went on to say that though he displayed symptoms, he was not planning to take the next step into adultery. It was too predictable, he said, an affair. He loved me, he said. He was unhappy with himself, he said. He needed *time* and *space*, those one-size-fits-all abstractions.

In fact, I'm sure he *was* unhappy with himself. I had no doubt that he was still unhappy. I knew he loved me, in some way, although not the way either of us would prefer. "I want to be *in* love with you," his voice spoke for the thousandth time on the merciless reel to reel in my mind. I had been attending to that line in order to ascertain the inflection, as if it were the key. I *want* to be in love with you. I want to be in love with *you.* He'd been *in* love with someone *else,* and that explained everything. And when even his baby's birth hadn't particularly rallied his love, that lack must have been the unbearable convergence of guilt and despair. Our summer separation now made sense to me. He was willing to miss the first few months of Lily's life in order to save his own.

My husband came clear to me there, but my own situation seemed instantly a swirl of murk and confusion. Why was I a thousand miles from home, standing on top of a mountain, listening to a woman I'd only met two months previous telling me about the state of her ravaged body and broken heart?

"I feel faint," I said, unexpectedly. "Would you take the baby?"

Startled, Sarah immediately began helping me unstrap the front pack. We both were surprised at my assertive neediness.

"I have to sit. Careful with her neck." I lowered my head between my knees, attempting to gain back my peripheral vision, my requisite oxygen, my sense of balance. I stared at a tick as it crawled onto my boot. Lily cried in Sarah's awkward arms but I couldn't worry. For the moment, for the first time in months and months, I was thinking only of myself.

I replayed my pregnancy like some beloved mysterious film, the highlights, the major scenes, the tender moments and the surprising ones, and then I revisited the small incidents, and all the minor players. Now, I was trying to guess who my husband's lover had been, what young girl or old flame. Was his lover more like nefarious Beth or foolish Melanie?

It incensed me that he'd had a lover, he who'd had dozens before we married, he who was supposed to have sown his oats, he for whom I was in line to be the second, trophy wife. His first marriage was supposed to have been the messy one, the one where he got things wrong, the test run, the mistake. I was still in my twenties, for godsakes; if anyone was going to commit adultery, oughtn't it have been me? But mostly I just suffered the humiliation of having been duped, betrayed, left alone with a faith in our happy life like the lone member of an abandoned religious order, its pathetic last nun.

I hadn't felt quite this alone since my parents had died. Orphaned, again.

I decided I wasn't going to wait for my husband to want me once more. I would go home regardless. I said good-bye to Sarah Siebert and Joel Metcalf. Never had I met two people more adamant about retaining those separate last names. They were sad to see me leave, their confidante, their audience, their dramas as yet unfinished. I donated money to their clinic, the newsletter of which I would read religiously, once home.

I took with me a baby who could hold up her own head and who smiled dazzlingly, faithful as a light switch, whenever she saw me. I had a good tan and calf definition. I had new knowledge, gained at the rare intersection of isolation and exposure, focus and leisure, a four-cornered limbo. It was captured there in my parents' picture, embodied in my friends' secret love lives, manifest in my husband's misery, waiting in my own future fate. You wanted two conflicting things. You wanted to be sitting in a comfortable leather recliner sipping fine wine and reading a passage of exquisite prose to your wise spouse for your mutual amusement, and you wanted to be having demeaning speed-demon sex in a seedy dorm room with a gorgeous soulless youth. You wanted a savvy, possibly unscrupulous business partner, and you wanted a devoted fool to pray at your feet. You wanted something solid; you wanted something fluid. They could not be reconciled except by a giant leap of faith. Between them lay the great paradoxical gap, the miserable marriage.

The image of Palisades I'd carried with me for so long, my parents in their racy embrace, was swapped for this year's model. Now, when I thought of that small mountain retreat, I would remember the couple I'd spied on the cliff, my secret desire to see them take each other's hand, and sail off.

➣ *Loose Cannon*

*A*ll of a sudden John Gamble was the responsible one. What happened? In his family he was supposed to be the black sheep, the pothead, the lazy, dirty, unemployed, undependable, immature, unserious one. Now his sister Lynnie was usurping his role.

First she'd wrecked her car on the way to his little southwestern village, calling him from the radio phone of a tow truck to ask him to come get her.

"*I* don't have a car," he'd told her.

"Me, either," she singsonged.

"I don't even have a telephone," he said, but of course she'd known that, since she dialed his neighbor's house.

"If you don't come I'm going to hitchhike." Their father had recently died, he who had prohibited foolish things like hitchhiking, things like riding ski lifts or dismantling television sets or balancing on the back legs of chairs.

"I'll come."

Responsibility was more bureaucratic than John Gamble might

have suspected. He was thirty years old but at the Avis counter at the airport he discovered, for the very first time, that a person had to have a credit card to rent a car. His neighbor Hernando Peños— who'd given him a ride the twenty miles into the city, who'd answered Lynnie's phone call, who'd provided an antifungal powder when the skin on John Gamble's feet and hands had begun mysteriously shredding away—lent him his Visa number, and soon John Gamble was driving to Dalhart, Texas, in a Chevy Impala with automatic windows. He hadn't been behind the wheel of a car in months. It wasn't until he switched on the stereo that he realized he'd forgotten his marijuana. Already, his reckless habits were abandoning him.

His ex-girlfriend would have been surprised, he thought. She considered him juvenile, though in a charming, harmless way. Near the end of their relationship she'd let herself get pregnant without consulting John Gamble, giving birth the previous winter to a little girl he had yet to meet. "You are nothing but Mr. Sperm, boy," Hernando had told him, clapping his own pelvis with his hands. "You are the spurt in the dark, just an X and a Y, isn't that so?" John Gamble supposed this was true, but he did not share Hernando's vexation. After all, it was Polly who'd chosen to become a parent, not him. Should he begrudge her that?

In another time, John Gamble might have talked with his youngest sister Lynnie about his feeble fatherhood. But she seemed to have misplaced her personality: all the good parts had vanished, leaving simple three-letter emotions—sad and mad—and a lot of empty space. She rode home with him from Dalhart in unsullied silence, John Gamble afraid to mention the sharp object in her duffel bag—lying between him and her on the seat—that was poking him in the thigh.

And so she came to live with him in El Oro, New Mexico, in the defrocked old church John Gamble rented. Because Lynnie made no comment about the crumbling adobe walls and slumping meatloaf shape of the place, because she failed to mention John Gamble's assortment of broken toys and pile of metal rebar lying in the cyclone-fenced yard, because she seemed to have become *incapable* of noticing his seedy eccentricities, John Gamble pointed them out to her, explaining about the grave markers he'd been creating from the rebar, rusty crosses adorned with plastic dolls or toy trucks that Hernando sold to tourists, netting John Gamble drug money.

"And I had an idea for a nursery business," he said of his hundred potted dead plants, dried sticks in their buckets, some dismal orange foliage like doll hair. "But I'm lousy with living things." Lynnie just looked at him vacantly as if waiting for the punch line.

Their mother, the widow, alone in the huge barnlike house in Kansas, paid to have a telephone installed at John Gamble's. These symptoms of Lynnie's—the crying, the despondency, the drunken anger, the carelessness—she had seen before. Her eldest daughter Joanne had tried to kill herself once; their mother wasn't going to take a chance on Lynnie's doing the same. She wanted to be able to hear Lynnie's voice. Despite John Gamble's misgivings—he was in principle antitelephone—he discovered he was relieved to have a connection to the outside world. He believed he might have occasion to call for help, whether professional or familial.

In the evenings, Lynnie drank too much and then phoned her friends long distance. She drank a sweet pink wine John Gamble associated with college sorority girls, with fingernail polish. Listening to her laugh and chat with her friends, he could convince himself she was fine, just fine, simply taking a break from her life. But in the mornings, when she woke groggy and listless, her eyes shadowy from lithium, her hair stringy and her attitude sullen, his faith in her sanity evaporated. She was nothing like a sorority girl; her fingernails she'd gnawed bloody.

After three weeks of tenderfooting around the issue, John Gamble finally asked what was wrong, exactly. Having to ask embarrassed him: he'd lost his brotherly hip. Lynnie studied him a few moments, distilling her problem, then said, "Nothing matters to me, not one thing in the world."

"So this started when Dad died?"

"No," she said, sneering. "This started a long time ago, like it does for everyone, when I was a kid. Didn't you ever lie in the dark and kind of *spin*? And really *know* that nothing meant anything?"

"Sure. But you get over that."

"No you don't. You start pretending. Well, I'm not pretending."

He was honored she'd chosen him for her collapse, but uncomfortable with her ennui. Where was it going? Over the phone, his mother said, "I feel like we're waiting for the other shoe to drop." John Gamble instantly conjured two boots—generic punk black—one fallen, the other dangling by a lace. He woke from nightmares about Lynnie, propelled from bed by panic to check on her, to climb up the church loft and listen for her sedated breathing. When their sister Joanne had tried to kill herself, no one had been prepared, no one had believed such a thing could happen. For weeks and months they'd simply been stunned. To this day, John Gamble couldn't pick up a kitchen knife without imagining his oldest sister drawing one up the length of her inner arm.

So with Lynnie, he was ready—perhaps too ready.

Winter came to the Rio Grande valley; leaves fell, frost glazed the ground every other day, and heavy bunches of mistletoe hung, green and lascivious, in the bare trees. Wearing a ski hood and work gloves, John Gamble left for his job at the pecan grove before the sun rose, before Lynnie woke, always muttering to himself a little prayer as he closed the front door, that she would allow herself to live through the day, until he returned home.

He walked to work on the empty highway, thoroughly resensitized to the world. The calls of birds had become distinct and isolated—starling, owl, dove—instead of artless noisy clatter. Since Lynnie had moved in, John Gamble was having peculiar moments of clarity. Her presence had given his life a sort of purpose—each morning, there was the same strategy to devise. She was his signpost, his crux. This clarity felt like adulthood, at last. And it also felt like congestion in his throat, the stuff of tears or the common cold.

There was little evidence to suggest Lynnie did more than sit idly at John Gamble's church all day long while he was away. He used to do this himself, skip work, get high and listen to music, study the covers of old record albums, forget to eat. But since Lynnie moved in, he hadn't missed a day at the groves, too ill at ease with her placid company, or perhaps trying to establish himself as a role model. Sometimes he arrived home to discover her holding a mirror in her hands, staring at her miserable face. Sometimes she colored in a coloring book. Sometimes she was still in bed, wearing their father's old pajamas. The building was dark—lit by the mute colors of stained glass, by the discrete disks of light thrown from floor lamps. Dirty dishes tottered in neglected stacks, water dripped patiently into the sink, and the air smelled of illness, of animal left too long indoors. Her ailment seemed to have sent her into hibernation: for hours she would gape from the open church door at the clay roads of El Oro like a bear from a cave, daunted by the sun.

He tried to give her things to do each day outside, "chores," he found himself calling them, the thin deceptions of a kindergarten teacher or camp counselor. He led her around his trashy yard, instructing her on feeding the two peacocks who hid out in the brush or watering the desert plants, but she was unreliable and John Gamble could never tell whether she'd done what he asked or not. Every now and then he realized he was about to say things their father might have, and in the same vaguely disappointed voice: "I thought we had an agreement." Or, "I don't want to have to make a scene." When the teenager he bought marijuana from came by with a lid, John Gamble sent him away.

Then basketball season began. Though John Gamble was not a sports fan, his boss at the groves wanted to reward him for turning into a reliable employee—the only English-speaking crew boss, holder now of a key to the indoor bathroom—and gave him season tickets for the university team twenty miles up the road.

"Look at my raise," John Gamble said, flapping the sheet of tickets at Lynnie, wondering what he could sell them for. Jokingly— maybe desperately—he asked if she wanted to go to the first game.

"Sure," she said dully. She pulled on her clothing—a pair of wool navy pants, a large flannel shirt, a soft, stained deerskin jacket—all of it having once belonged to their father. Usually John Gamble's three sisters would harass him about his clothing, his dirty corduroy pants or his torn T-shirts. Every Christmas they bought him new clothes and then couldn't believe how quickly he wore them out. His ex-girl-friend Polly had wanted to lend him the clothing of her old lovers, trying to make him presentable. Now he stared at Lynnie, dressed in their father's things—which, aside from the spilled coffee on the lapel of the jacket, showed no real sign of wear—and wanted to ask her, in the baffled tone of voice his sisters and former girlfriend used on him, *why?*

The basketball team was ranked twenty-first in the country, according to the program notes. In a stadium packed full of people wearing red—thousands and thousands of *fans*—the mood was fre-netic. John Gamble's boss had reserved the same prime seats for a dozen years, near one of the baskets, a few rows up from the floor. His boss didn't like to come to games anymore because of his sciat-ica. Also, he told John Gamble confidentially, because the students used nasty language when they cheered, nothing at all like students of his day.

John Gamble bought popcorn for Lynnie, and she sat beside him holding the unopened bag on her lap, her fingers swollen shiny, the nails bitten beyond the quick. She looked around her with a frown as if searching for someone in particular among the crowd. Its noise and number did not appear to intimidate her.

"What happens if there's a riot?" John Gamble yelled to her. But she just stared blandly at him, her thoughts elsewhere. This empty gazing always made him acutely lonely for the sister she used to be, the one who so effortlessly entertained his qualms and habits, who'd leapt into his odd cosmos without a second thought. Where had she gone? And would she be back?

Because John Gamble was slight in build, he'd never played much basketball. He hardly understood sports at all. His sister Natty, the one who'd gotten all the useful family traits—perkiness, popularity, a way with children, good luck—was an athlete. The rest of them didn't have the requisite capacity to care enough about winning. Their father, in his old age, had taken to watching football on the television, but only with the sound turned down, and frequently just as backdrop to a nap. In their family, you mostly read books. You were disdainful of things brutish or physical. Back when their father was a history professor in Kansas, he'd led the protest when the baseball field was carpeted and the library wasn't.

The home team basketball players—so huge and menacing—were introduced to great foot stomping and applause. Their names all seemed to be nouns: Hill, Saylor, Pott, Needles. The visitors were booed, as in a melodrama. Both teams clustered at center court and swatted at the ball. John Gamble tried to pay attention, tried to empathize with the fury on their faces. Whistles were blown, fouls called, profanities exchanged, the ball thrown in, out, over, sweaty black men hurled themselves from one end of the court to the other. On the side, the coach jumped up frequently, motioned with his arms, gnawed on a towel, slapped his players on the butts. Cheerleaders were flung high into the air, where they jackknifed spasmodically and then fell earthward into the arms of grinning, thick-thighed white boys, who formed circles like firemen to catch them. A band, dressed in red striped shirts and topped by Santa hats, moved their horns back and forth as they played peppy tunes. Grown men stood on their seats and shrieked, "Pull your head out, ref!" High in the stands, a huge lighted gun belched smoke whenever the applause reached a raucous-enough pitch. John Gamble felt like the spectator of an alien culture. He tried not to spend too much time locating fire exits.

But Lynnie never quit staring at the court and players. It was the first thing in two months she'd concentrated on with any degree of interest; her eyes seemed sharp and intelligent once more instead of muddy and dumb. At the end, when the visitors had beaten the home team by six points and gotten showered by a slew of empty drink cups as they left the court, she asked if she and John Gamble could come back for the next game.

In January, after the Christmas season had mercifully passed, after the anniversary of their sister Joanne's failed suicide attempt had come and gone, after John Gamble's daughter turned a year old without yet knowing her father, after it was clear Lynnie would be staying with him from now on, after the conference games had begun and the home team had an 8–2 record, a woman showed up at John Gamble's door one evening.

"I'm Kit," she introduced herself. "Maybe Lynnie told you about me?"

They were preparing to go to a game; the state rivalry was tonight. An unusual precipitation fell from the sky—not snow, not rain. John Gamble turned his face up to feel its coolness. Lynnie had never mentioned anyone named Kit to him. "Come in," he told her.

She stepped in from the wet front stoop—a pretty woman with thick glossy hair, her clothes the wholesome colors of cooked vegetables—and took a long look at his church. No member of the sane world had been here for a while. John Gamble could see anew the strangeness, the little piles of sand where the adobe was disintegrating, his sparse belongings shoved against the walls in between the stained glass windows, the dark wood floor undulating like a body of water all the way to the refrigerator, which was bright turquoise and tilted precariously where the altar had once been. John Gamble himself ran his tongue over his dead tooth, the top one that was turning gray, worrying about it for the first time since September, when his sister had arrived.

Lynnie came down the ladder from the loft, wearing her father's clothes, her hair cut a few nights earlier with dull scissors by weak light. Her friend's obvious shock made John Gamble lose confidence in what he'd taken to thinking of as Lynnie's progress. Maybe she'd put on a few pounds since September. Maybe her bruised-looking eyes made her appear beat-up instead of metaphysically exhausted.

When she saw her friend, Lynnie's mouth fell open. John Gamble had seen the phrase in books; now he witnessed it: her jaw dropped.

Kit cleared her throat—John Gamble would discover she did this frequently—and said, "I brought your dog."

"Rebel," Lynnie said thoughtfully. She nudged her way close to John Gamble, her gaze on the floor, a perfect parody of the Shy Girl Upon Meeting Her Blind Date.

Nobody said anything. Finally John Gamble asked Kit if she wanted to come to the game.

"Game?"

"Hoop," John Gamble said. "Basketball. Great team, lotta fun, come on."

"You want me to let Rebel out of the car?" Kit asked. "He's got to pee, if nothing else." John Gamble had not thought of Lynnie's old Irish setter until this moment. Good old Rebel, Lynnie's dog for eight or nine years, since high school. How could she have left him behind?

Outside in the cold slush, Lynnie put her hands to Kit's car window and looked her dog in the eye. His tail flew in a circle where he stood on the seat, his breath fogging the glass.

Lynnie turned away. "We could take *her* car to the game," she said to John Gamble, as if Kit weren't present. They'd been borrowing Hernando's car to drive to campus.

"Okay by me," said Kit. "What about Rebel?"

Lynnie wiped her damp palms on her father's pants—pants he'd worn in the navy, on a ship in the Atlantic fifty years ago. She said to John Gamble, "If you put him in the church, he'll eat your stereo speakers."

"He's been sitting in the car all day," Kit said.

"Then he's probably getting good at it," Lynnie said, climbing into the backseat with her dog. "Scoot over, you old fleabag." Rebel's joy at seeing her made John Gamble's eyes tear—that, and the cold weather.

They sloshed along on the back highway instead of the interstate, John Gamble directing Kit past cotton gins and chile fields, pointing out to her Staley Pecans, where he worked. Lynnie didn't like interstate highways; she'd become opposed to most things contemporary. She rode crunched against one window, fending off the aggressive affection of her stinking dog. Her single conversational nugget was on the virtues of being a good passenger. "Most people sit there driving even when they aren't," she said, unaccountably angry. "Like when you stop at a corner, they lean their big fat heads forward to see whether it's clear, and they stomp the floor like they have a brake, and they tell you how to get places faster. A good passenger just shuts up and rides."

Neither Kit nor John Gamble disputed this, though John Gamble found himself studiously *not* watching for oncoming traffic or giving instructions at the stadium entrance. He noticed that Kit kept peering into the rearview mirror and squinting, as if to reconcile her image of Lynnie with the reality. Her fretfulness made him fretful; was Lynnie really in such trouble? Had he just gotten used to it? The fact that she was still alive had seemed like respectable improvement to him.

The car scraped the ground into the parking lot, which was simply a large muddy field that in the summer held a Ferris wheel and a merry-go-round run by moth-eaten types. A cold striation fell from the sky, angled lines illuminated by the high bright lights on the roof of the arena. Lightning flashed over the mountains.

"Was that lightning?" John Gamble asked his companions as they walked through the wetness. "Is this sleet?"

Lynnie ignored him; Kit said, "I didn't see any lightning, and there's not enough of this to be sleet."

"Yet it's not snow," John Gamble went on.

"Sneet," Kit offered, and John Gamble relaxed: she wasn't going to judge him or his sister. Hustling along behind Lynnie, she seemed like a good sport.

At the gate John Gamble had planned to buy a general admission ticket for Kit but, instead, discovered the three of them being pushed through, flashing only the two passes, indebted to the excitement of the weather and general fan zest for keeping everything confused, though he also sensed that Lynnie's complete absence of ego made her nearly invisible anyway.

Inside, everyone shook water from nylon jackets and cowboy hats; in New Mexico, nobody owned an umbrella. Lynnie sniffed John Gamble's hair—her moist breath electric at his ear—and said, "You never yet met a pet as wet as they let this wet pet get."

Kit giggled and Lynnie frowned at her. In the vivid stadium lighting, John Gamble could see Lynnie's thick, chalky makeup. Was she covering her sallowness or emphasizing it?

They forged through the crowd, then bumped down the bleacher steps to their place, where they sat their three butts on two bench numbers, John Gamble crowded between the women. Kit told them, cheerily, "I've never been to a basketball game before."

"Oh, goody," Lynnie said flatly. Depression permitted her certain liberties. John Gamble recognized the style; she might have learned it from him, since fuckups and crazy people shared a fine line. But he didn't feel comfortable reprimanding her—he wasn't her father, after all, and she wasn't any longer a child. He would hold his breath and hope her next utterance was polite.

Kit cleared her throat—a kind of decorous purr—then asked, "So, what's it like to live around here?"

Lynnie watched the teams warm up, her eyes following the balls as they collided and fell—like sand in an hourglass—through the baskets at either end, and just as John Gamble was about to provide some generic answer to cover her rude silence, Lynnie said, "*Around here,* hereabouts, there are a lot of trucks driving around with refrigerators in the back of them."

Kit laughed nervously.

Lynnie said, "Have you noticed that, John Gamble?"

"No."

"Well, there are. Around here."

"I'll keep an eye out," Kit said. She proceeded to quiz John Gamble on statistics—rent for his church, types of local industry, numbers of ethnic people, of restaurants, bookstores, movie theaters, miles to larger cities. He answered without thinking, concentrating on Lynnie's deliberate lack of interest in her friend. It occurred to him that Kit was a former lover of Lynnie's, though how he concluded this, he couldn't quite say. There was something in Kit's manner of leaning over John Gamble's lap toward Lynnie, of eyeing the place where his thigh met with his sister's, of clearing her throat and trying to remain jolly and optimistic in the face of Lynnie's surliness. And, mostly, in the unmistakable leverage Lynnie still held—unattractive and abusive as she was—the leverage of the one who loves less. In John Gamble's former personality, he might have asked, point blank, what the story was. But he'd had that personality stolen away from him.

A drum roll signaled the national anthem. Just before the horns started, a fan yelled out, "Pumas *suck*!" and others hooted approval. Four ROTC students were marching midcourt where they would hoist a flag and shoulder rifles. The crowd rumbled and stirred; the band struck up the song. Lynnie stood reluctantly with her hands in her pockets—John Gamble had had to hold onto her elbows and lift her to her feet the first few times. Men flapped their billed hats over their chests; women chastely covered their left breasts. A surprising number of people sang, wavering thinly on "the rockets' red glare," building at the end to trill out "brave."

"I hate the national anthem," Lynnie growled as they sat amid the cheering. "Did you hear that jerk before the song started? Is a moment of silence too much to ask? Nobody can keep their big mouth shut."

"She hates everything," John Gamble told Kit. "But she loves basketball."

Lynnie gave him a cold glance. She had learned all about basketball; she read the sports page religiously, making daily forays now to the Kum-N-Go near John Gamble's church to purchase the local newspaper. If Lynnie was John Gamble's guiding focus, then basketball was hers.

"These guys are an outlaw team," she explained to Kit over John Gamble's lap. He liked her ease with the native tongue, though Kit obviously did not care what the phrase signified. She nodded eagerly, happy to have Lynnie's attention. "Hired guns," Lynnie went on, "JC transfers all the way. The Cowboys have had five twenty-win seasons in a row so there's pressure on the Hawk, the coach." She pointed out a prematurely gray-haired fellow wearing a gleaming green suit and wide necktie.

John Gamble, who enjoyed the gossipy elements of the game, added, "That's his lucky tie. Wait'll the second half—he chews up Styrofoam cups when the heat's on."

"Why are all the players bald?" Kit asked.

Lynnie didn't answer. She did not care for personal assessments of the players. When John Gamble had mentioned that one of them had been cited for drunk driving recently, she wouldn't talk to him for the rest of the day.

"Bald makes them look tough," John Gamble told Kit. He had grown accustomed to the military appearance of the home team, but the visiting players, most of whom were white—"Anglo," you said in the Southwest—reminded him of chemotherapy.

"White people have uglier heads than black people," he said.

"I was noticing that," Kit answered.

"Pumas think they're so cool 'cause they graduate sixty percent of their players," Lynnie said of the visiting team.

"Only sixty percent?" Kit asked. "Isn't that kind of low?"

"That's high," John Gamble told her. "Our team hasn't conferred a degree in three years."

"Oh."

The man and his young son who had the seats beside John Gamble's and Lynnie's were scowling and scooting; they wanted to make sure John Gamble understood what an inconvenience Kit was, squashed in illegally. John Gamble smiled at the son, a big dim-witted child who oftentimes ignored the game completely and stared at Lynnie as he chomped his corndog.

Kit, warming to her subject, said, "Why don't their shorts fit? Look at number five."

"Will Hill," Lynnie told her. "Great hands."

Kit said, "Let's hope he's got great cheeks, because those drawers are going to drop."

John Gamble laughed, but Lynnie was busy muttering things at the same moment the refs' whistles blew. "Traveling," she would say. Or, "Reaching in," "Lane violation," "Over the back." She sat in her baggy clothes, elbows on knees, concentrating fiercely on the players, the ball, occasionally the big lighted scoreboards hanging from either end of the gym. She had taken to sputtering her lips when unhappy with a call; her new haircut was of the variety intended to prevent tangles and knots in young children. His sister had become a character, John Gamble acknowledged, and it was his job to shield her.

"Here comes the wave," John Gamble said. Around them, fans were rising and sitting, their arms flapping in a kind of genuflection. His neighbors joined in the first time it went by, and John Gamble and Kit lifted their hands the second time.

"I hate the wave," Lynnie commented.

During a time-out, two men wearing huge papier-mâché heads chased each other around the gymnasium floor. One was dressed in chaps, his big mask topped with a ten-gallon hat the size of a garbage can, decorated with peacock feathers. He was a Cowboy, and he walked bowleggedly, firing off an obnoxious popgun. His opponent was a Puma, who wore yellow fur and plastic eyeballs that made him look deranged. From his gash of a mouth lolled a lewd rubber tongue. The cowboy smirked, brandishing his toy gun as around they went, kicking each other's pants.

"I hate the mascots," Lynnie said. She looked as if she might spit.

Just as the action started up again, the dozens of blinding lights hanging from the high ceiling dimmed. Instantly every gaze in the building was riveted upward, as if in sudden rapture. The crowd oohed as a unit, the lights dimmed further—the drain somehow affecting the mood, slowing time to the buzzing hum of stray current for a few seconds, making everyone for an instant afraid—then resurged, sending the crowd into another round of applause.

"Must be the weather," Kit said, still looking up.

"Must be," John Gamble said, wishing their seats were nearer an exit.

Lynnie had reflexively glanced up when the lights faded but had quickly resumed interest in the game. Basketball had given John Gamble new insight into his sister. For instance, she was genuinely indifferent about victory; a home team drubbing of the visitors did not please her. She seemed to be in it solely for the smooth motion of the ball, the magic that incited it from one end of the court to the other, from behind backs, through legs, into the air, sideways, crosswise, by trick or talent—at least, John Gamble *supposed* that this was the source of her fascination. These big clunky boys could, in a group like a singular living organism, moving full speed and without apparent plan, perform a miracle, pull a rabbit from a hat.

"Oh, they're into the bonus," Lynnie informed Kit and John Gamble.

"*Nice shot, asshole,*" the crowd chanted after each opponent's free throw fell.

Kit looked alarmed. "They sound dangerous," she said.

"They *are* dangerous," John Gamble told her. He had begun to find the fans' passion disturbing: the hatred that flowed from them onto the court, so uniquely affixed on the opponents. He could see why his boss no longer enjoyed the games. But Lynnie had explained to John Gamble that people required somebody to hate, enemies. It was temporary malice; she wasn't worried—though she also seemed serene with the prospect, say, of being fired upon by an automatic weapon. Not caring had that advantage.

"You know what all this random violence is about?" Lynnie said now. "It's so we'll have some disaster to rise to the occasion of. People are good under stress, they like to be heroes. They're good at it, they really are."

"I know what you mean," said Kit, delighted to have a chance to agree. "Like when there's a flood and people row boats around saving each other. Or when a child falls in a well or gets lost in a forest and everyone—"

Lynnie cut her off by slapping a fist into her palm. "No way was that a foul!" Others around her shouted their disapproval.

"And what you're saying," Kit went on, "is that people create their own disasters so others can be heroes."

Lynnie filled her cheeks with air and blew a raspberry. On Kit's behalf, John Gamble felt like pinching her.

Opposite them across the court, an older woman in the stands waved long underwear on a stick like a flag. "There's the pantaloon lady," John Gamble told Kit, turning his back on his sister. "There's the psychopath," he added, pointing to the young Indian man who leapt up every time the ref's whistle blew and jabbed his finger, cursing, his fury far out of the realm, even in this crowd. "He gets ejected every few games."

"I hate the fans," Lynnie said loudly.

At halftime, the Cowboys led by three. Small girls in fluorescent orange tights marched onto the floor and began turning cartwheels to a scratchy recording of unintelligible rap music.

"Well," John Gamble said, stretching. "How'd you like the first half of your first basketball game?"

"Fine," Kit said cheerfully. They both looked at Lynnie to make sure she wasn't going to be snide.

Below them, cheerleaders were throwing rolled T-shirts into the crowd. A man dressed as a turtle was soliciting maniacal applause so that he could give away a pizza. A TV cameraman panned the crowd, motioning with his free hand to work the students into a lather.

In the midst of all the action, the high lights dimmed once more. Once more the crowd interrupted its chaotic fun to stare heavenward as the stadium went from bright to brown. There was a fizzle of electricity, a surge and fade. John Gamble could feel the power of the drain, the way it pulled at the atmosphere, the way it frightened everyone. Afterward, the announcer came over the PA system and said, "We're having a little technical difficulty, folks, so in the event of a blackout, let's all keep our seats and our heads. Let's don't act like Pumas, huh?"

Light safely restored, the mob of people cheered and jeered. This was what it was like in a city with a redneck attitude and a ranked basketball team.

"Must be the weather," Kit said again.

"Wust me ma meathei," Lynnie mimicked.

John Gamble cringed, though it hadn't used to be his nature to want peace. "Can I get you some candy or something?" he asked Kit. "Nachos or a wienie or Cracker Jack?"

"No, thanks," she said, sighing.

Over John Gamble's lap Lynnie registered Kit's hurt feelings. Then Lynnie's own face lost its anger, its snottiness, its everything. She was empty, a fleshy sack of blankness. John Gamble knew she hated herself, and it was a terrible thing to know. He wished he could seize it away from her and endure it himself.

Instead of apologizing to Kit, Lynnie slapped at her own eyes with her palms, one and then the other, hard.

"Don't!" Kit cried.

John Gamble grabbed Lynnie's hands, forcing them to her lap. They were icy cold. The father beside them directed his little son's attention away from Lynnie, and John Gamble tried to give him a sheepish perplexed look over Kit's head to signal his own bewilderment, as if he might find affinity, father to father. Lynnie's hands were limp under his.

"Let go," she said. "I gotta pee," she added, rising.

John Gamble hesitated, then stood to let her pass.

"Talk about me while I'm gone," she directed him and Kit. "Tell each other how fucked up I am. Could you move your . . . *feet*?" she asked the little boy.

John Gamble watched her saggy pants go up the bleachers and disappear at the top, on the busy mezzanine. Would she be back? He half rose, as if to follow, then sat, unwilling to humiliate himself at the women's restroom door.

"Should I go with her?" Kit asked.

"I don't know."

They looked at each other. Kit said, "She didn't even tell me she was leaving Wichita. She just asked me to pick Rebel up from the vet's office one day and that was the last I heard until I called your mom."

"Mom never mentioned Rebel," John Gamble said. "It's hard to believe Lynnie would abandon him."

"She abandoned everything," Kit said. "A lease, for example. A job interview. A fridge full of rotten food."

You, John Gamble thought, then said, "I just don't think she's surviving Dad's death very well." He had trouble himself, a phantom longing to set some undefined thing straight. On the telephone at Hernando's, listening to his mother give him the news, John Gamble had begun grasping for firm images of his father: they were flying away as he spoke to her, so fast! Yet the shock remained potent: he would never see his father again, simple as that.

The band played "New York, New York" and their conductor sang into a microphone. Next, they started in on "Minnie the Moocher." In the bleachers adjacent to Kit and John Gamble, a large woman stood up and danced a striptease without actually undressing. Students shrieked and whistled. She spun her jacket around a finger while shimmying her generous chest. And two rows above her sat Polly, John Gamble's former girlfriend. On her lap she held a fat baby.

"Whoa," he said to Kit.

"What?"

He pointed upward, to Polly and her baby. "That's my daughter." The word had a striking sizzle, still warm on his tongue.

"What?"

John Gamble watched Polly lean over the baby's shoulder, her expression stern and preoccupied, parental. Where had she gotten that expression?

"You're divorced?" Kit was asking.

"Separated," John Gamble said, aware that what he was suggesting by claiming separation was some knowledge of his little girl. The fact was, she had nothing to do with him. He was honing his fathering skills in reverse order, first the gloomy undergraduate, maybe later the terrible twos. His baby threw her head against her mother's chest so abruptly that John Gamble flinched, automatically put his hand to his own sternum.

"You must miss your baby," Kit said.

"Oh," John Gamble said, scratching the skin between his shirt buttons.

Kit frowned, then directed her gaze across court, to the dancing forms of seven bare-chested young men with giant white letters printed on them, front and back, their skin painted red. They were supposed to spell COWBOYS one way and EAT PUMA the other, but they couldn't seem to get synchronized, two of the middle young men consistently turning at the wrong moment.

"So inept," Kit said.

John Gamble said, "Lynnie hates all of it."

"Yeah, I heard."

He tried to explain to her what he thought about his sister. "It seems like she's pissed off at Dad for dying, but I think she was pissed off at him before that, so she ends up being pissed off at herself, and then guilty." John Gamble was sweating. All these accumulated bodies and their heat. No wonder the cheerleaders wore nothing but bathing suits. Kit's pretty face was flushed, like a little girl's. If he were his sister, he supposed he might also resent her, her sweetness and light. He might want to provoke. "His dying was so fast," he went on, "nobody had time to get ready. He had a heart attack and just went. It was totally unexpected. Totally."

"I don't mean to belittle your grief or anything," said Kit, "but I can't believe that's the whole reason for Lynnie's losing it." She crossed her legs, accidentally kicking the man sitting in front of them. "Sorry," she told him.

"Yeah." John Gamble nodded thoughtfully. He didn't mention his own complete faith in this reason as sufficient for breakdown. Instead, he told her, "She wants to die, that's the way she feels." Did it matter why, really?

"She was my girlfriend," Kit said. "I thought I was still in love with her, but I can't tell. I feel sorry for her, and angry at her, too. She's not exactly herself."

"Actually," John Gamble said, "actually, I think she *is* herself, the unexpurgated version."

They both turned to look up the stairway to the mezzanine. The fans had started the wave again, kowtowing madly. Polly and the baby had disappeared in the sea of swaying hands.

A horn sounded and the second half began, Lynnie still gone. John Gamble went to look for her, his heart thumping. He purchased a Coke in order to have a prop, and sucked at the sweet unfamiliar fizziness while studying the faces of hundreds of strangers. None of them resembled his sister. None of them looked unsure.

He considered going down to the courtside table, where the announcer sat unfolding notes and notifying the crowd of illegally parked cars or player fouls. He could page Lynnie, but what good would that do? She wasn't a lost child, crying for her parents. If she read the letters of her name, scrolling across the scoreboard, above the team logos and below the La Costa Bank sign, it wasn't likely she'd respond.

"She's a loose cannon," his mother had told him on the phone, and John Gamble pictured a tossing ship, the huge loaded gun rolling on its deck.

And then there she was, sitting on an upturned bucket, out here among the cigarette smokers and program hawkers. Clearly she was waiting for him, like an abandoned little girl. Her eyeliner had run like ink down her pale painted face; she was a pitiful mime in her father's big coat.

"John Gamble," she said when he knelt before her. "I'm bad," she said. "I'm bad, bad, bad."

"You're not." He wanted to put his hands on her—but where?

"Don't lie to me! Don't bullshit me! I'm so *sick* of *bull*shit!"

From the stands came a great roar. "Tri*fecta*!" shouted the announcer. "Three points," John Gamble told her helplessly. All along, he'd felt that he must possess the way to reach Lynnie, that she wouldn't have chosen him if he didn't. He'd thought she contained her own indigenous wisdom in coming to him. He'd operated under the assumption that there was a future wherein she would no longer feel like dying. The important thing was ferrying her safely from here to there. He tried to recapture his clarity, the prompt that assured him the future would arrive.

"How are you bad?" he asked. "How?"

But she just shook her wretched hair, looking over his shoulder at the back of the stands. Did this qualify as failure? he wondered. Was he failing Lynnie now, unable to prevent her slipping irretrievably away? He followed her gaze. More cheering erupted. Whistles blew. A technical foul was called against the home coach.

"Let's go see," he begged his sister, lifting her by one elbow to lead her around the mezzanine. A plan was circling his brain, one that might involve locating Polly and her daughter, *his* daughter, the one-year-old child whose name, he discovered at this very moment, he had never troubled to learn. His sister followed alongside him as if she were being led to punishment. She didn't wipe her black-stained cheeks, and people—those who weren't engrossed in the acrimony on the court—stared openly. Some seemed sympathetic and John Gamble saw an amazing kindness in their faces that he would never have expected.

Back at their seats, the father and son clambered up to make way for Lynnie—as if her tears had something to do with them.

Kit hesitated, running her eyes up and down Lynnie, then patted the place beside her.

This time Lynnie sat in the middle. She snuffled and wiped her nose on her father's deerskin jacket sleeve. John Gamble realized that those coffee stains on the lapel had been made by his father—who knew how long ago?—hot drops fallen from his cup or mouth. John Gamble tried to envision the spill—the slight tremor as his father brought the coffee to his lips, his mustache that moved when he ate or drank—but saw instead a closing door, clicking gently shut again and again, his father having disappeared on the other side of it.

On the court, the Cowboys were engineering a comeback, their desire to win rousing them into the state of grace that had always seemed to most enthrall Lynnie. In swift and spastic play, the Pumas lost the ball—suddenly it popped into the hands of the Cowboys—and lone Will Hill flew downcourt to receive it and then sailed off his feet into the air, twisting around the ineffectual hacking of a Puma, to jam the ball behind his head through the ring. The bleachers shook, pom-poms flew, smoke belched forth. Thrown rolls of toilet paper unraveled and fell, an empty tube landing on Lynnie's lap. Everyone else was on his or her feet, even Kit, inspired. The Cowboys had tied the score.

Kit laughed, clapping along. "I suppose you hate that?" she called out to Lynnie. The teeter-totter of control between them had either seesawed or vanished entirely. Lynnie didn't look capable of hating anything, right now. She was unmoved by the excellence of the play, staring instead at the invisible screen between her and the world.

Then, above them, the lights dimmed once more. The crowd turned its adoring gaze from Will Hill, down below—who had been fouled and had just stepped to the freethrow line—to the distant, metal-raftered ceiling, waiting in a surprised hush.

The lights grew dimmer, the buzzing tension of waning power upon the enormous space, and then suddenly went out altogether. Nothing! John Gamble shut his eyes to test—dark within, dark without—and reeled, as if untethered. Around him, there was a stunned intake of breath while fourteen thousand people were left in a deep, black, boundless void. Were their hearts pounding like his?

Beside him, his sister pressed close. He reached to reassure her, but she found his ear first and breathed into it. "I don't hate this," she said. "This, I kind of like."

Happy Hour

*W*hen she went to her lover's house, she carried a little feather pillow she'd slept on for twenty years. It was small, so she could stuff it in her backpack where it made what she hoped was an unremarkable lump. Soft down, no heft whatsoever. Like a princess, she required this pillow and no other.

These excursions out the door with her backpack were supposed to be to walk the dog. The dog obliged by trotting along on a leash, slashing the air with his yellow tail. Andrea walked a few blocks, then stepped into the pickup truck of her lover. The dog, accustomed now, hopped in after, at her feet. The truck bed did not interest him.

Behind Andrea, in her pink house, she imagined her three children and her husband receding in the distance, growing tiny as she sped away. After their days at work and school, they arrived home disgruntled, ready to fall apart in front of people who would let them cry. They would be watching television, eating comforting crackers, her husband having the first of a few harmless beers. It was just possible that her husband sat there berating himself: here he was watching cartoons like a big silly boy, drinking beer, while his wife went walking for the health and sanity of all.

It *was* healthy, Andrea thought fiercely, to have an affair now. She didn't think the health part was obvious; there weren't calisthenics involved. Hardly any muscles, except her heart, of course, which rose and fell and pounded and swelled and would no doubt end up broken, sooner or later. Still, this secret destination every few days seemed indubitably good for her. Thinking of her lover made life pleasant, and not only for Andrea. Everybody benefited from her obsession: in the mornings, when she used to be resentful, she now woke cheerfully to indulge the children's sullen sleepiness. She let her husband lounge in bed while she whipped up French toast and whirled around the kitchen and bedrooms finding socks and shoes, stuffing three different brands of chips into three different sack lunches, vigilant with the various schedules each child kept, the allergy medicines, the favorite cereals, trimming the crusts off her son's sandwiches while reminding the youngest girl to go potty before sitting at the table. In love, as Andrea felt herself to be, she was a model mother. She sat among her beautiful children and felt stunned: to be a member of this exclusive club, one she'd never dreamed she'd be allowed to join. In order to win their approval and to amuse herself, she made the pets talk, get some of their complaints off their chests while the children laughed. In love, she had a lot of extra energy and wit. She was the life of the party. She lost some weight. She gave her husband a blow job, just out of joy.

Before she'd fallen in love, things had not been so good. She sometimes arrived home from work and began drinking, not stopping until she'd fallen into bed, head on her little feather pillow, unconscious. Drinking, she could just barely manage her life in the evening. Things proceeded fuzzily. There was a large degree of guilt, but an even larger degree of helplessness. She was unhappy and restless, her life seeming to leak away from her. And drinking, at least, put some sort of plug in that. Fortunately, her husband seemed to recognize her state—not its source, but its persuasive strength—and did not chastise her. In fact, it was he who suggested getting the dog, taking the walks. And it was his friend Robin who pulled up in a blue pickup truck, in the reddening sunset, and smiled sadly as Andrea and Rip hopped in.

Happy hour: in ancient Europe it was called the hour between dog and wolf, when the pacing canine shadows outside the city walls could not be distinguished, friend or foe? You had to shut the gates to keep the wolves on the other side, domesticated animals within. Andrea's west Texas town didn't have a wall, but within its confines all was green and fertile and mown, while all around lay the vast brown desert, prickly with danger. All the roads flew away from the city, like a spoked spinning pinwheel. Get on one and drive into the unknown.

"I wanted to show you something," Robin said shyly as they sped down the street out of Andrea's neighborhood. Even after a few months of being in love, the two of them were nervous with each other. It was sizzling nervousness. It probably burned calories.

"Okay," Andrea agreed. She liked to ride around in Robin's truck, although she worried occasionally that someone would see them. Alternately, she hoped someone would; and when it was reported back to her husband, and he asked her about it, she would blink, as if trying to recall the episode, then, oh yeah, Robin had given her a ride home some hot day. From one of those long walks she'd begun taking, walks that were responsible for her weight loss and general fitness and inordinate happiness.

Tonight he wanted to show her some ostriches just outside the city limits. He liked his tidbits, the odd things he found or saw and then offered up to Andrea. It was what had drawn them to each other to begin with, oddness. Every morning, when she read the local terrible newspaper, Andrea was looking for the funny headline, the foolish letter to the editor, the number of stars her horoscope held for her day, the hilarious lost or found or stolen or destroyed item in the police blotter. She knew Robin was drinking his coffee, in his trailer, reading the same newspaper. They were laughing together, she thought, across town. Was there anything more seductive than a sense of humor?

The ostriches stood in their fence, which was enclosed by another fence, as if someone might want to steal them. "Where's its head?" Andrea asked of the darker bird. Could it be that she would see an ostrich with its head buried in the sand? Could Robin actually produce such a thing?

"It's our angle," he said. "The head's over to the side. See, he's waving." The dark bird did appear to be waving. Its wings were astonishingly large.

"You'd think they could fly with wings like that."

"It's the tiny brains that thwart them. No imagination."

Andrea reached across the truck seat and took Robin's hand. He swallowed. The dog emerged from the floorboard to stare, transfixed, at the big birds. What were they? And how did they concern him? Outside, the second ostrich sat placidly on the bare dirt of her double-fenced yard. She looked like a grotesque nesting hen, calm, stuck. How did Andrea know this one was the female? She just did. Although if she wanted to make an analogy, if she wanted to see her life in the life of these birds, she would have been the one waving her wings, knocking her little head around, looking ready to get the hell out of the pen.

"Now what?" she asked Robin. This was what they always said. She'd said it first when he came to visit her at her office downtown for no real reason. They'd made small talk for a while, then he mentioned that he ought to be leaving, then he didn't leave, then they didn't talk, they just sat in two chairs casting glances at each other and looking rapidly away. Neither was very adept at flirtation. They'd been social dorks in their respective high schools, all those years ago. They both liked Andrea's husband a lot, too. Still, something began then. "Now what?" Andrea had asked, and Robin had shrugged, smitten, desperate, helpless.

*   *   *

They both liked to drink quite a lot. This was perhaps related to the social awkwardness each felt when sober. Self-conscious. Unattractive. Lubricated, their truer natures surfaced: sweet, silly, erotic. They blushed very readily. They made each other blush constantly. Andrea wondered if they were really that much alike, or if she were simply doing what she often did, adopting the personality of her intimates. In her desire to fit in, she'd unintentionally slip into the gestures of her friends, take on their inflections, talk, act, laugh like them, remember stories from her past that were like theirs. It was all her— just a different take, her life viewed from a vaguely distorted angle. Her best friend in college had humiliated her by pointing this habit out to her. Up to that moment, she'd often wondered why she never recognized her own voice when she heard it. It was always changing, camouflaged by the presence of whoever she happened to love just then. Now she loved Robin, and now she seemed to have become like him.

They drank beer from a can that reminded Andrea of a container of motor oil. Heavy, so big as to require two hands. Robin's trailer sat in a court surrounded by a very thick wall. Andrea's joke was that the trailers wanted to escape, but the wall was preventing it. The trailers conspired while the people were away, shifting on their cement blocks, muttering among themselves, ready to scoot off when the wall wasn't looking. The road that wound through the trailer court was called Rusty Lane, and at the end of it, at a T, was Bridle Path. "I'm a rusty bride," Andrea sometimes said, because she was older than Robin, just by three years, but that was enough to make her feel vulnerable about her breasts, those faint stretch marks like fish scales at her pelvis. Oughtn't he to have found a strapping twenty-five year old, one free as a bird, ready to dedicate her life to him, swing his hand publicly as they crossed the parking lot to attend a matinee, kiss him at the mall in front of God and everyone?

Robin held the doors for her, the truck door, the screen door, the wood interior door. He had touchingly good manners, a kind of bumbling politeness, as if his parents had forgotten to give him instructions and he'd had to train himself.

"Here," he said, removing Andrea's backpack. He reached into it familiarly, around the water bottles and purple bandanna, the Walkman and cellular phone, the sunscreen and lip balm, and retrieved the little feather pillow. He carried it, plumping it as he went, to the bedroom, following Andrea from the tight quarters of his living room, through the narrow passage of his kitchen, and into the warm space of his rumpled bed. This was happy hour, right here and now.

Why then did she cry? She always cried when she made love, especially with Robin. His bedroom was the sweetest place she had ever lain, and her feelings, so enormous and guilty and passionate, overwhelmed her. This room, at the end of the trailer, was not unlike the club car of a train: windows panoramic, and outside them big old cottonwoods, their leaves shimmering in the early evening light like coins, like water. Small brown birds, plain and unremarkable, twittering. Andrea thought of herself as plain and unremarkable—and then sometimes exotic, singularly beloved. Robin adored her, and the knowledge filled her like a drug. In his trailer, she was reminded of the Ozarks, swinging lazily in a hammock, her grandmother or mother or some other childhood comfort, of being swept away. The sensation made Andrea teary, yet delighted. She felt full, then, after Robin had kissed her, and held her, and fucked her, and then held her again, then kissed her some more. The best part was the second round of kissing. There was something so fatigued in it, fatigued and satisfied and full and flush. These manners of his, the way he remembered to adore her afterward. His funny trailer with its old trees, enclosed by its heavy stone walls, by meandering random Rusty Lane. The fading daylight through the windows, like a train, like a trip to some distant nostalgic place.

Outside, Rip had his exercise, gamboling madly. Up and down

the paved driveways he went, spurting from one scent to another, tail like a propeller, legs bounding sideways in his enthusiasm. Because the dog had to come home from this excursion exhausted, as if he'd been on an hour-and-a-half-long walk in the desert spring heat. So one of the risks built into the evening was Rip's freedom outside the trailer. He gleefully roamed the roadway, which was lumpy with speed bumps, then halted abruptly, drawn to an odor or movement in a yard. He had begun to see the trailer court as his personal park. He peed on its trees with a new bravura. There was a swing to his gait that let you know he'd been here before.

Andrea made love with Robin always anticipating the sound of a car hitting her dog, the screech of brakes, perhaps the yowl, or, worse, the sick silence. That would be her justice, her punishment. And how could she sacrifice her dog this way? How could she lie here, her face on Robin's pale freckled shoulder, thinking so calmly about the death of the family dog?

Because she had the relentless desire to shake her life by its shoulders, until its teeth rattled and its organs unhinged, until there was hell to pay.

She could lose that dog; the wall wasn't high enough to really contain him. All the possible dangers, discovery, betrayal. All these things just to find a moment of happiness.

And then the hour of the wolf. Into her walking clothes, skin red where it had made contact with Robin's, chest, navel, neck. A faint chapped feeling on the lips and chin. They shared lip balm in the truck cab. Headlights were necessary. The dog reeked, damp from who knew what foul puddle or toxic drain, or perhaps he'd eaten something dead, roadkill, vermin. He went savage, left to his own devices. In the dark, he might scale that wall and disappear into the untamed desert surrounding the city. At the intersection three blocks from her home, Andrea did not want to get out. Adamantly not. Beneath her the seat vibrated warm as a washing machine, as a

heart pulsing in a solid chest. Every time, every single time, she forgot how terrible this part was. You'd think she'd learn. You'd think
she'd prepare herself with some strategy or other. The streetlights
above them hummed, ready to flare into their green fluorescence.

"Casual sex," a friend had recommended when Andrea complained of feeling trapped, ready to explode, self-destructing at a rate
that alarmed her. "You need casual sex." Now she understood the
phrase as a profound oxymoron.

"If you stop loving me," Andrea had told Robin, "I don't know
what I'll do. If you come to my office someday and say you want to
just be friends, I'll slap your face. You'll have to buy a different car and
then not tell me what it is, so I won't be seeing this blue truck everywhere."

"I'm crazy about you," Robin said now, looking not at her but out
the windshield, toward the trailer where he would return alone.
Every few days they had to abandon each other. He meant that his
love was making him crazy, and his eyes were wet.

"Andy-pants," he called her.

Andrea leaned across the space between them to put her nose
into his neck. She ran her tongue over stubble. It was this sensation
she would wake later in the night to review, lying beside her sleeping
husband, Robin's hot textured throat on her lips. "I'm in love with
you," she told him now, miserable. Ahead of her lay a few drinks,
wine or perhaps gin, the bedtime rituals with her children, the tired
sad friendship she shared with her husband, dishwashing, door lock-
ing, videotapes. She had forgotten her little pillow, she realized as she
pulled away from Robin, and when she woke later, mouth cottony,
dizzy with dehydration, her back would also ache, a flare in her
shoulders from sleeping wrong. Sleeping all wrong.

"That dog stinks," her husband would complain.

"He has wild desires," Andrea would explain.

She stepped out of Robin's truck into the dusk, the lonely post-
happy-hour walk to her house full of evening, indistinct shadows.

Goodfellows

*A*nybody who ever worked for long making minimum wage at a little business knows how the family thing gets going: you all play a part. Somebody acts like Mom, keeping track of your tardiness, commenting on the black circles under your eyes, tsk-tsk-tsking. And then there's always Dad, the guy who can have you fired, whose nasty masculine office you have to visit to get a reprimand or a paycheck. Around you swarm your coworkers—younger, older, dumber, prettier—with whom you compete and spat and ally yourself, like siblings, like a gaggle of goslings. On the fringes, in the back, at the odd hours, are the eccentric in-laws, uncles, and other random black sheep.

The summer I was eighteen I worked at Goodfellows pizzeria. We were the prairie outpost of a Chicago-based chain, pioneering westward with our cornmeal crust and blend of four cheeses. Our product cost twice what the competition charged, yet the Kansas customer never quite bought the logic that it also weighed twice as much and fed twice as many. A pizza, the plains state consumer reasoned, was a pizza. Goodfellows was destined to go belly up after only one summer.

But for that summer I was employed at my first real job. Good-fellows had advertised for "those interested in ground-floor entry to an exciting new business!" They were moving into what had most recently been the Szechwan Palace: out went the fragile screens with dragons and Asian women coyly waving their fans, in came the Chianti bottles and red-and-white cafe curtains. I was interviewed by Marvin as he stood on chairs cutting tassels from light fixtures, collecting the Chinese characters in his left hand. He hired me because he didn't care whether the business made it or not. He was a sort of reluctant, distant Dad figure, one I recognized from my real-life family. You felt like you needed to snap your fingers in his face sometimes to bring his gaze into focus. He'd been sent to Kansas against his wishes and he missed Chicago. Mostly, Marvin was not a career pizza man. He planned to return to school for a master's in math as soon as he made enough money, and his true vocation, the one he kept looking toward, lay elsewhere.

"You like Bob Dylan?" he asked me as he leaned over the jukebox. "I got six Dylan records in here, so you better like Dylan."

"I can learn to like Bob Dylan," I said. At home we were never allowed to hate our food; we could only claim to be learning to like it.

"Raise your right hand," Marvin said. When I did, he grinned. "Nah, I'm just kidding around. You don't have to pledge allegiance." His assistant manager, however, had dedicated himself to pizza the minute he got the job. This was Steve Two. Steve Two was a fat guy just a year or two older than me who'd leapt into service for Good-fellows the way some boys join the army: with a righteous passion to go kick ass. The only thing that could distract him from pizza was racing hotrods. He built models and brought them in to decorate the restaurant kitchen. They were elaborate replicas, painstakingly glued and adorned, ridiculous but impressive, the way all minia-tures are. It was hard to imagine Steve Two's broad stubby fingers capable of such intricacy, but there they were, complete with tiny steering wheels and hubcaps, occasionally a minuscule driver in a yellow helmet. On Friday nights, Steve Two's one night a week off, he would return to Goodfellows after the races in Augusta or Chanute to tell us what had happened, his enthusiasm sending the spit flying while the rest of us maneuvered around him, closing the store. He wore his racing outfits on these nights, dirty white jump-suits with too many pockets, and black protective eyeglasses held to his large round head with a rubber strap—dressed like a great big two year old.

Nobody really took Steve Two seriously except Annette, who put on a perplexed frown as she listened to him through the order window dividing front from back. Instead of leading him along his ludi-crous yet entertaining narrative concerning the night the way the rest of us did—oh, those Kansas City boys and their hot shit engines, their hooker babes and their leather bikinis, the crack-ups and the anguish—Annette tried to compete. She was a kind of trashy twenty-five-year-old beauty school graduate with a sour outlook. She cut hair for five dollars and did not like me, even after I tried to get on her good side by letting her trim my bangs. Her own hair was a dramatic gleaming black, waved in one large stiff S-curve with a bright white stripe painted up the middle like the tail of a skunk. "Scary," Marvin had commented of her. Her jeans were faded white and stringy, and she'd taken her hair scissors to her green Goodfel-lows polo shirt, snipping fringe up to her navel. "Guess what these clippers cost," she challenged me.

I appraised them carefully, wondering aloud why they were ivory colored, and learned they were made of the same indestructible material used by NASA on the space shuttles.

"A hundred bucks," I guessed, aiming high so she could reveal her shrewd bargaining powers.

"For *these*? You couldn't touch 'em for less than three hundred fifty, and *I* got 'em for three even." Annette was always very busy catching people trying to rip her off. Most everyone fell into this cat-egory, grocery checkout clerks, insurance companies, the guy who owned the beauty parlor where she rented a station and from whom she'd bought the space clippers. While Steve Two told us about car crack-ups, Annette listed the offenses perpetrated against her that week by Hector, her other boss.

Our other boss was Steve One, the district manager, a large pear-shaped fellow who arrived apologetically every few days to check our percentages. Mumbling, he worried around the kitchen, his clip-board wedged against his big STEVE belt buckle, counting and weighing and adding, taking notes, then spending an anxious hour in Marvin's office on the second floor. Finally he would trundle heavily down the stairs, his computations showing us to still be, mercifully, operating in the black. Even though it didn't matter to Marvin how we fared each week, he had the good manners to fret a little while Steve One lowered his head over his calculator upstairs. Marvin seemed to respect Steve's limited expertise, his infinite stability. My mother's dull but reliable younger brother was just like this: instead of aspiring to become a medical doctor, he'd settled for driving around with a trunk full of drugs representing a pharmaceutical company.

On opening day, while Annette and I had filled pitchers of Diet Coke and Fanta, she told me she was sure Marvin would hit on her, it always happened, wherever she worked, that the boss came after her for sexual favors. She would have to watch her step. Favors, I kept thinking. "Also," she added as she cracked rolls of change into the cash register, "did you know there are more diseases on those forks out there than on this money? It's a common mistake to think money is dirty." She carelessly licked a quarter for emphasis, then pocketed it. When I pointed out that she'd misplaced the coin she began hating me.

So maybe I was the tattletale sister. Or maybe the family baby, as I was the youngest employee. At home, my other one, I was both. I'd been born late, after my parents' excitement for toddlers had worn thin, after the toys had broken and the dog had died. Everyone was gone—college, marriage, the West Coast. There, like here at Goodfellows, I most often felt like the ugly duckling, somehow never properly at home, honking when I should have been quacking. I honestly *wanted* to fit. They fascinated me, I liked them, all of them, and wished to imprint.

Closing time made my heart pound: the dark vacant parking lot where trash blew under the vapor lights; inside, the loud jukebox, turned up using a crooked dime to a volume unsanctioned by Midwestern Sound Emporium; and the steady expressions on the faces of my new friends as they labored to restore order. There was something hellish and unreal about the empty business. It was my job to clean the salad bar, to wipe up coagulated dressing with a damp cloth diaper, to take buckets of dirty, half-melted ice to the sink in back.

One night a girl my age appeared at the locked front door and began pounding to be let in. She was banging with her wrists.

"We're closed!" I shouted at her over the din of the music, Annette's furious vacuuming. The girl wailed alarmingly on the other side of the glass, her skirt blowing around her thighs, their shape clear and beautiful beneath transparent material. I stared at her legs, mesmerized by their perfection, and somehow missed the blood, sticky and opaque, now on the glass.

"Hey!" I yelled, "Help!" I backed away as she held both wrists against the glass, flattening them white, the blood momentarily stanched—I thought of a stingray sliding eerily up an aquarium wall. Then she resumed pounding with the hands, smearing her blood between us. I had the greasy diaper at my mouth, the sweet-tart smell of Thousand Island in my face.

It was Marvin who let her in, Steve One who dialed the police, Luke who took her by the elbows and guided her to a seat, while I stood quaking, unbelieving. Her boyfriend had left her; she'd used a broken beer bottle. "A serious suicide follows the vein," Annette told me after the girl had been taken away, tracing a line from her own wrist to the soft inside of her elbow. "That chick just needed attention."

"She sure as heck got it," Steve One said, his hanky mopping his forehead. "You okay, Jane?"

I nodded, though I wasn't okay, and finding it hard though somehow necessary to hide my bewilderment. Steve Two muttered at being assigned to clean the glass; in the process he managed to drop and break the bottle of Windex, its clear shards on the concrete seeming an invitation of some kind. I never again reached for the Goodfellow's door without thinking just for an instant of her standing there in her skirt, beautiful, stricken, a catastrophe.

An interesting fact about the microcosmic job site is that you inevitably choose someone to love, even if you wouldn't give that person a second thought on the outside world. This, in my case, was Luke. He and Marvin had met at a used compact disc store buying jazz. Marvin was ecstatic to find a kindred spirit here in the milquetoast Midwest and hired him on the spot. Luke was wasting time between semesters, beginning graduate school in the fall, and decided he could save a lot of money by both collecting a paycheck from Goodfellows and eating three meals a day there. I was eight years younger than him, hopelessly tongue-tied in his presence, unable to speak a word that illustrated my maturity. He wasn't good looking (stooped, skinny like a crane, and embarrassed by it), and his sense of humor you had to coax like crazy. Unlike Steve Two, Luke was not actively seeking a girlfriend. He was more interested in pianos, in science fiction, in bantering with Marvin on a constantly evolving range of topics including *Star Trek,* Spinoza, chaos, microbreweries, garlic therapy, hockey, William Casey, Thomas Merton, Bob Dylan, and many many others. I listened entranced, unable to enter. Annette, oblivious, never thought twice about tossing in an anecdote, as if all conversation were equal, every word its own gem, but I could not fathom the real rules of the game and would not try to play without knowing them. Only occasionally would Luke acknowledge me, leaning through the window separating front from back to ask me about an order I'd taken.

"Black olive?" he'd say, "or peppercorn?" I would look past his finger at the letters I'd scribbled.

"B.O."

"Sit or split?"

"Split," I'd say, pointing at the arrow I'd drawn at the bottom of the paper. I could never have explained to my friends how thrilling these exchanges were, the weight placed in a single acronym, Luke nodding eagely when everything had been deciphered. Only his barely quivering finger ever hinted at the possibility of his nervousness in my presence, and that gave me hope.

Though Annette claimed to have to fend off Marvin's interest in her, it was actually the reverse. She worked at getting his attention in a strategy directly opposed to my own in getting Luke's. She took every opportunity she could to touch him, to brush past and swat him, to lean through the window (her feet off the floor) while he sliced pie with a cleaver the length of his arm just under her face. These blatant overtures offended me. I felt my winning, subtle approach much the superior one. Of the two types of restaurant employee, she fell into the careerist category: she would stay in the service industry. And, as I mentioned before, Marvin was merely a tourist, like Luke, like me. I did not believe romance would transcend the line.

The four of us, plus Steve Two, constituted the late afternoon and nighttime Goodfellows staff. A large morose girl named Cherie (Cheri Amour, everyone called her) was the daytime waitress. It was she I relieved at four every afternoon, she whose African boyfriend leaned sucking a soda straw at the front counter each day, waiting. He was a striking molasses-colored man whose friendly expression seemed unshakably serene and self-satisfied. Cherie was not at all pretty, and I attributed her boyfriend's undiscriminating taste to the fact that he was foreign, never once thinking Cherie could have had anything to do with it. She hardly smiled until he was around; they walked out hip to hip, ambling in a frankly sexual manner. Steve Two would grab the mike in the back and make kissing noises over the sound system. The daytime cook told us her boyfriend had been waiting for her since Goodfellows opened at eleven.

"Nothing to do in the whole wide world but wait for that ugly girl," Steve Two marveled, rocking on his heels.

Steve One, in the back checking our percentages, shook his head disapprovingly. "Watch your mouth," he told Steve Two.

Steve One had been in the Goodfellows business since he was sixteen. It had been his idea originally to open a Wichita branch; his wife was from here. His reprimand of Steve Two reminded me how unattractive Mrs. Steve One was, a woman so altogether fat you couldn't tell she was eight months pregnant on top of it. She never spoke when she visited the store, sitting at a table with her huge legs crossed, smoking cigarettes and drinking aspertame-filled, caffeinated Diet Coke in spite of her pregnancy. Fat couples always made me imagine comic sex.

"Jane," Steve One said. "Jane? Jane?" Finally I realized he was talking to me. My real name, Roberta, had lately begun to seem frumpy, so I'd asked everyone at work to call me by my middle one instead. Although I'd originally had the reputation of someone bright, the fact that I often forgot to respond to my own name made my coworkers suspicious. Luke thought I was being sly, which endeared me to him.

"Could you get me a water, Jane?" Steve One asked. He was sweating earnestly, weighing our bags of meat pellets and mushrooms. No one except the two Steves worried how Goodfellows fared. Annette could get temporarily excited by a profitable week, but she mostly was on the lookout for fake phone orders, ones designed by malcontents and misfits who wanted to humiliate us. We were located in a strip mall in a semiseedy neighborhood and much of our clientele made her suspicious. Wichita did not know what to do with our concept: gourmet pizza served on plastic tables, video games twirping and bleeping in the corner, waitresses who made you fetch your own meal and condiments, and prices higher than K-Bob's. Was one expected to leave a tip? Not without good reason did Goodfellows go under.

The thing was, we served great pizza. I ate pizza no fewer than five times a week that whole summer and never grew weary of it. Luke stopped by in the mornings to make little pizza dough rolls for his breakfast; at noon he had salad and a My Pie (pizza for one). He and I took our break together around eight, after the dinner rush, and split a small pizza in the back room while the Hobart rumbled in the corner. Eating with him made me happy. Occasionally I will still try to imitate that Goodfellows flavor, but it can't be done. Something secret—a nonsequitous spice or lost baking tip—keeps me just this side of reviving it.

I looked forward to my job, bathing every afternoon before I went, washing and blow-drying my hair, making up my face. Despite the fact that I would stink of oregano and canned tomatoes five minutes after entering Goodfellows, I laundered my polo shirt every day, hoping to pass near enough to Luke early on so he could smell my cleanliness like a wafting breath of innocence. I liked our carryout rushes best, the times when I was asked to help in the back, working the assembly process with Marvin and Luke, Steve Two scurrying around doing the gopher jobs, fussing and muttering, Annette pacing the front in her surly predatory manner, squelching jokes by taking everything literally, telling long tedious anecdotes about her day, which revealed her as the person other people *thought* they might pull something over on. She was our mother, a necessary wet blanket, a source of constant conversational white noise.

"Wild Man," she yelled through the kitchen to the back one busy Friday night in late June. "You have three messages." Our day cook was Waldman. I never knew his first name, and hardly knew his last. Everyone called him Wild Man, though he seemed to me quite dull. He rarely spoke but always wore a quirky delighted grin like someone unabashedly stupid. He had long blond hair that Marvin, ever the inefficient Goodfellows manager, did not require be kept in a net, so Wild Man—or, *the* Wild Man, as the male employees called him—had to forever shake it from his eyes. He moved like a hoptoad pull toy I'd had when I was small, a kind of burping lurch that probably had to do with music, with the tiny headphones in his ears, two black buttons with a slack wire across the back of his pimply neck. He had stayed to wash pans that night, leaning over the big sinks, his long simian arms silver from the aluminum, marked with red slashes where he'd burned them pulling out pies. A mysterious woman kept phoning him and leaving urgent messages that he call. He wasn't responding.

"She's a nurse," Steve Two told me now, standing beside me feeding dough into the Hobart that flattened it. "I can't see why he won't even call her back. Man, if a babe wanted me that bad . . ." He popped his lips, leaving the thought unfinished, baffled by it.

Luke looked at the ceiling. "'Babe,'" he said. The previous Saturday night while Steve Two was at the Augusta track, Luke cooked a model car. It had had a Playboy bunny on the fender, tiny naked breasts just over the front wheels, flames and smoke on its long phallic hood. The car melted into a puddle of shining primary colors, the exhaust fan switched on high to suck up the fumes. Luke had put the mess in a to-go box with Steve Two's name on it, and Steve had had to accept it as a joke since Luke and Marvin were friends.

That evening, when the ringing phone wasn't a takeout order, Annette, who'd picked up, announced for all to hear: "Wild Man, I'm not gonna talk to that woman again! You think I'm your goddamned mother?"

Marvin clanged on the stainless steel shelf in our window with his huge class ring, and I jumped. "Hey," he said to Annette, "let's watch the language here." Marvin's temper was of the volcanic variety; he would preside sedately and then surprise us by exploding over nearly nothing. From my father I'd learned how to manage this kind of anger, staying out of the way, placating.

But Annette sparked right back at him. "Shit," she hissed, rising through the window. "He can get the damn phone back there!"

Marvin narrowed and then closed his eyes, twisting his head side to side to pop the joints in his stiff neck. He rolled his shoulders. When he opened his eyes, he was no longer mad. "Get the phone," he called out to Waldman. "Wild Man, pick up."

I went around back to find Waldman gone, the pans still dripping beside the sink. I picked up the rear extension. "He's gone," I told the nurse. She sighed over the line, as if she were heartbroken. It amazed me Waldman could elicit such feeling. I mean, he never washed his hair. Then she asked if she could leave him a message.

"Sure," I said, eager to keep her hopes up. She sounded nice.

"Just tell him his test was negative, okay? He'll know what it's all about."

"Negative test," I said, as if writing it down. "Okay," I added, and hung up. "Negative test," I said to Luke, back at my post beside him, our hands plunging in the cool, colorful toppings before us. As I was about to repeat myself for everyone to hear, Luke stopped my left hand with his right, and, putting an onion-dotted finger to my lips, his whiskery chin near my ear, warned me that this might be information best kept to ourselves.

Steve Two was saying, awed as always by the ways of women, "Those nurses and their white panty hoses!"

When I relayed the news to Waldman, the following night, he pulled the little speaker buttons from his head and peered at me, his mouth open.

"Say what?" he said.

"You had a message that your test was negative," I told him, trying to remain discreet, having stopped him before he entered the kitchen. HIV, I had decided, though it could have been anything.

He shook, like someone chilled, from his hips to his hair. Like someone who'd been given back his life. "Thanks," he told me, the only thing I remember him ever saying to me. I had nothing to do with his good news, but the pleasure I had in being its bearer carried me for days.

*   *   *

Even though we lasted only a summer, Goodfellows managed to attract regulars, a few of them. There were the guys from the 7-Eleven around the corner, the women from the Laundromat two stores over, a few families in the neighborhood who ate salad bar once or twice a week. The most faithful regular was an older bag lady who stopped by to have coffee every evening around five. She wore dense glasses like twin magnifying lenses, her eyes behind them big and runny as two raw eggs. Mrs. Crow. Some evenings she brought her grandson Donny, who was also a regular. With her he was always well-behaved and humiliated, but later, when he returned with his friends, he revealed himself as a ten-year-old thug. The graffiti on the mall walls was undoubtedly his and his friends', and Marvin's generous policy of providing free soda refills had bought us a clean storefront.

Donny had bad eyes, like his grandmother, but he worked around his disability rather than wear glasses. Not that he had any call to read anything, though his Asteroids game seemed hindered by his having to put his nose to the screen. Over the course of the summer, Marvin and Luke had tried to tutor Donny without his catching on. This included thinly-veiled lessons in the solar system using pepperonies and Canadian bacon on a twenty-four-inch circular heaven of tomato sauce, or more complicated three-dimensional structures involving toothpicks and pineapple chunks to illustrate the construction of a molecule or floating suspension bridge. Donny liked Luke and Marvin. He was smart enough, and young enough, to give in to their foolishness. His grandmother couldn't keep him away from his friends, and his friends wouldn't let him quit being their leader. The cleverest part of Marvin and Luke's teaching was really the simplest: they let him hang around. Steve Two would have been the boy's idol under other circumstances, but because he was quick enough to see that Luke and Marvin did not entirely approve of Steve, the boy held his esteem in check.

Donny's interest in me had to do with my breasts. He made no secret of his fascination, constantly staring in his unfocused way at my chest.

"Just slap him around," Luke suggested.

Marvin illustrated. "*Fa-thwack, thwack*," he said, flipping his hands.

"But be kind," Luke said. "Gentle. He's our mascot, after all."

I suspected Donny of stealing from us, but that was probably because I myself had been taking a few things. For example, I loved those old-fashioned shakers we had filled with Parmesan cheese and what looked like crayon shavings, red pepper flakes. Filling the flakes jars made me sneeze, and suffering was the excuse I used for taking a shaker home in my purse. Sometimes, more than a few times, I balled a twenty-dollar bill in my palm and stuffed it in my jeans pocket. The price of a medium pizza was $19.98, so I'd just punch NO SALE and refund two cents, hanging on to the twenty. I felt I deserved a little bonus now and then.

We talked a lot about where our money would go. It's not an unusual topic anywhere, what you'd do if you won the lottery. Marvin was saving money for school; so was Luke. Annette wanted to own her own beauty salon, but I don't think she really thought she'd ever do it. Steve Two saw himself operating his own Goodfellows someday, though of course it wouldn't be in Wichita, and he'd get rid of a couple of things, like the self-serve aspect of it and the jukebox. "But really," he began backpedaling, "I love Bob Dylan."

Annette snorted. "That man's the biggest crybaby I ever heard, all that whining around like a car stuck in second gear. '*Buck*-ets of rain, *buck*-ets of tears,'" she imitated, badly, then added, "Needs a fuckin' bucket to carry the tune." Marvin and Luke plugged their ears. Somber Steve One never talked about what he did with his money— or what he'd do with more of it—but he was the only one of us with a family, the only one with a baby on the way. I myself was being sent to college by my parents in the fall; paychecks were supposed to be for luxuries, but I had already purchased some antiques on layaway at the junk store across the parking lot. The day I made the final payment on my first piece I had the store owner deliver my rosewood and crushed velvet chaise longue to Goodfellows, where Cherie and Wild Man and Steve One came out to stare at it beside the cigarette machine, bewildered.

Cherie sat down on it and said, "Kind of uncomfortable."

Steve One just turned around and went back to work in the hot kitchen, swiping at his forehead with his hanky. But Luke thought my purchase funky and amusing. He and Marvin approved. Later, during our break, Luke and I sat on it and observed our empty parking lot. Still later that night, he followed me home in his truck to deliver it to my parents' living room. My fifteen-year-old niece Lydia, visiting from San Diego, was still awake watching television. When I introduced her to Luke, he bowed a few times and started backing out the front door.

"What a dweeb," she said when he was gone. "And *why* did you buy *that?*" The chaise sat in the middle of the rug like an old red swaybacked horse.

"I don't know. I've always wanted a chaise longue."

She laughed, invoking the family joke for strays. "Yes, but does it eat much?" In my bedroom I set it beneath my window, and after work at night, when everyone else slept, I would sit on the rough nap smelling the unknown past that had infiltrated the cushion. I looked at the neighborhood I'd grown up in, through the tree leaves that had always trembled between me and it, working on my future nostalgia for the view. At these times my aloneness would come at me, like sad music, like heartache, like the dim knowledge of death, and I would welcome my own pale version of despair.

A few weeks later when I arrived at work there was a police car out front. My heart went banging: my thefts were discovered. Inside, up in Marvin's office above the kitchen, I could see a menacing black-uniformed officer through the curtained window. Luke was at the front counter, watching my feet as I walked in.

"What's this?" I asked.

"Money's been disappearing," he said, shrugging. He stared at me, but how was I to take it?

"How much?" I said, coming around the counter, waiting to hear footsteps on the ceiling, waiting to hear Marvin summon me by my alias to his office.

"About five hundred," he said. "Cherie's been making off with our lunch rush, such as it is."

I sighed, shivering the way Waldman had to hear his life was safe. "Five hundred?"

Luke nodded, wiggling his eyebrows.

"How did she get caught?" I asked, afraid suddenly there might be more arrests.

"Steve Two," Luke said. This made sense; Steve Two had a fervent crusading attitude toward Goodfellows. Whenever I'd taken money, I'd made sure he was nowhere in sight.

"What do you call those?" He pointed at my feet.

"Clogs?" I said.

"Clogs," he said thoughtfully, leaving me at the front. Later Cherie went away with the cop, her boyfriend conspicuously absent. Marvin hated having to have her arrested. "If it was up to me," he said as we shared a Sprite at the counter, "I would have just let her go, but once the Steves were involved . . ."

"It's a drag," I said. Cherie had been saving her money for a waterbed. My purchasing furniture had reminded her of her own goal. She told me she was getting a king-size one with a heater and a black lacquer headboard with bookcases and built-in reading lights. I'd lied and said that sounded cool.

Steve One's wife gave birth in August during a tornado warning. Everyone in the store except me was outside looking for funnels. I was honor bound by my real parents to behave in a levelheaded manner and keep away from windows. Acts of God were not dalliances.

So I was there to take the news. Steve One gave me an earful: his wife's thirty-two-hour labor, the baby's inability to move into the birth canal, the C-section that had resulted, "Apgar!" he kept insisting, some test his baby had failed. I tried to make encouraging noises at the right moments, though I was sitting on the floor stretching the phone cord under the front counter to avoid taking glass slivers in the face should our enormous window implode.

"Congratulations," I said without thinking, sitting on the sticky floor, noticing the greasy filth accumulating behind the soda canisters, the pennies permanently adhered to the linoleum.

"Her name is Ashley Cristolyn Damascus," he reported proudly. I almost asked, "Damascus?" before remembering he had a name other than Steve One.

"Congratulations," I repeated.

"Thanks, Jane," he said, and I could picture him wiping that earnest sweat from his brow with his handkerchief, then folding the hanky twice and returning it to his rear pocket where its white corner would hang like a tag. From outside I heard the all-clear sound. "Man, I'm tired," said Steve One from St. Joe's maternity ward.

"Tell your wife congratulations," I said.

"I'll see you guys right soon."

We hung up as everybody came back in, all of them disappointed at seeing nothing. I gave them Steve's news. We baked a celebratory pizza with the baby's first name spelled out in green pepper slices. Nobody else was in the mood for Goodfellows that night—bad weather, plus our novelty had worn off, our prices were still high, and the walls of the mall had been spray painted with skulls and crossbones and phalluses, which seemed to discourage business.

School was scheduled to start. Goodfellows was clearly about to end. My fun there was almost over; my dorm room in Lawrence at the University of Kansas, three hours away, waited for me. On the last night I was to work, Marvin and Annette came in together, holding hands, Marvin not only not embarrassed but silly with happiness. I was stunned. Annette told me they'd spent the day together in bed. She went to work like it was nothing, filling beer pitchers, slapping orders through the window, running toothpicks along the crevices to collect gray scum with which she threatened to top somebody's pizza. I listened to Marvin and Luke with profound disillusion, wondering what Annette's conquest really meant. Was Marvin using her? Was this possibility worse than the other one, that he actually liked her? It made me unusually forgetful and incompetent that night. Somehow the restaurant seemed dirtier, less like home and more like a failing business in a strip mall.

Then the phone rang and we got the news that Steve One's baby wasn't expected to live. Things had not been going well, but we'd all thought they were normal baby dilemmas, jaundice and colic. None of the rest of us had children; I know I hadn't given the baby's illness more than passing consideration. Now it was "extreme failure to thrive." On the telephone—Marvin talking in the back, me listening in the front—Steve One told us from the hospital he wouldn't be in to check our percentages this night.

I was eighteen. I said to Steve One, the father of a baby about to die, "Maybe it was her smoking," meaning his wife's. She'd not quit during her pregnancy. It was perhaps conceivable this *was* the reason the baby would die, but so what? I was eighteen. I had no idea what I was saying. The line went quiet, the two men waiting for me to hang up. I did, burning in shame, in anger, happy to be leaving this life behind me.

At closing, Steve One appeared at the glass front door, his head lowered as he searched his heavy ring for the right key. I held my ubiquitous damp diaper, recalling as usual the young woman who'd stood there earlier in the summer bleeding. When Steve One entered everyone clustered near him. His daughter had died two hours earlier. His wife was drugged. Having nowhere else to go, he'd come to Goodfellows wearing his saggy pants and company shirt. When I tried to apologize for my previous insensitivity, he merely shook his head, forgiving me in his uncomplicated way. He had no reason to care what in the world I ever thought or did. Hundreds of waitresses would pass this way; I would be replaced, superseded, forgotten.

After we closed I went home with Luke and spent the night at his apartment, sitting on the couch watching his fish aquarium and letting him read rhymed couplets to me. Why wasn't he touching me? Why weren't we kissing? His apartment was unexceptional, except that it was his. I drank it in from the lumpy fake-leather couch. The support system was shot, so we'd slid close to each other. Luke smelled of scorched cornmeal pizza crust and cigarette butts, though we'd separated those two trash categories as we cleaned up, leaving the edible in Goodfellows boxes out by the Dumpster, as we did every night. This was at Luke and Marvin's insistence. It seemed to me that everyone I knew, *everyone,* was better than I. When Steve Two heard the baby had died, he went directly to Steve One and gave him a hug, laying his round Charlie Brown head on Steve One's chest. Annette had burst into tears. Where had this come from, I wondered? Where was it in me? The only time I'd ever cried at Goodfellows was chopping onions.

Luke's poetry was unfathomable, his apartment still and stuffy. We sat together so long not touching that by daybreak I was rigid with nerves, my face sore from wearing an interested expression all night. When it became abundantly clear that he wasn't going to do anything, when the sky outside his dirty shades started to go purple with daybreak, I finally stood to leave. Instead of a kiss, he gave me a Xeroxed sheaf of sonnets written by a manic-depressive friend of his in Wyoming. I thanked him and left, sleepy, edgy, dissatisfied.

My role in the Goodfellows family meant that I hovered uncertainly, watching it fall apart, unable to do a thing except abandon it the minute I drove out of the parking lot. Luke wrote to me but I only skimmed his letters and didn't respond, my shame—of him, of myself—thereby confined to a place and time I'd put away. I never saw any of those people again, not even accidentally, though Goodfellows could have been the proving ground for my next job, my next little family, and the next one, and the next, and all the others that were to come.

⌒ *The Unified Front*

*J*acob's wife liked to blame his hair, which had gone white as Santa's just after he turned forty. Now it was six years later.

"You're too old-looking to be anybody's dad," she said. He knew Cece didn't intend unkindness; she was trying to keep her chin up. After all, she had wanted a baby her whole life. She'd used to pretend to breastfeed her dolls, lift her shirt and smack a hard plastic head against her own flat chest. She had been the champion of younger, rejected neighbor children, had held the plump hand of her little sister, then her cousins, then a nephew, then godchildren, now great-nieces. When was her turn? Where was her baby?

Jacob held *her* hand on the 737 bound for that big theme park in Florida, the oasis in the orange groves, the giant golf ball and the mouse. Cece needed a holiday; she'd picked the unlikeliest place on the planet. "Did she think we don't know math?" Cece demanded of him before takeoff, apropos of nothing. He knew which "she" was meant; there was another "she" they didn't discuss. "Did she think we couldn't add up for ourselves how old we'd be when the child was sixteen?"

Jacob lifted the armrest between them and scooted closer to his wife, who lurched away to look him up and down: was he feeling sorry for her? In the aisle, a flight attendant mimed pleasure as she demonstrated the oxygen mask without mussing her makeup. One of the other flight attendants was pregnant, and behind them sat a mother and toddler, evidence of the cruel way life rubbed your nose in your misery. And, Jacob thought as he recalled his and Cece's destination, the foolish way you rubbed your own nose in it.

"We're being punished," Cece said, seeming to decide Jacob's sympathy was bearable.

"We did nothing wrong," he said. "You buckled?"

"Like a seat belt would do any good in an airplane crash." She might scoff, but she buckled, pulling the excess tight. She was forty-one years old and no larger than a young girl, optimistically wearing shorts, in Chicago, in mid-November, as a gesture of belief in the balmy reputation of Florida. Since she hadn't had a baby, her lap lay flat as it had fifteen years ago, when they'd married. Jacob had told her then, whenever she worried before the mirror, that he would welcome stretch marks, those wavering luminescent scars, the pearly opalescence of nearly torn flesh, those private hieroglyphs between them. Jacob kissed her cheek. He closed his eyes and let himself imagine the face of the woman who'd told them they couldn't adopt a baby, that they were too old. For himself, this offense hardly registered, but on Cece's behalf a dark rage bloomed deep inside him. He wanted to take cartoonish revenge against Adoptive Services: hit the woman—who was *pregnant*, smug fertile creature!—and tip her desk on its side, scatter her files and forms like confetti, bash together the heads of her assistants like coconuts, toss a brick or sizzling stick of dynamite through the plate glass agency window, write huffy letters, and make anonymous obscene phone calls.

"Kill the messenger," Cece encouraged him. He was fuming, but she accepted the news calmly; she'd learned to expect precisely the worst. There were a few reasons she believed she deserved no baby: she'd kept faith for too long, been too confident of her own reproductive fitness. She'd not come on her knees to the threshold of adoptive services, had, in fact, steadfastly shunned them, and now she was to suffer for her own arrogance: where once those administers of babies might have welcomed her, they now cavalierly closed the door.

And there was Crystal, of course. Crystal's child—the baby who'd been most clearly their destiny—would have been three years old now. Crystal had jumped from Jacob and Cece's fourth-floor balcony in her eighth month, surviving herself but killing the baby. She'd tried to reach Jacob and Cece—had come to their apartment to wait for them, used her key to let herself in, drunk a full bottle of gin, eaten whatever food she could find, then opened the sliding glass balcony door. Jacob and Cece had been in the Ozarks. That was the last vacation they'd taken, and they'd taken it to escape Crystal. Jacob could not think of that part of his life without wondering what would have changed had he done something differently, just a minor yet crucial contingency in the events. A little gesture the size of a note or phone call might have safeguarded their child, and Jacob sometimes feared that he'd brought the disaster upon them by not wanting that child enough. He'd known Crystal better than Cece had; he should have predicted her reaction. And perhaps he *had* predicted it, perhaps he'd taken advantage of it—he literally squirmed to think so. If the baby had lived, it would have now been the approximate age of the one sitting behind Jacob on the plane, the one kicking steadily into the region of Jacob's kidneys.

Cece tugged at his sleeve and said, "Remember that kid I told you about, the girl on the trip home from Germany?" This was an old story, one Cece did not realize she had told far too many times. Jacob imagined that she thought of it more often than she actually admitted, that she sometimes resisted telling him. Years earlier, before the airlines got technical about it—before some parent sued, Jacob assumed—Cece had been given the charge of an eight-year-old girl for the duration of a flight from Frankfurt to Chicago. "The mother picked me because she thought I was the most reliable-looking person in the waiting area," Cece said, now. She had some good stories she'd only told Jacob once; on occasion, she surprised him with a brand-new one, an incident from her past plucked like a fruit, handed him to delight him, fresh and delicious. But he'd heard about the German girl a dozen times. Cece loved having been chosen; she'd loved the little girl, who spent the flight explaining her family troubles—the divorce, the new step- and half-siblings, the intercontinental visits. Cece always concluded the story wondering whether the girl—Hannelore—remembered her, that and the fact that the child's father, in America, hadn't bothered to thank Cece for her transatlantic pampering.

"She was such a sweet child," Cece said now. "I always wanted my daughter to be just like her, smart and funny."

Jacob grunted.

Later, when their 737 hit a pocket of weather, the cabin's interior rattled as if to shake itself from its exoskeleton, and Cece grabbed Jacob's hand. He'd been dozing, having visions of children, great swarms of them, their faces hissing up at him like a cave full of bats caught in a sudden light.

"As if this might help," Cece said, squeezing the blood from his flesh, not letting go of him until the air smoothed once more.

"I never saw so many fat white thighs," Jacob commented twenty-four hours later. "People are ugly animals, aren't they? I'd give away my three-day pass to see just one alligator." Jacob talked because Cece wouldn't; someone had to fill the silence.

Not too long after, they sat on a ride through Never Never Land. "There's your gator," Cece told him.

What was *she* looking for? Jacob wondered. Clearly she had something in mind, the way she moved from ride to ride, choosing long lines, buying popcorn and then throwing half of it away, sitting listlessly on the tram and monorail, then hustling as fast as possible to the gift shop to purchase a bag of presents, leaving Jacob to trail behind. At the end of the first day, they soaked in the not-quite-hot tub at their hotel and listened to children playing in the swimming pool.

"We could adopt an older girl," Jacob said, so physically relieved to be sitting rather than walking, so comforted by the darkening night sky and the dull images behind his own eyelids in place of the garish ones he'd been blitzed by all day long, he said whatever came floating through his mind, his lazy familiar thoughts leaking out his mouth. "Plenty of older children need parents."

"I'm a good person," Cece responded with her own weary refrain, "but I'm not a saint. I could only love a teenager when I remembered it as an infant. Besides, we don't want to inherit problems."

Actually, their next step was to go to another country. Jacob knew this was coming, an inevitability mushrooming on the horizon. They would find their baby far south of here, a doe-eyed brown child. He was not unhappy with that scenario; he preferred not knowing the parents, nor the language, nor the shaky lawfulness. But it exhausted him, the anticipation of the work involved. "You like Florida?" he asked.

She sighed. "Do you?"

"I do." He did; the weather was his friend, gentle and humane, utterly unlike the weather of his homeland. "I may discover I hate winter, if we stay here much longer."

"Is my bathing suit frumpy?" Cece asked. Jacob opened his eyes to look at her. She was so small only her head showed, and Jacob couldn't recall what her suit looked like, under the bubbling water. She said, "I feel a funk coming on. There are about a thousand different ways to hate this place. I thought everybody would be happy, but nobody's happy, everybody's miserable."

"Not me," he told her. "I like the palm trees. Palm trees make it an official vacation."

"All the crying children," Cece said, "they make me sad. And all the angry moms and dads, so mean to their children. Plus, now my hair's all rank from this chlorine, and my bathing suit is so old and cruddy it could stand up without me."

But this was Cece's personality, to choose Florida and read a guidebook about it and make the trip and then complain. She complained so that Jacob would play the other role, the promoter, the endorser. She would summon the black cloud so that he could point out the silver lining; she would despise it so that he could enjoy it. He remembered there were fireworks. "Let's go back to the park," he said, though he had no interest in making the trek again. "We'll watch the fireworks."

Jacob didn't need a baby; since the horrific year when Cece had befriended Crystal and convinced her not to have an abortion, the idea of a baby always brought with it a queasy dread. Besides, he had Cece, although he knew that wasn't a fitting attitude to broadcast to the world. Popular sentiment had it that marriages ought to be between equals, but Jacob hadn't ever known an equal in love. It was always somebody feeling more than the other, somebody protecting, somebody requiring safe harbor or permission or simple compliance. He loved Cece in the sheltering way of a parent; he wanted to cover her eyes and ears from the unkind news of the world. He loved her the other way, too, the way that made him want to bite her on the thigh, hold her naked shaken body. She was everything to him, a little person who bought her clothing in the boys' section of JC Penney, flannel shirts and Wrangler jeans, her fingertips reaching only as far as her hips. Something in her composition made her thumbs stumpy like the heads of turtles and her arms abbreviated—simian, it was called, the telltale crease cut straight across her palm so she could fold her hand in half like the mouth of a puppet. Traits left over from the apes, traits found in five percent of the normal population. "Five percent of the *normal* population," Cece would always emphasize. He loved that emphasis.

In front of the hotel bathroom mirror Cece shedded her dreadful suit and studied her naked body in the unforgiving light. "My breasts are shrinking and I'm sprouting facial hair. Maybe I'm turning into a man."

"I don't think so," Jacob said, cupping the two halves of her clammy rear end in his palms.

"Okay then—a neuter. Give me that, will you?"

"Let's get to the fireworks."

"Why do I like those things, anyway?"

"They remind you of sex," he said.

At the grand explosive close of the fireworks display—the lance-like lasers and rapid flaring lights, the dizzying volley of music and mobbing patriotism like the end of a war—Cece shouted into his ear, "So, have you come yet?"

Jacob dreamed of Crystal. Of course. Crystal Lake, the girl with the preposterous name, the psychopath who'd detonated in their lives. She'd been his student in the required senior class, peer leadership, a mediocre student held back a year, an indolent girl with a bad reputation and a sly smile. This was no excuse; he'd betrayed the central edict of his profession by sleeping with her. He'd had sex with her and she'd become pregnant, though it wasn't so elementary as it sounded. In the first place, she'd slept with so many boys that the odds of the baby's being Jacob's were low. (Hadn't he and his wife, by the way, been found infertile?) Secondly, she'd blackmailed him. While Crystal stoically refused to tell whose baby it was, so that neither her parents nor Cece had ever discovered the affair, this muteness on her part left Jacob open to whatever impulse might seize her. He'd settled for halfhearted gratitude, wholehearted hatred. Cece pitied her and Crystal soaked it up like a sponge. She had not told the grown-ups, but Jacob had read the knowledge in his other students' eyes, and as an enduring murmur in succeeding classes, a rumor just wild enough to be true.

In Florida, in his dream, Crystal was throwing a party in Jacob and Cece's hotel room. The cookies she'd made in the microwave were delicious. Jacob kissed her, then moved his hard penis between her legs. By then he'd figured out it was a dream, that there wasn't any harm in having sex. And it felt good to slam against her, to hurt her this way because there wasn't any other way to do so. At home, there was that punishing patch of ground where'd she fallen, a place Jacob's eye strayed to when he rounded their building for the underground garage. He did not love her, he did not desire her: he wanted honest release.

When he woke, he still had an erection. Cece was already up, strategizing with her pamphlets and a pencil, devising a game plan. The sun shone through gaps where the hotel room curtains didn't meet, beneath the door, in a piercing ray of white from the peephole in the door. It was aggressive, this sunlight. Outside on the balcony, the season could easily have been summer—palm trees, green grass, people in shorts and shades, the soothing sound of lawn mowers. In the bathroom, Cece had left her monthly discreet sanitary wrappers: not pregnant, again. Her gynecologist had explained that Cece's eggs were tough-skinned things, inpenetrable. At the fertility clinic, the doctor had injected Jacob's sperm, hoping to boost infiltration into the resistant, fickle egg. Jacob had sat in a chair beside Cece during this procedure, tempted to make jokes, loathing the man whose head and shoulders disappeared under the tent created by Cece's raised legs.

Cece claimed not to blame Jacob for the one child they'd conceived, a baby long before they were married, before they knew they would marry, before they knew even the easiest secrets about each other. But Jacob had been the one to suggest the abortion, and then couldn't go with her. He'd just begun a job and didn't feel he could ask for time off. At the clinic, they'd let her sleep afterward. When Jacob picked her up she was still too muddled by anesthesia for her grief to show. And then her younger sister had come to town with *her* baby and Cece had had to pretend there'd never been a pregnancy, otherwise wouldn't everyone feel awkward and squeamish? And Jacob stood by like a gawking stranger, only beginning to comprehend the tenderness Cece could bring forth in him, while Cece held her nephew in her short arms and grew damp eyed. When she'd bled, later, Jacob was at work—a job he'd left after only three months, a job that amounted, in the end, to nothing—and her sister took her to the hospital, bringing along the baby nephew, who slept in his cloth bag on his mother's chest, and though Cece lost a lot of blood, she was fine, but after that there simply weren't other babies, as if Jacob and Cece had been given their chance and squandered it.

"If we hurry," Cece told him from the made bed as he returned with a flop to the messy one, "we can see the parade." She tapped the metal ring of the pencil eraser on her teeth, which made Jacob's tonsils wobble. He thought about Crystal, about the phone messages she'd left on their answering machine, about the mess she'd made when she finally came over the evening she'd leapt from the ledge. There was drinking, smoking, crying, phone calls to anyone whose number she could remember, there was even the cutting up of Cece's dresses with pinking shears: a sick party with only one guest. She'd been an unreliable caretaker of their child, a deranged baby-sitter from a bad movie, a child in a grown-up suit upon whom real grown-ups had made grown-up demands.

"Parade," Cece said, pulling Jacob's toes.

Jacob stared straight up. Above him, the fan looked like a giant starfish glommed to the ceiling.

Cece ate mouse ear-shaped ice cream and mouse ear-shaped pancakes. She bought a mouse hat and a mouse shirt for herself, and a pair of mouse pajamas for her youngest great-niece. She sat on benches in her mouse clothes like a ten year old, dangling her legs and letting the sun turn her pale skin a bright pink. Most of what she saw she absorbed in silence, though in the darkened cars as they passed by Indians or mobsters or spacemen, she held onto Jacob's arm. Jacob felt like Gulliver in the Lilliputian theme parks; they had not been designed for tall men, and he kept cracking his head against roofs and doorways.

On the fourth day Cece pointed out a double stroller carrying twins. The girls sucked pacifiers and wore mouse bonnets on their big heads. "Cute," Cece said.

Jacob followed Cece, who followed the twins, whose parents had three other children. There were two more girls and a nearly teenage boy whose head had recently been half shaved—for reasons of fashion, evidently—leaving scabs. The mother leaned on the stroller as if to prop herself up; she had a stout disposition to go with her body, and she never quit talking, a flowing litany of instructions to keep the family machine functional.

Cece said, "She's a breeder," and Jacob realized the woman was pregnant, on top of everything else.

Originally, Cece and Jacob had held three-day passes, but Cece had wanted more and Jacob had made this fourth day a gift to her. Jacob, utterly depleted, exhausted, had to keep remembering his selflessness. His nose had sunburned and his feet had blistered; he was weary of sunshine, having discovered he could not entirely trust it when it shone so single-mindedly, and the music that surrounded them made him long for the common noise of his dark gray city. Though he had tried, he could not find the dirty underworkings of the park. The bathrooms were spotless, the trashcans almost empty, a whole fleet of men in jumpsuits scurried around with scoops and brooms whisking away the waste. You presented your passport and they let you in; they kept all the unpleasantness on the other side of the gate. It was a bright seamless world as insidiously seductive as a drug trip.

"Cece, do you remember hearing about some sort of accident here once? Some horse that bolted?" Jacob recalled that a bystander had happened to videotape the event, that his camera had been confiscated, his footage destroyed, his teenager's college education guaranteed as part of the cover-up. Or something like that. "A scandal," Jacob said. "Remember?"

Cece listened impassively; people in line frowned at him. They shuffled forward and she leaned close to his ear as if to kiss it, saying, "You don't care about having a baby, do you?" Although they knew each other well, it sometimes became necessary to ask a plain question.

"Only because you do," he said, it being impossible for him to lie to her.

She stepped away. "Is that because you're a man? Is that why? If that's why, then I'm glad I'm not a man. I wouldn't be a man for a million bucks." Her eyes were suddenly wet and the people in line frowned once more; what had Jacob said to upset his wife so?

Jacob was thinking he wouldn't be a woman, either, not one like Cece. Maybe some other woman, but he couldn't have endured the longing she suffered, the consuming desire to give birth. He wondered if he shouldn't be wounded, that he wasn't enough for her. She, after all, was enough for him, a fact he'd discovered during his affair with Crystal.

They boarded their boat and began floating through a long maze of animated figures all singing the same song, a song that proclaimed harmony in the world, happiness, equity. Just one boat ahead rode the family with twins. Their parents held them up, as if to push them even closer to the spectacle, and the babies' arms waved, their big heads turned to look from one side of the canal to the other: all those blinking, dancing, spinning, smiling dolls. Jacob was reminded of a horror film, but the children seemed pleased.

From the boats, they followed to the gondola, where the canned yodeling and the wait in line gave Jacob a headache. A wasp circled the crowd, making people bat their hands and duck their heads. It was the only piece of ungoverned nature Jacob had seen here, and, as a result, he cheered it on, hoping it would sting somebody. Cece stared at the family, whose sullen son had dashed away to a more dangerous ride. The older girls begged for trinkets—the same souvenirs Cece had been buying for days—and the mother threatened them. If they didn't stop complaining they were never going anywhere again. The father thought the girls could have one prize each. The mother argued that simply *coming* here was prize enough and, furthermore, that her husband should back her up, regardless of the issue, when they were with the kids. "Unified front," she said, as if anything but blind compliance would not be tolerated: whether he disagreed was irrelevant. One twin fussed, thrashing her arms, tossing her pacifier to the ground while the other watched placidly, pacifier bobbling between her lips. The wasp circled.

"Which one of those babies would you want?" Cece whispered to Jacob.

Neither, he thought. "The calm one," he said. This baby sat blinking, sucking. Jacob believed that he himself might appear contented—overwhelmed, stunned—to be pushed around in a stroller among the life-size stuffed animals and bright whirling gadgetry.

Of course, Cece would prefer the unhappy baby. "That one will take no shit," she proclaimed.

Way up in the gondola, Jacob rested his sore heels on the opposite seat where Cece faced him to watch the gondola car bearing the family, ahead of them. Jacob looked out over the park, hoping to catch a glimpse of something beyond it. As a child, he'd been taken annually to a small amusement park on his midwestern city's outskirts, and one of the pleasures there was the high ride into the sky on the Ferris wheel. You could spin downward into the clownish chaos of Joyland—organ music, sickening cotton candy, black-toothed carnies—then up for a serene vista of the surrounding farmland, the fat slow river shining gold in the sunset, the distant orange earthmovers riding over the lumpy jumble of the city dump.

But here there was nothing but park, far as the eye could see, beyond the rides the lakes and highways and mouse-eared traffic signs, a country unto itself, manicured as a golf course, pristine as idealism, perfect as plastic. It was undeniably grand and attractive, but it did not, finally, appeal to Jacob. The swinging basket he sat in suddenly made him aware of being off the ground, that he could fall. Again, he thought of Crystal.

Crystal probably believed he'd escaped feeling guilt. There wasn't any way he could convince her otherwise, he knew. Cece had insisted she not have an abortion—despite her immaturity, despite her ostracized life—and then Cece and Jacob had both promised to be available, to be pregnant with her. True, she'd taken advantage—borrowing money, spending all her time on their couch, blackmailing Jacob for favors and attention—but that was no excuse. When they left without telling her where they were going—escaping to Missouri, to a little cabin near the water, just for two nights—she'd behaved like any neglected child. They'd reneged; so would she.

He could not imagine what her life was now. He had heard she'd finished high school and gone on to college out west. She had never revealed her affair with Jacob to Cece, and perhaps the whole horrible ordeal had made her a better human. Jacob wondered if he himself was a better human than he'd been then. His seduction of Crystal, his single infidelity, had taught him that he would never betray Cece again. Humans erred, this was central to Jacob's knowledge of the world. He'd erred, and Cece would have forgiven, had she ever discovered his offense. And he'd not been entirely unhappy to have Crystal's baby disappear from their lives, no matter how much it meant to Cece.

This infidelity, he knew, Cece would not have forgiven.

The gondola ride ended after no more than four minutes. "The time ratio, waiting-to-riding, is not good numbers," Jacob told Cece, shaken by the trip through the air. "Roughly ten to one, as I figure it. And this is the off-season. Imagine this in July." He saw the whole place in his mind's eye as a melting structure, a magnificent birthday cake left too long in the sun, a whim of the tyrannical rodent with his pinched, shrill voice.

Cece trailed after the twins, whose father carried both girls downstairs while their mother led, angrily bouncing the stroller on each step. Outside again, they stopped to get their bearings, then headed toward the long line winding around the enclosed roller coaster. The building was supposed to resemble a space station. Their gloomy, ugly, half-bald son waited in the middle of the line, staring dispassionately as his parents and sisters approached.

Cece, following, said to Jacob, "Watch the people standing behind him in that line."

Sure enough, there was grumbling when the family cut in. But the big mother ignored it, preempting with conviction, busy reconfiguring the doublewide stroller and ordering her son to seek out hot dogs for them all while they held his place. Cece occupied herself locating sunglasses and a map of the park, standing alongside the line without actually being in it.

"That mother's going to go on the roller coaster," she predicted. "Even though she's pregnant." A sign outside this ride warned various types to beware: people with back or neck injuries, small children, pregnant women. "She's so hardy she doesn't think twice," Cece added. Had the woman wanted to, she could have heard the remark, but she was haughty with bottles and powdered formula: motherhood made her oblivious. One of the older daughters was sent to a drinking fountain for water. The husband was given the task of smearing sunscreen on everyone's face. When the son returned, they ate their hot dogs quickly, the mother sucking mustard off her fingers.

The two older daughters were left with the babies while Mom and Dad and brother stepped into the cool dark of the building. The girls each took a handle of the fat stroller—the kind designed for jogging moms, bicycle-wheeled and expensive—and steered it toward the shaded exit ramp on the far side of the roller coaster. They sat on a curb and ignored their sisters, one of whom cried and the other of whom sat looking around like a sated toad. Jacob felt his feet had never been so fatigued in all his life.

Cece was gone, on her way over to the children, striding fast on her short legs, leaving Jacob alone to watch. She waved at the big girls, exclaimed over the little ones. She asked to hold the noisy one, reaching out without waiting for permission.

Jacob steeled himself. If Cece took that baby, he would not only have to hire a lawyer and come up with bail money, but first he would have to pluck the child from her arms. Possibly he'd have to streak after her through the crowds, dashing among the rides and costumed characters—all this nonsense that his wife wanted so badly to claim a share of—and bring her to the ground. Security here, he was sure, would be exemplary, quick and efficient, sovereign. It would be of no interest to anyone but Jacob that she had waited for a twin to kidnap, waited for a baby who wouldn't be *as* missed.

It was hot and Jacob's head seemed cooked. The setting was surreal and thoughts of Crystal Lake had made him feel crazy. Sense was abandoning him. He focused on his wife, who was rocking the squirming unhappy child. She had a way with babies, a rhythm in her hips, a friendly smile. Babies had been stolen from her and she'd had no recourse. Her desire was larger than his, she alone understood its power, the force it had to make her behave less like a saint and more like a human. Watching her now, dizzy with sun and loyalty, Jacob pledged himself to her anew: if she ran, he would not stop her. When she ran, he would come along.

⌒ *One Dog Is People*

*O*nce there were two, and now there was one. In the process of dealing with diminishment, that central fact kept targeting me like the ray of a stun gun: I'd had a husband, and now I had none.

He died on a snowy night, an unusual desert storm, the highways obsidian in the moonlight, drivers skating down the frozen chute of New Mexico, from the mountains of Santa Fe along the ridges of Albuquerque into the basin of Truth or Consequences under a full moon on black ice. Because I had always believed the worst could happen, Thomas's truck tires had been recently rotated, his engine winterized, and in the cab he had stowed a candle, matches, flashlight, extra batteries, blanket, water bottle, Fix-a-Flat, emergency flare, and a cardboard sign the size of his windshield that blurted SEND HELP!! He hadn't himself slid off the road, but instead, had stopped to help the frivolous Miata driver, the one traveling too fast, the college student spun off on a curve, unscathed. On the sportscar floorboard, Mr. Stud Muffin Delta Chi had tossed his beer cans; the truck driver, bringing RCA nineteen-inch color televisions to Texas, had taken the curve too fast, too, everyone reckless except my husband, who died instantly, the full weight of a heavy load coming down upon him under the influence of inertia, the impossible pitting of machine and man, matter and spirit, body and soul. It was the trucker who sent me an apology, all the pertinent words misspelled. *Greif, flook, quilt,* by which he meant guilt. The college student had been, no doubt, counseled by his family's lawyer to keep his foolish mouth closed.

When the newspaper ran Thomas's photo, the phone began its ringing. Strangers sent cards and claimed to be saying prayers; Tupperware tubs with mysterious contents arrived anonymously on the doorstep; and in the yard, someone left a life-size St. Francis, birds on his outstretched terracotta arms, his brick-colored eyes mournful. My son believed the statue was a headstone, that his father had been buried out front beside the palo verde tree. My daughter, three years old, continued to ask when Papa was coming home.

In every tragedy there is the sorting of events—by the police, by the family, by the public—the pinning down of facts so that those few moments leading to disaster can be brutally inventoried. The ironies and coincidences must be noted: Thomas had first passed the stranded Miata, then circled around, off one ramp and onto another, making a time-consuming, backtracking, heroic effort to rescue the drunk boy. It's possible he recognized himself in the trouble, his former hapless strandedness, the many nights he'd been flung from the road for one foolhardy antic or other. The trucker had just finished speaking to his wife on his cellular phone, who told him she was worried, that she'd been watching the Weather Channel, tallying the jackknifed big rigs across the Southwest. And the college student's aunt turned out to be a woman I went to high school with, a girl who'd once driven me home from a party when my boyfriend had told me to get lost. I'd been inordinately grateful for her rescuing me then, as I was drunk and stricken; she'd seemed like a savior. Lois Freudenthal. She told me she hadn't been on speaking terms with her sister, the boy's mother, until this accident. Now they were talking again, reunited in our tragedy.

After my husband died, I received predictable advice, much of it contradictory: honor my feelings of sadness, someone would suggest, while another would exhort me to get on with what she called my life. To our daughter, Thomas could be described as in a deep sleep from which he would never wake. Or: his ascent to heaven could be detailed, his panoramic vision of her, and her brother's, life assured. "I go *with* him," she cried, "I want to go with him!" and her brother, wise second grader, recipient of harsh playground folklore, punched her in the stomach.

"You can't," he sobbed. "*No one* can go with him!" And we were then a trio in a weeping heap, me without any inclination other than to hold my children, hold them tight.

My friends and family, a large and mixed group, waited a few months before offering the most alarming advice: date.

"You need to move past this," my older sister told me, as if there were some obstinate bovine creature preventing me from crossing the street. My sister lived two thousand miles away, but felt the need to keep track of my life as if we were nextdoor neighbors. To this end, she phoned every weekend, probing at the small details—was Tavia's croup better, had Jed been promoted to fourth grade math, had I gone to my group meeting—in order to claim intimacy. I was lonely, so I allowed it. For once, *I* was the subject of our conversations. In our previous relationship, we discussed her, or, in lieu of her, my failure to quite meet up to her. She had used to consider us in competition, herself always in the lead, but now I had finessed front-runnership. She was not a widow, she couldn't even blatantly aspire to it.

Widow. I went to a few group meetings hoping for fraternity. Parents Without Partners and Bereaved Spouses both have chapters in our town. But even there, people echoed my friends and family, spending a shocking amount of time discussing replacement. In fact, many in attendance were on the lookout for another mate. I couldn't begrudge them that—the off-kilter absence, after all, I felt directly—but I, myself, seemed unprepared.

My true intimate was my husband's business partner Barton. Barton's bereavement mirrored my own: he was now the sole survivor in a partnership that, practically speaking, required two members. He, like me, carried on doing more than one person should have to do. And he missed Thomas in a daily way, in the startling way of perpetual surprise: sabotaged by suddenly forgetting our friend was not there. He missed their jokes and coffee breaks. He missed Thomas's easy company. My husband, quiet and calm, had always provided the balance at our house. I might explode, slam doors, hang up on irritating solicitors, yell at the children, kick the dogs, but Thomas would be there like a faithful force of rational composure. The Big Picture never escaped his vision; he could grasp the essential and, Zen-like, let loose the rest. In his and Barton's nonprofit theater business, he had been the same. Distributors preferred to phone him; projectionists went to him with their complaints; food service suppliers showed up on mornings when he was scheduled to be in.

Barton, like me, was the hotheaded idea man in the business. Like me, he'd proposed the alliance; like me, he worried most about its success. I'd been forever pondering our suitability as a couple, fretting over the long silences that punctuated the marriage, on occasion lapsing from him to test other waters. In eleven years, I'd had two affairs, and each time I'd returned to Thomas chagrined and grateful, rededicated and more certain. He'd found out about the second affair because he asked me, and I confessed. The first, I knew, would have upset him more because it was such a thoughtless fling, one that didn't reflect what Thomas liked to think of as my authentic character. I slept with a stranger, a one-night stand in a hotel room. We met at a state conference of special ed teachers, ate dinner together and had drinks, then went to bed. I can't explain why the idea seemed like a good one. At least in my second affair, I had fallen in love and agonized over the ramifications. But in the first, I simply acted on a weak impulse, in a role that wasn't my own except for that one night. I could offer reasons, but they would be lies. I might as well say that the moon was full, and so I howled, atavistic and unstoppable.

Probably there are not many married individuals who don't contemplate, momentarily and in anger, a spouse's death. During my second affair, there were a few months where I was convinced no other solution was possible: Thomas had to die. If he died, I could marry Gene. If he died, I wouldn't have to hurt him, I wouldn't have to live with what I was doing to our son (our daughter, then, was not yet even an idea). If he died, then everyone would *want* me to fall in love anew. And sure enough, I had been right: everyone wanted me to fall in love. But now that Thomas was dead, it didn't look like I would be able to comply.

My son Jed took the death hardest. He told me, a couple of months after the accident, that his life had gotten sad after his papa had died, that he just couldn't be happy the way he had when he was six or five. He cried, wanting to reclaim what he perceived as his youth. Of course, I would have preferred he be spared, that I might take all his anguish and suffer it myself. But I also saw the way his character would benefit by this early grief. What doesn't kill you makes you stronger, right? He had had some layer of superfluity excised; he knew what mattered and what didn't. When his friend Nikko mistreated him at school—wouldn't sit beside him, wouldn't share his Oreos—he had the ability to put it in perspective. It simply couldn't fully bother Jed. He had a hole in his life where his dad had lived, and in there developed a new self, a private self that made him more interesting, I thought. At home, we understood something among us, even Tavia, whom Jed and I counted on to sometimes wail, to note in anger the unfairness of her father's absence. Jed now stayed up later in the evening, later than any of his school friends, reading or watching television with me, curled quietly next to me, two warm bodies, until he was physically tired enough to combat all the scary stuff that creeps in at night. He probably wasn't getting enough sleep, but he didn't like lying in the dark being sad any more than I did.

But there were times when my mourning couldn't include the children, any more than our sex life could have when Thomas was alive. There were grown-up, private parts of marriage. I missed Thomas's affection for my underwear, his once-annoying habit of idiotic pillow talk. He'd learned all his sexual banter from B novels and movies. It had irritated me when he was alive; now it amused me, made me miss him more profoundly. Who would ever sweet-talk me again? Who would I ever know well enough to trust non-sense with again? Masturbation became another wretched hazard, sexual solitaire, morbid yarn spinning; a fantasy ought never to have as its object a member of the dead.

A year passed. Time had begun bothering me, during that year, and I took my aggravation out on the kitchen clock, foolish white-faced simpleton. Its placid continuation tormented me, so I moved it from its exalted spot above the stove to a lower berth beside the door. I demoted it, in other words, and it, in turn, stopped keeping time. Fine with me.

Otherwise, life went on. I persisted in mainstreaming the mentally handicapped, my job seeming like cover-up, deception, the pretense that these children could assimilate. I began to question the assumption that assimilation was an ideal goal, that blending was preferable to being uniquely themselves. In their quirks, I found a kind of comfort, one that had eluded me previously.

Another new thought was the realization that I would have settled for Thomas in a diminished state, similar to my retarded children's; I would have welcomed whatever piece of him I could have returned to me, so long as it was the genuine article. In the past, my snobbish preference had been for the able, the whole; I wanted to leave my work at work. Now I imagined Thomas in a wheelchair, amputated or deformed, bedridden or brain-damaged, comatose. I would have fallen gratefully on his living form, no matter its short-comings and eccentricities.

The first anniversary of those dreadful days came and went: the accident, the wake, the funeral. On television the fifth evening, I watched a show about separating Siamese twins. There, finally, was my metaphor. Even though it was late, I phoned Barton. He wasn't home, so I left a horrifyingly maudlin message on his machine during a commercial break. In the show, a surgeon was making two people out of one, a Korean twin set. The girls were connected at the sacroiliac, the vagina, and anus opening between not two legs but three; they ambulated with surprising dexterity, their midleg foot splayed, three toes on each side of it. Their bladder had to be divided, their pelvis cracked, their shared leg bequeathed to the larger torso. After the surgery, the two girls lay on separate gurneys, physically stable but angry with each other. They wouldn't speak; they wouldn't even make eye contact. Three years old, they each resented being abandoned by the other. And before they could reconcile, the smaller one, the one without the advantage of the shared leg and bladder, died of infections.

I was the surviving twin, grown healthy in Thomas's presence, now whole in his absence, walking on two legs, at least one of which was rightfully his. How could I think Barton would have really understood? He, like our other friends, had moved on, found ways of surviving, lived willingly under the militant organization of standard time. On the sofa, I sniffled, so relentlessly alone. The surviving twin was destined to go on and lead what her neurosurgical team spokesman labeled "a normal and productive life."

I didn't want to be productive. I didn't care that much, anymore, about being normal—fuck assimilation. I wanted to have extraordinary experiences, sex, and fun. I wanted to laugh at someone else's misery. I wanted to get on with things, whatever they might be. I was tired of being the victim of poetic justice, of irony. I was exhausted from feeling like the one who should have died.

Because that was the real trouble. The black sheep always uncover the saintly, don't they, and marry them? The martyrs redeem the sinful, the generous embrace the greedy, the logical soothe the hysterical. Otherwise, how would the world go 'round, sun and moon, Greenwich Mean?

A few days later, I was sitting in traffic after dropping the children off at school. I relied on their disappearance every day; I could not stand such thorough neediness. And yet, as soon as they'd been swept into their buildings—third grade, Montessori—I missed them. I fell under the heavy weight of guilt: how could I not be grateful? How could I not cling to what was left to me, cling and cherish?

In front of me, in the sparkling blue monster pickup truck, a beautiful golden retriever paced the bed. Beneath its smiling gold face, on the truck's bumper, was the sticker reading THIS VEHICLE INSURED BY SMITH & WESSON. Poor dog, I thought, beholden and devoted to an idiot. The animal was clearly a male, his big square head and broad back and sweeping tail well over the lip of the generous bed. He didn't seem accustomed to traveling outside the truck cab—his movements seemed nervous, as if the corrugated metal beneath his toenails unsettled him. Beside his truck, in the right lane, in a beat-up subcompact with dark tinted windows, someone was whistling. I could hear it not through the thick glass of my consummately safe Volvo, but through the motion of the dog, as he paced and approached the source, paced and considered, his ears lifted, his tail waving, his loyalties tempted, his intelligence tested. He seemed to be weighing the appeal of an interior ride, a new owner, raising a thick yellow foot to the metal wall of his container, then thinking better of it.

Suddenly from the driver's window of the subcompact came a hand holding a donut, a white circle with a bite missing, dancing tantalizingly in the air. The dog considered his leap only for a moment. Then he was down and in traffic, off to meet his new friend in the next lane, just at the instant the light changed to green. The car behind the subcompact, its driver apparently unaware of the drama that had just unfolded before him, lurched at the green light and struck the dog, who thumped to the pavement.

Its yelps were unbearable, and they penetrated the Volvo's glass.

The dog's owner, the driver of the blue truck, had pulled away, also ignorant. How could everyone be so perfectly oblivious? The subcompact with the donut-eating driver had driven off, too. Cars behind us—"us" meaning me and the driver who'd hit the dog—squeezed around on either shoulder, leaving the two of us and the shrieking animal. Who wouldn't stop shrieking, shrieking, misery's suffering siren, let loose in the atmosphere, his hindend dragging as he whooped, working his front legs like useless fisted arms, a beached mermaid.

I was out of the car without realizing I'd opened the door, let alone unfastened my seat belt and shoved the gearshift into park. The street had cleared with the green light, but I couldn't get near the dog because of the noise. It was his pained noise that made me stand helpless, screaming myself—another unrealized feat.

The other driver was a large man, thankfully, and he'd popped from his car like a jack-in-the-box. He managed to wrestle the crying animal into a head lock, disable those useless forelegs, his own pants' knees ripping on the asphalt. I hurried to the tail end, lifted them, wet with urine, with motor oil, and helped lay our heavy load in the rear of the man's Blazer.

"Let me come with you," I said, quickly parking my car, leaving the emergency lights flashing. I didn't hesitate to hoist myself into the stranger's passenger seat. His car was full of cigarette smoke, the smell of something besides cigarette burning, too. He'd left his butt in the ashtray where it had melted a dent in the plastic.

"Where did he come from?" the man demanded. He was sweating, hair unplastered by his effort. When he tried to drive, he made the engine roar, having forgotten to shift into drive, then forgetting his parking brake. "First thing I saw was a goddamned tail under my tire. Hold on, boy," he called back to the dog.

I told him what I'd seen, the donut, the truck. Behind us, in the far rear, the animal whimpered, a pained hum, one I associated with childbirth, with the lying idea that breathing correctly would lessen one's agony.

I directed him to my vet's office, the place where I'd taken our sibling dogs for eleven years. Now twelve years, I recalled, now longer than my marriage. We'd gotten the dogs two weeks after our wedding. My husband had wanted only one—"One dog is people," he'd quoted his wise hillbilly mom, "but two dogs is *dogs*." I'd won that argument, advocating for companionship. And when it was time for children, I got my way then, as well, and we made a pair of them, too.

The parking lot was empty; the office opened in five minutes. By now the golden retriever sounded like a whickering horse, lifting his head only because he was terrified. The man—Jim Selby—and I stood by the open Blazer door watching, helpless. The dog turned his pleading liquid eyes our way, as if asking us to put him out of his misery. Jim Selby's face wore the look of most men in fear, in self-blame: angry. Curt. Likely to kick something, hard. He had my sympathy. I missed masculine habits, the way my husband's confusion or unpreparedness had always displayed itself in this same mad fashion. Jim Selby shook his head, cursed, attempted to put his hair into some kind of order, never mind the mess his pants were, the puddle of blood soaking into the carpet of his rear hatch.

By the time the vet and assistant arrived, there was nothing to do for the retriever but put him down. From his collar, the vet found a rabies identification number, and promised to handle notification of the owner. Under the cold fluorescent buzz of the office light, we all four shook hands, our clothes covered with blond hairs, our wrists and forearms scratched, small rusty spots of blood. There wasn't much blood, because all the real damage had been internal. We sighed, and separated, the assistant giving me a ride back to my car, whose lights were still blinking patiently on the parkway. I was exhausted, and sat behind the wheel for a few minutes collecting myself. It was only 9:30.

That dancing donut tormented me. My anger resided in that image, the thoughtless adolescent temptation the driver had offered the dog, a mortal seduction. I thought of the college student who'd killed my husband. My rage would not abate, in fact grew as time passed. Finally, a full week after the accident, I phoned up old Jim Selby. In another story, I suppose he and I would have become a couple, united in our shared ordeal, purged of our pasts and ready to ignite a blazing future. But Jim Selby didn't interest me, his pomaded hair and padded buttocks. In some other story, he would have been handsome instead of overweight and unbearably soft, his anger would have been compelling instead of merely predictable. And my own distress he would have met with in sympathy, earnest understanding. Instead, he said, "I'm the one who hit the damned dog. How do you think I feel?"

I said I thought he'd behaved admirably, that he'd been the victim of circumstance, et cetera. For some reason, I wanted to keep him on the line, despite the fact that he obviously had no interest in talking to me. I sat alone in my kitchen, feeling still as if I were the only unbalanced aspect of my life: two dogs, two children, two full sets of grandparents, everything paired and complemented, morning and night, the sun and the moon, hot and cold, inside and out, even the light switches with their bright option and their dark.

Jim Selby, of course, knew nothing about my past. Only my present. "Why do you want to waste your energy on that other car?" he asked, rhetorically. I could hear children in the background at his house, or maybe a television. "You did the right thing," he said. As if I'd called to be told that.

"Really?"

He sighed impatiently. "Sure." Maybe I had been tested—and my first impulse had been correct, to help. I had not driven away. There I had been in traffic, aiding at the site of an accident. And now this total stranger seemed certain my character was intact.

"I gotta go," Jim Selby said, his shrieking children louder now, the ordinary annoyances of the nuclear family. "You take care," he added, casually, reflexively.

"I'll try," I said, sincerely. When I hung up, I simply laid my head

188 · A N T O N Y A N E L S O N

on the kitchen table and wept with thankfulness: I no longer needed to believe myself the unworthy survivor. I no longer needed to hate that donut-tempting driver in the next lane, nor the college boy in his zippy Miata. All a person could do was the right thing.

In the kitchen that night I hadn't any clue about the future; perhaps my life would right itself, arbitrarily, invisibly. Tomorrow waited like any road: unknown, riddled with firm destination, as well as with flimsy happenstance. Treacherous. Merciful.

The Other Daughter

*W*ho," my father asked me, "would pay fifteen bucks for that crap?" We were waiting for my beautiful sister in the masseur's lobby. Before us towered shelves of oils and creams, anemic blue bottles with labels in French script. It was a crowded little anteroom. Price tags hung on gold thread. Lutes played, seagull sounds. "Better be the frigging elixir of the universe, worth that much," he grumbled. "Right, Patty?" he prodded, looking for me to agree.

I shrugged, though I did not doubt the value, only my father's false, old-fashioned innocence about it. On the glass table against which our knees were jammed there lay fanned-out business cards. Made of heavy paper, they were designed to look torn, and although the address they specified was on a rue in Paris, France, this was First Street, Wichita, Kansas. An air conditioner went on and on; everything smelled of essence of almonds and had a slippery quality to it. My sister had introduced us to places neither my father nor I would ever have reason to seek out on our own, offices without signs, without receptionists, whose business hours seemed arbitrary and crooked. Now she was in the room beyond the closed door, beyond the window and its slender sealed blinds, lying naked on a table.

A man named Ascenzo, emaciated with a rotten tooth, would be running his thumbs up and down her spine locating pressure points and meridians. If I was thinking this, knowing it, what was my father thinking? I moved my knees away from his. Of course he would be thinking of Janice, too, his beauty. This summer he was unemployed—like us, Janice and me, free from high school—bored and self-hating, waiting for prime-time TV. Every afternoon he would step onto the back porch of our house to tell her, as she tried to tan in the muggy sunlight, that her skin was so perfect, why was she ruining it with ultraviolet rays? She wouldn't even look at him, just yanked her tube top higher, adjusted the inside elastic of her thong, and listened to him plead.

"Thank you, Father," she would call indulgently. "I wear screen, you know." But what she wore was a chemical designed to turn her more quickly orange, a stain that smelled like soy sauce. Over her eyes sat a green plastic device like two spoons. She accepted neither parent's advice, though she was far kinder to my father than to my mother. The hostility between Janice and Mom was our family's crux, the thing we all orbited and negotiated: who was tormenting the other more? And whose displeasure could we better endure?

Our mother most often lost. She was no fun, especially in recent times. "Menopause," Janice diagnosed. My father greeted Mom in the mornings with the same stale line: "Look who took her ugly pills," seeming to believe it so outrageous as to be endearing. It was true she woke up with rumpled face skin and liquid eyes that leaked unchecked. True she muttered and bristled and wished most sincerely to be left alone. None of us was who she wanted. We had turned out wrong.

Dad and I could have read magazines while we waited for Janice, but I was afraid of what I might find in their pages while sitting next to my father, all those bodies in clothes, and out, girls not like me but like Janice. His reason for not reading them might have been the same. Our mutual shame left us staring at the svelte bottles for sale on the shelf, signed by Ascenzo, the masseur, containing pricey oils used to anoint bodies like my sister's. In the company of my father, even these benign vessels made me look aside blushing.

When her hour was up, the inner door opened just wide enough to let Ascenzo escape. He squeezed out and closed it softly behind him, showing his gray tooth as he greeted us. I watched his hands, which shone with oil. He continued to wipe them on a towel as we made small talk and waited for Janice to dress. It was a stubborn oil, like cooking oil, and Ascenzo had to run the towel between his fingers, rub down his wrists. This scrubbing was the only movement in the room, a vaguely masturbatory massage of his own. I knew my father was watching it as closely as I, thinking of those smug hands, that oil, on Janice.

My sister clattered out of the inner room, trailing her purse on her injured hand, as if to draw attention to it. She was a teenage model. Her hair was a glossy white curtain she swung with exaggeration, as if it were heavy, though in reality it was thin hair inclined to stringiness. She had to have just this moment brushed it for it to swing as it did.

"Ready?" she asked us, leaning into Ascenzo's open arms. Their embrace was for us to witness; they were dear friends, this gesture implied, dear and sympathetic like kin of another plain. Janice gave me and Dad a little glance, just to make sure we beheld her worldly, uninhibited, un-Kansan affection.

I was like my father, shy, embarrassed by my own presence, as if I were large or ugly or uninvited, though I was none of those things. But my sister was superior on all three counts: lithe, pretty, welcome. And damaged, her right hand shredded and ruined.

She held it up to slide her leather bag onto her shoulder. Where her three fingers had been were cherrylike buds, suture scars along the rims. Only her forefinger and thumb remained, so that she appeared constantly to be making a point.

"That's eighty-seven eighty-seven, even," Ascenzo told Janice, "including the co-pay and drops," handing her several bottles of his oil. My father made out the check, crossing his sevens with a terse jerk of his wrist, and then leaving the paper on the table instead of in Ascenzo's open palm.

If I'd been brave, I would have answered my father's earlier question: "*You* pay fifteen bucks for that crap, that's who."

"Drink water," Ascenzo advised Janice. "I thought those kidneys would never clear. I had to do some *talking* to those fellows," he told me.

It was July, and though Janice glistened with massage oil and smelled of almonds, I sweated. In the car, she rode up front while our father drove us to her next appointment. She cracked her neck, side to side with her eyes closed. I wondered where *my* kidneys were, my liver, and all the rest. How had she become so exotic? My life had sprung from the same source, fed on the same kibble, been exposed to the same midwestern rays, and yet—the chasm between us.

"What did you think of Ascenzo?" Janice had asked my father and me after the first session, in June, her hand then a white plaster-cast club, a big wrapped drumstick stuck on the end of her slender arm.

"His name sounds like somebody sneezed," I had answered, without thinking. She'd given up expecting much from me. When she was whole, we'd spatted; it had been fair to do so. But now I felt a chilling, dumb guilt for the injustice done her.

My father said, "Uh-huh," trying not to sound judgmental. Later, when Janice wasn't around, he said to me, "That Ascenzo was a fairy." He made declarations of these sort only occasionally, as if to release dangerous pressure, and only to me, as far as I could tell. Why? Because he knew I was thinking the identical thing? But shouldn't he have had the befuddled respect for me that he did for Janice and my mother, the same masculine mock impatience, the same restraint? Instead, something about me generated confidence in him, as if I were his son instead of younger daughter. The other daughter.

Today my father leaned his elbow on the ledge of the open Falcon window, holding a cigar in his fingers. He'd done this so regularly, for so long, that the paint on the door had worn away, revealing a smooth silver beneath. I always thought the whole car might have looked pretty, rubbed down to this hue, a blinding chrome. At the tip of the cigar, his wing window glass had a halo of unctuous brown smudge. In the back, I smelled myself. I shook my head to see if it hurt. I tried to focus on the painted lines of First Street to quell carsickness. Had I ridden in the front seat since Janice's accident? I had *driven*—learning, in the graveyard; later today, I would finally take the test for my license—but had not been a passenger up there.

"You girls want some lunch?" he asked us as we passed Pitt's barbecue.

"Frozen yogurt," Janice answered, gazing out her window as the crowded, shimmering parking lot of Pitt's disappeared behind us. "Salad and a Diet Coke, don't you think, Patty?"

I shrugged; nothing sounded appetizing, though I would eat more than she would, once we arrived at the table. They consulted me as if they might actually take my advice, my father looking in the rearview, my sister turning her ear in my direction. I might have mediated between them, if it had been called for, having a foot squarely in each of their worlds. But it was never called for.

"I could circle 'round to Pitt's," he said, edging the Falcon toward the right lane.

"Grease," Janice said, motioning with her good hand for him to swim back into through traffic. "I'm nothing but a greased pig myself. Let's don't eat one, too."

"What do you want, Pats?"

"Nothing, a Coke, some Tylenol. My *hair* hurts."

"If we eat at the yogurt shop, I'll have fries," Janice said. "If the air's not greasy, I could eat some fries and yogurt."

"Air-conditioning," I agreed. The yogurt shop appeared in my mind like a mirage, bright green and white.

My father did not belong in a yogurt shop. He belonged at Pitt's, where he could bring in his cigar, not here where little stickers with puffin penguins on them declared the place antismoker. Janice ate a yogurt cone with her left hand, her tongue moving concentrically, sexily, around the white cream. I couldn't seem to maintain my posture in my seat, slumped and suddenly chilled by the rush of Coke up my straw. That icy ache flew to my forehead. My father pulled a hairy mound of bean sprouts from his avocado sandwich and left it on his plate. ("Bean sprouts smell like sperm," he'd declared to me once. Was I supposed to know enough to praise such an insight?) We all checked our watches; Janice's next appointment was at the Danish furniture store where she would be photographed displaying teak end tables and high-tech chairs that looked like praying mantises. This shoot had been delayed for two weeks to allow her stitches to heal and her gauze to be removed; I was just happy not to have to anticipate seeing her in bras and underwear in the Sunday newspaper pullouts.

Why had they waited for her? I studied her to try to learn why, what people saw in her that commanded their submission. She was not merely beautiful. That wouldn't have been enough. And now she would have to tuck away her right hand, behind cushions, in her pocket, leaving perhaps her thumb poised outside like a cowgirl. She was blessed with something far better than simple beauty, a kind of fickle, charmed affection that made you feel lucky when she turned it on you, and flawed when she withdrew it. She would choose to leave you, and you would deserve it.

Men stared at her here, as they did everywhere, and Janice did not seem to differentiate between those who ogled her intact, and those who fixated on her sudden deformity. She ignored them all unless it became necessary to do otherwise. "Take a picture," she would say. "It'll last longer." If only I could have adopted her assurance, I often thought, but of course it was inseparable from the rest of her. She had earned her indifference.

After lunch we returned to our wretched hot car. Later I was going to drive it around with a stranger and obtain my license. Dusty bits of the old cushion stuffing would stay like fine sand on the examiner's pants. Janice sat in the front again and brushed her hair with her clumsy left hand. "My shoulders are killing me," she told us. "My relationships are a wreck, Ascenzo said, that's why they hurt right here." She stretched to tap her right shoulder blade with her hair brush.

"Which relationships?" I asked, as I was supposed to. The air was so hot that my words seemed to come out composed of a gaseous substance.

"All of them," she said. "Family, friends, lovers, all of them."

Dad snorted and relit his cigar. He only made it through one or two of them a day, constantly extinguishing and tamping, the butt end in his mouth growing soggy, its leafy origins becoming grotesquely clear, little remnants like lawn debris on his tongue.

"Who'd believe insurance would cover this stuff?" he announced. Janice and I had heard this before; I listened as if in a trance. He digested topics of conversation like a cow, constantly bringing them back up for a chew. "*I* wouldn't believe it if I hadn't seen it with my own eyes. This *Ascenzo,* the guy with no last name, or maybe no first name, who has the Blue Cross Blue Shield–okay, this guy knows from your *back* you have trouble? He consults with your kidneys, they say 'send water'?" But Dad wasn't really annoyed. He found Janice gratifyingly mysterious, and her fierce defense of the bizarre amusing. He tolerated all manner of what he called *flakelore* as long as it came from her. He'd allowed her to glue a large, many-spired crystal right in the center of the dashboard, stuck there with a green substance like Silly Putty, because she said it would protect his ride. The crystal was almost exactly the size of the fat compass that used to be attached to the windshield, its slow watery slosh something to focus on from the backseat when I grew bored, the green letters slipping serenely from N to NE to E. This had been my mother's compass, something she'd ordered by mail for no apparent reason; she never traveled anywhere she might have needed one, and besides that, she'd stuck it in our father's car instead of hers. Also for no apparent reason, the compass simply dropped off one hot day, rolling to the floorboard and disappearing out the passenger door when Janice opened it, the plastic ball cracking open as it hit the parking lot pavement and spilling out its viscous fluid. Oddly, it fell off only hours after Janice's crystal had been affixed beneath it, as if they'd waged a turf battle in the stuffy, summer interior of our closed car. On the windshield where the compass had been remained a cloudy circle of leftover glue, something Janice picked at in traffic with her bad hand.

What had Ascenzo made of that hand, anyway, free from its bandages at last? Her mangled hand—I stared at it endlessly—those sutured buds like boys' testicles with their funny seams, three in a row.

We arrived at Danish by Design and pulled in behind the white panel van that belonged to Marty, Janice's photographer. "He's probably sleeping with that masseur fag," my father had said to me privately. Privately, while Janice had been posing for a girdle ad, a still for Macy's, the bottom half of a girl who didn't need a girdle. Red and black girdles, spread on our Sunday breakfast table, the newspaper sticking in the syrup. I'd never known girdles came in colors. But mostly, why did my father feel he could say things like that to me?

"You guys waiting, or coming with?" Janice asked. She had to reach over herself to open her car door, her right forefinger not yet strong enough to pull the stiff handle by itself. A yawn suddenly overtook her: her mouth flexed open wide like a cat's to reveal her impeccable teeth—as she shook her head, rolled her shoulders, cracked her neck—then closed with a little peep.

"I'll bring your stuff," I told her, unhooking the dry cleaner bag holding her pressed skirt and blouse. The blouse was silk, and she would wear it without a bra, her large breasts quivering like gelatin beneath. My father had already stepped from the car. He wouldn't sit outside waiting, "like a dog," as he put it, "a damned drooling dog."

Yet he reminded me of something ferocious and canine, a boxer or bulldog. And then there was me, the mutt. Janice led us inside where it was air-conditioned. Customers watched her as they moved on the periphery, fingering floor lamps that looked like microphones. I sagged in my poor-postured way onto an ottoman with Janice's clothes on my lap. Marty's assistant, Roid, was playing with his shields and reflectors, snapping them open like big round silver fans, then checking his light meter, retracting the reflector, checking the meter. Roid, like Janice and like me, was another South High student, a doper looking for a way out of class. Marty taught photography there, a buzz-cut redhead, tense and tangerine-freckled from top to bottom, also a doper. He'd brought Janice drugs when she was in the hospital, a French candy tin full of pretty pills that she'd given to me. She'd given me her legitimate meds, too, the codeine and Seconal. Marty had no patience for Janice's family, us, my father the watchdog and me, the gape-mouthed dimwit.

"Yo, Patty," said Roid, who only had clout here. His biggest function was to shoot Polaroids—hence, his name—in advance of Marty's real shots. At school, he was nobody.

"Scum," I said to him, not unkindly. "Freak."

Janice motioned for me to follow her to the back, to the closetlike bathroom where she changed. I had to button her blouse, zip her skirt, smell again the warm perfume of almonds. It was her dominant hand that was ruined; her physical therapist would train the other fingers to take up the slack. Soon, she wouldn't need my help. When I'd heard about her accident at school, during algebra, my first thought had been that she would die, that I would be a celebrity. My imagination was grotesque that way, greedy and ruthless.

"I look okay?" Janice asked me. In our previous life, I would have lied and said no.

"Great," I said, which was true, but which didn't feel true.

"Thanks," she said, dismissing me. I left her to apply her own lipstick and found a leather armchair to sink into, momentarily comfortable in its pristine coolness. Marty's lights had cast an overbright, beachlike atmosphere in the place, and I closed my eyes as if sunbathing. Through a drooping pair of eyelids I watched Janice's shoot. She floated through the showroom, caressing a teak highboy, sprawling over a cream-colored chaise, crossing her beautiful legs as she perched on a mahogany computer center shaped like a dressmaker's dummy, her bad hand behind her, supporting her. My father sat at a dining table across the showroom, reading Danish by Design literature, biting his damp extinguished cigar. Marty marched from his camera to Janice's knees and lifted her skirt. "Scooch," he told her, wiggling his own ass. She pulled the skirt higher. Roid giggled. "Thankee," Marty said, restored behind the lens of his camera. "Isn't that the way we say it out here, in Kansas? 'Thankee'?"

"That's right," Roid told him.

Janice said, "You betcha," without moving her smiling lips.

It was clear to me that Marty wanted to provoke my father. What would happen if Dad reacted? Janice would patiently hop down from the table and calm him. Marty would step outside to his van and take a toot, pop a diet soda, return when the air was clear again, red-eyed fox. Janice had taken several independent studies with Marty at South, leaving the grounds to visit developing labs and museum exhibits, to sit in his panel van and tell him about herself, to earn As by virtue of her sophisticated flat affect and her natural beauty.

Outside of Danish by Design's tinted showroom glass, a traffic jam evolved around the overheated engine of a red Celica. I watched languidly as the driver put his face in the white vapor, everything wavering around him like a dream. My driving exam was our next stop today, and I wondered if I were prepared to navigate a snarl like this. I ran groggily through rules of the road while Janice finished up with her shoot. Signal at a hundred feet. Two seconds space between your vehicle and the one in front of you. At breakfast—pancakes for the rest of us, milky coffee in a bowl for Janice—Dad had asked in his bright expectant morning voice, as he did every morning this summer, "What's on the agenda for today?" Janice couldn't drive because of her hand; I was useless unless accompanied by one of my parents. My mother worked. Dad had to take us. In better times, he was a general contractor. But his temper defeated him, over and over. He'd been supposed to supervise the construction of a car lot this summer—a sultry, asphalt-heavy prospect. A fight over his office space—the air-conditioned trailer parked at the site—had lost the job. This was what my mother called shooting his mouth and foot off at the same time. *Her* position at Southwestern Bell was secure—she *liked* to work; she liked it better than she liked us—and we got telephone perks. For example, Janice had her own line, her own unlisted number, and her own calls that came late at night to keep her murmuring in the room beside mine, her indistinct voice telling other people her secrets.

"Wrap, wrap, we gotta wrap," Marty sang out after an hour of flashes, to the tune of "Ding Dong the Witch Is Dead." Janice pulled down her skirt and shook her breasts. Roid lowered his head like an industrious mole and began collapsing equipment.

Janice and Marty were intimate in a different way than she and Ascenzo were. With Marty she exchanged little pecks to the cheeks, both of them, their arms not involved, like birds nipping seeds. How did one know these things, I wondered? What in his appearance led Janice to behave this way and not another? And to be always correct?

"See ya, Dick," Marty called to my father, who preferred to be called Richard, or, if one absolutely had to shorten it, Rich. "Pat and Dick," Marty continued, meaning me and my father, "the dead Nixons."

"Yeah," my father said. "Ha ha."

Marty raised both his hands as we left, two-fingered victory signs, "I am not a crook," he called, "I am not a crook."

"Later, babe," Roid yelled out to me.

Restored by my doze in the chair and by test anxiety, I climbed into the stifling backseat. Now we were headed for my appointment. Now it was my turn.

"You want to try to drive?" my father asked.

"Sure," I said.

"I meant your sister," he said. "I thought maybe she'd like to practice."

"No thanks," Janice said from the front passenger seat. "I'm happy just to ride. Let the munchkin drive."

"Nah, we're already going," Dad said, swinging the Falcon into traffic.

They did not wait for me. They relinquished the car because I had to drive it to pass the test, but there was a coffee shop down the block, so they walked there, my sister still in her modeling clothes, my father with his new cigar. Of course, the Department of Motor Vehicles was not air-conditioned. Old-fashioned floor fans whirred, orange streamers flying straight out as if to prove they were doing their best.

My examiner was a woman named Officer Davies. She sat in front of me as I took, and passed, the written and eye exams, and then, afterward, motioned with her fingernail at her own front teeth. "You have something right there," she said, looking cross-eyed at my mouth. A chocolate sprinkle, there since lunch, had lodged itself beside an upper canine. Then she asked me to lead her to my vehicle.

The Falcon was blistering. I felt obliged to explain the crystal, though she hadn't asked. "My sister's superstitious," I told her. "She thinks this crystal will bring good luck to the driver."

"We'll see," said Officer Davies. She buckled, I buckled. Before we even left the parking lot I had failed to stop at the sidewalk, and she had made a demoting little black mark on her clipboard.

I piloted my father's car slowly down the street, past the coffee shop where I dared not glance; would they see me, sailing sluggishly by? Obtaining my license was our last errand today, and if all went well, tomorrow it would be I who ferried Janice from doctor to physical therapist to voice lesson, and we would go in my mother's car, the one with a stereo and air conditioning, first dropping her off downtown at Bell headquarters. Everything would be different, once

I could drive. My father, with nothing else to do, would be obliged to call on his contacts in the world of construction. He would go to Pitt's barbecue and do some lunchtime hustling. He would lose track of Janice's commitments and adventures. Between tomorrow's errands and today's lay a brief but important fissure of time: my passing the test, and our waiting tonight for Janice while someone else took her away from the house.

My sister had two boyfriends, and this evening's date was with the college guy, Trevor. "How can she go out with him?" my father would ask my mother and me while we moved around the house in her absence. "Who can take seriously this *Trevor,* the boy named from a soap opera?" We would occupy ourselves in front of electrical appliances—TV, stereo, refrigerator, microwave—while we waited for her, rotating every thirty minutes or so. Before the accident, my mother would have predicted the hickeys Janice might arrive home bearing on her neck, the liquor on her breath, the tardy hour. Never mind that it was I who sneaked cigarettes (Janice wouldn't risk the stains or stench), or that Janice never went without her full eight hours' rest. These facts merely compounded my mother's annoyance. She seemed not to want a beautiful daughter, after all, nor an unbeautiful one, either. Maybe she wished she'd had sons.

Janice's other boyfriend, Teddy, was Janice's age, and my father preferred him. Teddy's parents had the same names as our pets, Max and Emma (dog and cat, respectively) and Dad liked this about Teddy; it kept him in a proper place.

But tonight was Trevor, and then when we all woke tomorrow things would be different. That's what I thought as I performed my head check before changing lanes, as I scrupulously entered intersections and on-ramps and parking spaces when Officer Davies instructed. Everything waffled in the miserable Midwest heat; the sky above us was featureless, not blue but simple empty white. Pets and children and red rubber balls all stayed put in their yards; wheelchairs weren't rolling into crosswalks, taillights weren't flashing on ahead of me unexpectedly. I drenched myself, jumping these mild hoops only adequately, but Officer Davies was going to confer my reward.

At our house it had always been I who'd come home marked and scarred and broken, from sunburn or wind chill, the V on my chin from the rock I hadn't seen, an apostrophe at my scalp line from which a fishhook had been pulled, the chicken pox and acne dimples, the fractured femur after skiing, the grisly flesh on my hand where the iron had once fallen, the bruised lips and genitals from boys I let manhandle me.

On the hot steering wheel, I tucked my three lesser fingers till they were hidden away. In my nightmares, it had happened to me, and I had deserved it.

Who had done this to Janice, our beauty? A stranger had, an ugly girl with no stature at our school, no notoriety until now. Now, she had plenty. She was the one who'd stood beside Janice in Mr. Tilbino's shop class, who'd been designated Janice's building buddy, who'd held the end of Janice's two-by-four as they used the radial arm saw, who'd shoved her sideways into the blade. There was jealousy involved, as you might expect, a boy this ugly girl loved in a sickening unrequited way, this boy who loved Janice in the same pathetic way, lonely desperation begetting lonely desperation.

Couldn't you sympathize with that luckless girl's desire to do damage? Couldn't you imagine the self-preserving instinct that would guide her lurching into my sister?

When we got our bodies, Janice and I, when we bloomed, my mother took me aside to offer consolation. Janice had gotten Grandma's big breasts and slender legs. She had gotten a confident swing in her hips and large clean teeth, a flare for higher math, a spontaneous wit, a knack for combining unlikely clothes. She'd gotten things I ought obviously to desire, and now she'd gotten something I could not have known to wish for.

Officer Davies said, "*Both* hands on the wheel, please."

It would become an enduring habit of mine: using my thumb and forefinger, I made my own gun.

☞ *Ball Peen*

*M*y brother Sonny taught me to carry a hammer. He wrapped
one up for Christmas when I was fifteen and he was twenty-seven;
then, I accused him of laziness, of forgetting the holiday and me, his
only sister. But later I saw he'd picked the gift on purpose, gone out
to get it with me in mind. Only eight ounces, it seems feminine, the
way some tools and toys are designed differently. Its handle is slender,
leather-dressed, the head sleek yet heavy, curved round exactly like a
penis, down to the ridge beneath. Its weight, in the palm, demon-
strates a specific pleasing gravity. For comfort, I often slip my hand in
my purse, as if in a pocket, to cup that smooth ball peen.

A hammer is useful. With it, I've loosened lug nuts, resoled shoes,
tenderized meat, destroyed a bike helmet, killed a crippled cat, not to
mention driving plenty of nails, a piece of upkeep endlessly necessary.

I wanted to take the hammer to the skull of my boyfriend. I said
so, anyway, and that was enough for my brother Sonny.

"Scrawny," he'd said of me, when he showed up at the front door.

According to him, both I and the cabin looked like five miles of bad road. He opened the cupboards and sniffed at the refrigerator. He patrolled the little house noting how his boots stuck to the floor and how I'd resorted to using coffee filters for toilet paper. He saw my weight loss for what it was: deprivation. My brother is a man of few words. He sometimes simply grunts like an animal. He'd frowned mightily, shaking his head as if to dislodge insects. What was I thinking, letting everything go to hell this way?

"Where's your vehicle?" he demanded.

"Gone," I said. Even my car had a sad name: Saab.

So first he gathered provisions, driving his big red truck rather than walking the four blocks to Main. He hadn't been to Telluride in at least ten years. Our hometown wasn't his kind of place anymore. His hoodlum buddies had all died or gone to jail, and now celebrities wandered the streets and wrote letters to the editor. I grew a headache waiting for him to return: the lack of parking space, the fruity clerks, the pretentious prices, the ridiculous offerings of edible flowers and free cappuccino, mayonnaise in tubes and oxygen in colored little canisters . . .

Sonny brought back potatoes, onions, sausages, a veal roast the size of his head. Corn chips. Baked beans. A frozen turkey. A can of Folgers. A box of red wine, a box of white, two cases of cheap diet beer. These supplies looked good to me, cheerily surreal, sustaining.

"Huh?" he said, looking for my approval. "Had to get us some food in our hidey-hole."

"What'd you think of downtown?"

"Pathetic," he said, dropping the turkey on the counter. "Place has gone to the dogs, and I mean *literally*. I saw a guy cleaning up dog shit on Main Street. I thought, Good lord, man, where's your self-respect? Scooping up shit behind a dog, Jesus God." He opened the freezer door, cleared the shelf of flavored coffee beans and hoary frozen yogurt with a single gesture, making room for his turkey, and then discovered he'd broken the countertop where he'd dropped the big bird onto it. "Now we got a project," he said, not unhappily.

*   *   *

We drank that first night. After the white wine was gone, we gradu-ated to whiskey. Sonny never traveled without a bottle of Fighting Cock in his toolbox. He also carried a Colt .45 in that box, rigged in a holster, casual as a drill. Back in Colorado Springs, he was a car-penter.

"I pretend she's dead," he told me, when I asked how he managed. His wife had divorced him last fall. I had been too far away and too much in love to really attend. His problem was like any other news received in Telluride: the planes fell into the oceans, hurricanes rose out of them, it was all so much faint splashing. But losing love had suddenly made heartache near and dear, nasty and damp; I wanted him to show me how he had survived these last six months.

"Dead," I said, laughing. But it wasn't a joke. I thought about it when I woke up later, hungover, mouth sticky, brain shrunken inside its casing. I went for water, and found Sonny asleep on the couch instead of upstairs in his old bedroom. The TV lit his face, the remote lay on his chest. Except for his boots he was still dressed, ready to spring to action should the need arrive. Dead, my former sister-in-law could only be grieved. Sonny had found the shortcut through the emotional morass—the rage, the jealousy, the self-loathing—to arrive at pure regret. It was genius, his brand.

While we drank, he plotted with a rusty measure. Our old shack had not one square corner, not one level surface. Nobody had ever bothered to slip in a foundation, just shims beneath the appliances. It smelled of a hundred years of wood smoke and cheap meals; the people who had lived here were miners, men willing to crawl day after day into a hole in the mountain with the dim dumb hope of dragging something valuable out. Sonny walked off feet in his steel-toed boots, knelt at corners with a meaty *thunk,* scraped at the grout, bemoaned the jury-rigged wiring, brought in floor lamps to light—and despair of—his task. Every move he made revealed the growing horror of the job. There were mouse droppings in the drawers, nail heads beneath the throw rugs, scorch marks behind the hot water tank, garbage in the crawl space. Water had leaked so long into the wood around the sink that the counters flexed like rubber. "What happened to the chairs?" he asked. Their pieces waited beside the fireplace, gone from furniture to timber one night I couldn't fully recall.

Meanwhile, I told him about my broken heart.

"He lives in a *tepee*?" he might interject. Or, "What do you mean, 'his family's a household name'?" My boyfriend was a trust funder, a fact I would have once hidden from my brother's scorn. Now I relished his curled lip. Like the town itself, a whole other kind of man would emerge as I saw him through Sonny's eyes.

Two weeks ago my boyfriend said he'd figured out what was wrong with us.

"What?" I'd asked stupidly, not knowing there was anything wrong to figure out. I liked our lazy love, its absence of ambition. We were languishing in his uncle's condo, watching a late spring snow fall sloppily on the balcony. The thermostat was set at eighty degrees so that we could pad about barefoot, drinking frozen drinks. As a wealthy person, my boyfriend could live wherever he wanted whenever he wanted—Colorado could be Bermuda, this carpet the sandy beach, the only snowlike substance around the heroin in its film canister in the fridge. Ski season had turned to off-season, which meant most locals were leaving on vacation. The lodge where I hostessed would reopen June first. Meanwhile, the streets looked the way they did in the museum photos, haunted, apocalyptic.

"The fun's gone out of it," he said, pulling on his jeans, tucking in his shorts. "We're not having fun."

"Speak for yourself." I'd thought we were headed for the bedroom. That's how unprepared I was. I will never forget those cold bloodshot eyes, appraising me as I dressed for the last time before them. It was as if they, too, had a thermostat, one he'd abruptly shut off.

I wouldn't tell Sonny his name.

"Rockefeller?" he guessed. "Mr. Rubbermaid?"

Even if he knew it, my brother would not be impressed by my boyfriend's name. He did not care. He would be my role model, I thought. He'd always been my third parent. The other two might have sent me to college—blindly, with the faith in higher education that only the unschooled can claim—but my brother was the one to truly protect me. It was he who'd armed me, once upon a time, with a hammer, and this visit, while on the surface a friendly checkup, perhaps a kitchen reclamation, had me as its real rehab project.

"Caulk," he proclaimed, wielding the blaze orange gun as he unpacked his stuff. "It's a wonderful thing."

In the morning Sonny rose from the couch, stuck his head beneath the faucet, shook, and then began tearing out the rotting cabinets around the sink. He muttered as he worked, drinking coffee until eleven, then switching to beer. He usually listened to the radio when on a job, but hated the local station, the volunteer deejays, the mopey playlist. Far away, down in Montrose or Grand Junction, someone was playing regular tunes, but we couldn't receive them up in the rarefied Telluride airwaves. We worked in silence, me removing the utensils and rolling pins and pans and bowls and napkins and candles just ahead of his crowbar.

"You okay?" I asked, of his heavy breathing. He snorted; only pussies blamed the altitude.

By noon we had a pile of what we'd salvaged, among the rubble an old Crock-Pot, one of my mother's fond housewifey implements. I recalled childhood for an instant: the bubbling stew, the steamy lid, crock resting squat on the counter chuckling all afternoon, then placed in the center of the dinner table for us to behold. Sonny cleaned it inside and out, later plopping his beloved hunk of meat into it and tossing on top some vegetables and a handful of salt and pepper. Over this he poured the red wine, holding the box to his face afterward for a swig, then whipped out his eyeglasses. He read the

Crock's dial. "On, off," he said. "Refreshingly simple." At the conventional stove he had a single cooking maxim: "Apply heat."

He'd come here to make sure I was alive. When my mother phoned, I had let the machine take the calls, day after day. I could have asked him to come, but we both preferred it the other way, where I didn't know I needed saving.

Our parents were no good at seeing us suffer. After having Sonny early in their marriage, they thought they were done. Then, just as he entered rocky adolescence, I showed up—not a plan, not an accident, just a fact. We were a house that held the combined forces of infancy, puberty, and midlife crisis. And, as I've mentioned, it's a small house. My father's hair went swiftly gray. My mother's teeth eroded. I had colic and Sonny turned delinquent. He stole a car at age thirteen to impress his future wife, who was then seventeen. He was too short to make a clean getaway, and ended up high centered in the San Miguel River. When she moved to Colorado Springs a few years later, he followed. It never occurred to me to find out if he ever finished high school. For years and years he had been, in my mind, perched high atop a building in a bigger city, nailing the roof back into place.

Meanwhile, the property on either side of our little house had become valuable, and my father sold it lot by lot after the mine closed. He had been a member of what was called the skeleton crew, patrolling the empty mill and harassing trespassers. Sometimes he worked the tailings, trekking over its yellow surface in a hose truck, hopelessly watering the toxic ash to keep it from blowing into town.

"Hippies," he would say at day's end, disgruntled. The word never failed to embarrass me. I liked the new people. They came from big cities. They brought music and skateboards and hot tubs and daiquiris. These boys didn't want to hunt elk or play football or drink Coors. They wanted to inhale cocaine and ski. They liked Nirvana.

Each wave of newcomer had more money than the wave before. Nothing was torn down, it was merely enhanced, tuck-pointed, landscaped, covered in gold leaf. The new buildings were required to look old, and the old buildings had to be retrofitted with the new amenities. By the time Telluride had become famous, my brother was long gone to the Springs. Eventually, my parents moved there as well. They were tired of winter, of altitude, of tourists. They wearied of being asked, by the new shopkeepers in the old shops, where they were from and how long they planned to stay. The last empty lot of the eight we once owned is worth a quarter of a million dollars— right there, just outside my bedroom window. On this parcel sits my old swing set, a spruce tree we planted when I was six, and the burn barrel my father refused to surrender when the practice was outlawed.

Sonny hauled out the foul kitchen debris and started a fire in that barrel, the first in twenty years. I witnessed the stinking blaze with a beer in my hand, certain that dire consequences would follow. Dusk was falling like a wet blanket. Still, I was alarmed when the air horn sounded from the fire station, the shrill civic shriek. "Busted!" I said to Sonny. But the volunteers weren't after us. First a fire truck bumped through the intersection three blocks away, its own smaller siren singing under the general alert, and then an ambulance took itself importantly out on the highway; we could hear their fading, competing cries as they left town.

"Car crash," I guessed. "Or a lightning strike," I said more quietly into the vibrant silence the sirens had left in the air. "My boyfriend burns down buildings," I added tentatively, as if to up the ante. I knew this wasn't wise to mention. Sonny grunted, unsurprised. My ex was an arsonist, when the occasion arose. Like most things he did, he only dabbled. The town needed an arsonist, because back in the seventies some stoned do-gooders had designated the whole place *historic,* thereby protecting every shed and shack, firetrap, lean-to, what have you. With treasure as valuable as an empty lot sitting just beneath, how surprising was it that you might hire someone to torch your hovel? For this service, he was paid in drugs. They were good drugs, and I missed them, too, in an ancillary way, insult to injury.

"He's a punk," Sonny said definitively, his face glowing as he poked at the embers. He had shadows beneath his eyes, stubble on his chin, stains down his shirt. He was built like a body guard, inside and out.

That evening, he made a list at the kitchen table. "Why," he asked rhetorically, "did we never have a garbage disposal?" Our parents had remained frugal, still thinking like poor people even after they no longer had to. "I'm installing you a disposal," he declared.

I shrugged. I had become someone who lived on fluids, the kind that lift you up and the kind that knock you down. What would that angry little machine chew on, below my sink?

The fire alarm went off again that night, late, just a single rolling whoop, an afterthought. Sometimes it did that following an earlier episode, as if to rouse us just long enough to let us know that our houses *weren't* on fire.

The noise hadn't wakened Sonny. He slept, once more, before the television, lit a sickly blue. Drinkers' sleep, sodden and senseless. The kitchen floor beneath my feet was gritty and the destruction, in the dark, felt desperate to me. "I don't think I can afford this," I had told Sonny cautiously, too late, of course.

"It's mostly elbow grease and sweat equity," he'd said, looking mildly around. My parents expected me to provide maintenance, pay taxes, prevent the pipes from freezing. I was just baby-sitting their unwitting investment. Until recently, it hadn't seemed hard.

But my bank account was low. I'd begun to think too much like my boyfriend, and he lived by other means, accounts accessed by computers and plastic cards, money exchanged without its ever touching his or anyone's hands. Elbow grease and sweat equity were not his style. He himself wrote checks.

My brother didn't believe in checks. Nor banks, nor credit cards, nor anything else as flimsy and thirdhand as those. He'd refused, for instance, to believe his divorce papers. *He* transacted only in cash.

Cash he understood; he kept it in a metal box. It was an ordinary gray box, complete with a little silly lock and a handle like a smile. It held a few thousand dollars, give or take. That was Sonny's money. Now his money box sat beside the television set on the buffet table in our living room. I kept imagining he'd left his home in Colorado Springs—his belongings, his creature comforts, his necessary mementos, his life like a stage set he could decide to rejoin—but in fact he had brought it all with him, tossed in the bed of a truck and carried along. Maybe he planned to move in with me; I wouldn't know until he just didn't seem to be leaving. Already he was dropping his laundry indiscriminately into the washer, greasy jeans, thick socks like plaster cast, even his work gloves. These sloshed around with my smaller items, then tumbled dry, all of it emerging crackling and constricted from the dryer. Our mother would have been appalled.

She wouldn't approve of the way I kept her old home. How the furniture had been neglected, shoved around and recruited for purposes other than its original design. The sewing cabinet now stood in as the end table, ringed with drink stains, the buffet as entertainment center, stuffed full of videos and cassettes instead of china and linens, the piano as bookcase for my trashy paperbacks, the rocking chair a place to throw rain gear and parkas and backpacks. We'd deposited our cruddy boots on her cookie sheets, right in front of the wall heater, where they sent up the odor of wet animal.

But I know she would be relieved we were together, Sonny and I. He'd come because my mother asked him to. He'd left his wife when Jane Lynn said please go. What deed, I asked myself, would I bid him do?

"I'll help," I had offered lamely, concerning the kitchen.

"Uh-huh," he doubted, finishing his last beer and crushing the can with a single squeeze. Usually I closed the curtains at night but with Sonny there it seemed unnecessary. Maybe my boyfriend would think I'd found someone new already, some masculine one moving behind the glass—bulky but nimble, big yet capable of dance, like a bear.

And now, just as I was retrieving a blanket to cover my brother as he lay before the TV while it flickered and laughed and sang, ready to return to bed, the fire department siren soared to life for the third time. It often seemed that one alarm would inspire another. For months there'd be nothing—then a car wreck, a fallen climber, a burning house all in one day. This was no false alarm, no leftover reflex, but an urgent summons. Louder at night, more menacing.

Sonny lurched from the couch, hair and eyes wild. "You okay?" he asked, as if the air horn was about me. We went to the porch. The smoke was from an old structure, you could tell by the smell. Something historical, downtown, was ablaze. We stood, me shivering, him clacking his mouth guard rhythmically, watching as the volunteers gathered, their headlights showing the light haze of smoke that was filling the town.

"Your boyfriend the dumb fuck do this?"

I shrugged; I was busy picturing him dead, myself graveside. Alternately, I had a repentant urge to rescue him from the flames. Wouldn't he have to love me, then?

"Wanna go rubberneck?" Sonny asked.

I shook my head. It had been at least two weeks since I'd been out, and I was afraid. Living alone in Telluride was dangerous but not for the typical reasons. For example, no one would break into your house. That was the problem: no one would break in. No one would comment when you didn't appear for days at a time or wash your hair or answer your phone. It was a place happy to forget you; some people came here just for that.

The liquor store delivered. So did the grocery. If you had a telephone and a computer and cable TV and a fistful of credit cards you might not be seen for months. If you had inner resources, everything else came to you, directly to your door . . .

Everything except the mail. Unfortunately, you still had to walk to the post office to get that. That's where people gathered, at the P.O., running their eyes north and south over one anothers' bodies, chatting, bragging about feats of physical achievement—the inclines

labored up and then plunged back down—and recounting their gloriously, passionately wasted weekends.

They gathered at the P.O. and, occasionally, on the ring of a fire,
the burning outskirts of a flaming building. The siren would sound,
the population would hurry to seek out smoke, then everyone would
flock to the light. Fire: we like to watch it.

"We'll hear about it tomorrow," I told Sonny as the ladder and
hose trucks lumbered dutifully across the intersection three blocks
away.

On and on the siren wailed, looping bravely through the smoky
air.

The next morning, I stepped into the living room as my brother was
fastening his pants. That familiar little ratchet, the way he sucked in
his breath and ducked his chin down and edged ever so gently back-
ward on tiptoe so as not to catch himself in the zipper's teeth . . . I
had armored myself against any number of surprise encounters with
my longing for my boyfriend, but I was kneecapped by that faint
reminiscent move. I had to flee to the bathroom, stand in the shower
for a good long while to bawl.

I was lucky to bathe then, because later in the afternoon we had
no water. I heard Sonny drop his wrench and begin cursing in the
babbling way a baby might—"Good goddamny damny fucking
fricking shit on a stick"—without inflection or anger, just trying on
the noise. Outside snow fell on the bright green grass, and a group of
cold juncos stood unhappily on our porch rail like uniformed children waiting for a bus. I'd been standing so quietly at the window
they had not noticed me. I was looking for my boyfriend through
the old draining wavery glass, as if he might come hunched over and
proud to my front door, smelling of sex and smoke, curious about
the truck in the drive, eager to tell me about the building he'd
burned. Sonny's labor took place behind me, distraction, sound
track, comic relief, company.

"What is it?" I asked, turning from the birds.

He was sitting cross-legged, awestruck. Beneath the sink he had discovered where the drain had been leading all these years: nowhere. Just straight into the ground, simple as rain from the sky. I turned on the faucet above him and we watched the water rush into the rich dark under our house.

"Wow," I said, impressed. How had it held for so long, this structure with its barely hidden feral traits?

"This kitchen is going to kick my ass," Sonny said as he struggled to his feet. "Goddamn if it don't."

When he went roaring away in his truck to consult the city about the sewer line, I phoned my mother. "Where's Jane Lynn?" I asked. "What exactly happened with them?"

"She's seeing someone else," my mother said. She meant that Jane Lynn had fallen in love with a man more easily lovable than my brother, someone simpler to behold, less taxing to care for. "I just can't imagine what she was thinking," my mother went on; of course, it was her job to fault Jane Lynn.

But I thought I knew how my sister-in-law must have felt. This was because I'd found Sonny two nights now, TV playing at his feet, empty bottles and cans everywhere, his hand still wrapped around the remote, held to his chest like a cross or dagger. He was too old to scold, too big to carry, too gruff to mollify. Jane Lynn no doubt felt furious, sad, helpless, as if someone were knocking her, continually, in the breastbone, battering away at the gates of her conscience.

If he stayed with me, I would someday discover him masturbating before the television or perhaps weeping in his whiskey. He would break a window or drive drunk into a pole. It would come to that, I thought. Loneliness left clues, and I would pick up his while he picked up mine, neither of us ever mentioning them.

"Is your brother drinking?" our mother asked, nearly in a whisper, reverent in her desire to be told otherwise.

"Why?"

"He didn't tell you?"

She told me what he hadn't: he'd been fired for drinking on the job. Beams might have fallen, walls could have collapsed, there would have been litigation. He'd exhausted, it seemed, the goodwill of every contractor in Colorado Springs.

"How are *you*?" our poor mother chirped. She could seem like a toy on a track, going 'round and 'round, making one noise after another at all of her appointed stops.

"Do you know where the sink has been draining all these years?" I demanded of her. "Do you have any idea what a *wreck* this place is?"

When Sonny returned he told me about the fire. An old crib behind the bank, one of the tiny shacks where the prostitutes used to take their men. "Arson," he said meaningfully. Best that an act of God would take your eyesore, but in its absence existed the arsonist. I could wish he'd never appeared; he hadn't always been around. In the old days, fires had been set by the volunteer fire department in order to practice extinguishing them, piles of tires, leftover outhouses. My father had been a fireman; Sonny would be one, if he lived here. But the arsonist was a necessary evil; he'd shown up on the same ship with the real-estate agents and the developers, a stowaway like a disease or nonindigenous life-form, set to thrive where it lands.

This was my boyfriend. The last words he'd spoken to me were to ask if I planned to turn him in to the sheriff.

"Anyone hurt?" I asked Sonny, hoping exactly equally for two totally different answers. He studied me before letting me know.

"Not yet."

Later, my help was required in wrestling the kitchen stove away from the wall to find the source of a tiny gas leak Sonny suspected. The wooden shims scattered and the linoleum split as the mighty appliance lurched stickily from its place. Beneath it, in its hideous fur of dust and hair and burnt matchsticks, lay two dead mice. With complete obliviousness Sonny picked them up, not even by the tail but by their ripe midsections, and flung them unceremoniously out the back door. If he didn't know about the hantavirus, his gesture seemed to say, then how could he be afflicted by it? To the dirty copper gas line he applied soapy water with a sponge, waiting on his knees for it to bubble up and confess.

"You don't smell gas?" he kept asking.

I shrugged. Maybe I did. Maybe my life smelled like gas. Or maybe it seemed as good a substance as any with which to fill the air—insidious, lethal, flammable.

"Your pilots are shot," he said.

"I know."

"Nah, I mean your stove." He punched me gamely on the shoulder, then steadied me like a coatrack when I threatened to tip over. He scowled into my face as if he would like to check me with his magnifying eyeglasses. "Let's go get the stink blown off us," he finally said.

Already we had consumed Sonny's roast and picked the bones of his turkey; naturally, the alcohol was long gone. Getting no satisfaction from the city, he'd tied the kitchen sewer line into the bathroom one, carving a path through the two rooms' floors with a pickax. The place looked like a crime scene, a bungled treasure hunt, the site of a natural disaster to which aid might imminently be sent, PVC pipes and rot and rags and cracked tile and grit everywhere, lunky white stove standing dumb and useless as a cow, coup de grace and centerpiece of the mess. Water dripped into a saucepan and cool air seeped up from below. Sonny blew out a long sigh like an EMT who'd lost the patient, although he claimed he was on the downhill side of the job.

I looked at myself, the hipbones I'd once thought necessary to exhume. I touched my face as if to check for features.

"Let's drive," Sonny said, slicking back his hair, stomping into his boots. It took longer to warm up his truck than it would have to walk, but I didn't object. Sonny was in charge and I was his rag doll.

He'd kicked aside the recycling bins that usually sat in our gravel drive so that he could set up his Skil saw and park his big cherry red rig. It was a '69 Ford, fitted with a gun rack and a toolbox and a little squeeze bicycle horn on the driver's side rearview mirror. Per usual, the truck shone, bright as a fire engine. It went without saying that Sonny would take better care of his ride than he did of himself. He'd found her in a field of maize, languishing out there, rats nesting beneath the hood, long black snakes living in the bench seat, flood debris washed under the chassis. He took his relic and remade her. He was good with his hands, capable of fixing almost anything. Now we eased over a speed bump, springs squeaking, wax job sparkling, heat whirring at my feet.

I recognized everyone we saw. The bagel baker and the marshal and the owner of the video shop. The postmistress and the mushroom dealer. The guy who drove the ambulance and dejayed the goth hour. One of the real-estate twins I went all through school with. And here I was, the sad-sack local lately sucker punched by the city slicker. What was new in that?

Sonny signaled a turn off Main and we ended up before the former crib. The day's snow had frosted the black mess so that it appeared to have been burned long ago, benignly historical. The air smelled of ancient things. Like our house, this one had been built on rocks a hundred years ago. Those stones had been kicked out of the way, scattered in the frozen stew of water and ash and black wood. Now you could see the Telluride Bank, behind, the thriving business that could use a parking lot and drive-through window.

"I think I had a friend who lived here," Sonny said. The crib was one of five in a row, absent now like a tooth.

"It had a wall made of license plates," I said. A few lay scorched and bent on the ground. Next door, the cribs still stood, blue paint blistered on the east side that faced the fire, plum on the west. Sonny shifted into drive and we rumbled away, back to Main, where we made a U-turn at the end and headed the other direction, into the sunset, which was a thin line of pink in an otherwise gray sky: clouds? Or merely the lack of color? Sonny popped his lips and gave me a crafty look. "You know what's wrong with this town?"

"What?"

"No titty bars."

True enough. There were a lot of bars in Telluride, more bars than churches, yet, like churches, different ones for different sorts: the old hippie bar, the new hippie bar, the cowboy bar, the Republican bar, the pool players' bar, the sports fanatic bar, et cetera. I directed him to the one I preferred, the one that used to be a gas station before those, too, were outlawed. Total Liquidation, it was called. The famous nature writer with the mountain lion spent her evenings there, and she sat as usual in the big bay window, the cat blinking sedately beside her. "God bless the mighty V-Eight," the writer said of Sonny's truck at the curb.

"This is Pansy West," I told my brother.

"Huh?" he said into Pansy's leathery impassive face. "You what?"

"Pansy West," she repeated, expecting him to recognize the name, boring into his eyes with her steady blue gaze. She had an expression like a sled dog's, unwavering and severe. I did not trust it in humans, as it seemed humorless, though I liked Pansy well enough. "It's my given name," she declared.

Then give it back, I knew Sonny was thinking. "Yeah," he said. She wasn't his type, but they would get along. Pansy, like Sonny, was a fearless drinker, and although they would disagree on every single western topic—would scoff at each other's ridiculously rabid stances—they shared a terrible weakness for the opposite sex. They had that vast vulnerability—that willful misery—in common. Maybe everyone at this former service station did; it was probably how others described the bar: the church of the dumped, whose members loved the smell of gasoline.

"I thought you were in Belize," said Pansy idly, looking me over. "But I guess not."

"Sick," I explained. Dying, it seemed. "Brother Bill," I greeted the bartender, who had been at some point in his life defrocked. "This is my brother Sonny. He'll want a beer."

"What kind?"

"Cold," said Sonny.

"Oh ha," said Pansy flatly.

"Tell him a joke," I said to Bill.

"You like jokes?" he asked, filling a stein for Sonny and serving me a G and T without my having to ask. "So this guy was eating a bald eagle. You heard it?"

Pansy said, "Not *that* one," but Sonny shook his head to indicate he didn't know the joke.

"The guy gets caught by these forest rangers, and they go, 'Yo, buddy, don't you realize it's a federal offense to eat a bald eagle? We're gonna have to lock you up.' So they haul his ass away, taking him to jail, driving along, and pretty soon one of the rangers can't help it, he leans over and says real quiet, 'Hey, just between you and me, what's a bald eagle taste like, anyway?' And the guy thinks for a minute, then he says, 'Something between a whooping crane and a trumpeter swan.'"

There was that beat, where everyone waits for ignition, and then Sonny laughed and laughed and laughed. "Hooo," he said. I remembered Sonny when he was young, when he'd been happy, infectiously so. You could tell from his laugh that he hadn't forgotten what it was to be happy. He wiped his eyes with his knuckles, like a kid. I remembered how eager to please he had been. He used to do errands for our tired, tired mother, pluck her list from her hand and run cheerfully downtown, sweep the steps, dig the weeds, hang the laundry. He'd do anything asked of him by the women he loved. *Any*thing. His laugh had made Pansy smile, grudgingly, and even her lion flicked its ear. His laugh made me smile, too. Just as I did so, my ex walked by the bar's window. Not dead, he looked smug, loping along, looking for someone or something to ruin. "That's him," I said, thinking aloud, still in the afterglow of the punch line.

Sonny moved like a creature catching a significant scent. "The robber baron?"

I hesitated hardly a second before nodding, my head swinging like the business end of that ball peen hammer, wreaking its own kind of havoc. "That's him," I repeated.

Brother Bill opened his mouth as Sonny stood abruptly, a man on a mission. He smacked a ten-dollar bill on the damp bar and told us he'd be right back.

Bill asked, "Where's the fire?"

"Good question," Pansy said, regarding me with her cool canine gaze.

Female Trouble

*M*cBride found himself at the Pima County psychiatric hospital in the middle of the day. "Don't visit me here," Daisy told him. She slid her palms over her frizzy white hair as if to keep it from flying off like dandelion fluff. "It embarrasses me, these crazy people make me ashamed."

"I thought you wanted to see me. I thought that was the point. Why else are you in Tucson?" Daisy, McBride's girlfriend of the year before, had been discovered on the highway near the Triple T truckstop carrying a portable typewriter, trying to hitch a ride. Native New Yorker, she'd never learned to drive; maybe that was why McBride had assumed she would stay in Salt Lake City, where he'd left her. He certainly preferred to think of that chapter as a closed one, a place he had chosen against.

Daisy said, "I want to see you when I'm normal again. I just feel like you're staring at me, at my flabby skin and everything." She began jerking her shoulders in some simulation of crying but her eyes remained dry. McBride did not wish to touch her. She'd taken on an institutional smell and her sweatsuit hid any physical charm. Her eyes had lost whatever snappish wit they'd once held, glazed with depression and the medication used to treat it. McBride reached to hold her and felt she was made of something more inert than her former substance, dull as clay, and pale as an albino, as if she'd been dipped in bleach. In the past, she'd been burnished, tanned twice weekly in a salon coffin, hair dyed golden and frowsily restrained with combs and barrettes, a Victoria's Secret kind of girl, pubic hair dyed to match.

Had his leaving her brought about such thorough transformation? He felt like asking her. He was sort of flattered, sort of appalled.

When she'd fallen in love with him she'd gone to his apartment and climbed into his bed and waited for him to come home. She was a free spirit with a crush, a mission, a taste for disaster. His roommate had greeted him in the kitchen that late night, wearing boxers and socks, whispering as he stepped daintily on tiptoes, "There's a *girl* in your bed" with such admiration and awe that McBride seemed stripped of very many options. A naked girl between your sheets was not a thing to take lightly.

"Drunk?" he asked, pulling off his own clothes.

His roommate had given an elaborate impatient shrug and shiver: who cared? Or: of course drunk; you had to ask?

Was she desperate? No—devoted. Spontaneous. Outrageous. A girl on fire, burning so that you wanted to stand in the radiating glow, a girl on the verge, confident in not caring. The prospect of death did not deter her. She was up for whatever.

And this had led her here, McBride supposed, later and after, immolation imminent. The Arizona desert was forgiving in February, springlike by eastern standards. They sat in the building's courtyard. A general wooden catatonia in the human population— patients and orderlies both—made the Adirondack chairs seem full of personality, resting at jaunty angles and in conversational clusters over the evergreen grass. Other visitors carried Styrofoam cups of coffee to other patients, crossing the lawn quickly, trying to be spry in the face of lethargy. McBride felt trapped by his past, and kept sneaking covert glances at his watch. His tapping foot ached for an accelerator.

What he remembered about Daisy was sex. Even when he'd stopped loving her, he'd wanted to fuck her. They'd been strangers their first night together, Daisy waiting for him drunk on that crowded single mattress. His roommate's awe, "There's a *girl* in your bed." Like a gift, like an animal in a gunnysack, and on fire, in heat.

Was there a word for the way you winced, recalling a former affection, that place in your rib cage that briefly collapsed, your glance that no longer lingered but skimmed over her face like a skipped stone over water?

Now Daisy said, "Look," and pointed toward the hospital entrance. "Family theater." They watched a woman wrench herself free of the guiding hands of an older couple, her parents, McBride guessed, the three of them sharing a lankiness. Their daughter was easily in her forties, long-limbed and angry, crossing her arms defiantly and refusing to enter the front doors. McBride was sympathetic to the parents, who looked harried and doomed, as if they hadn't slept in days. Daisy said, "Old farts just want to get rid of her." McBride supposed that was true but he didn't blame them.

When the woman suddenly sprinted down the walk toward the street the parents began shouting. The woman ran like a dancer, straight into the street without looking. Her mother screamed, putting her hands to her cheeks. Cars weaved around the daughter as she stood between lanes but nobody stopped driving. Nobody in Tucson ever stopped driving. The woman stood facing traffic like the oblivious prow of a ship. McBride looked to the orderlies, who'd jumped up yet made no move toward action.

"Help her," Daisy said to him, pushing his elbow from the chair arm. He rose and started reluctantly for the street, jogging in such a way that his teeth hurt. When he reached the woman she took his arm as if she'd been waiting for him, her partner on their dance stage. She stared at him with clear unmedicated eyes, startled like a deer, pretty and skittish.

"What am I doing?" she asked.

McBride told her what he'd seen as he escorted her up the walk. They passed her parents, who simply watched as if at a wedding.

"*You'd* never do a thing like this," she informed McBride as they entered the building's foyer. She held his arm lightly, with long shaking fingers. A group had clustered at the commotion and now drifted away disappointed at the tame outcome.

"A thing like what?"

"Like impulsive behavior. It's a feminine trait."

McBride recalled a similar complaint Daisy had made when he refused to try sushi or inhale an illicit powder. No, he wouldn't eat raw fish, or snort an alien drug. Nor would he bolt, barefooted, into traffic.

"Party pooper," Daisy called him. "Wet blanket. Coward." What was so brave about taking risks, he'd asked her. What separated it from stepping off a cliff?

"You step off holding my hand," she'd said, popping a pill, removing a garment, switching off the headlights at high speed on a dark highway. But he'd wanted a bungee, a net, a loophole.

The woman's parents had followed them inside and now stood deferentially behind McBride. The woman let loose of his arm, surrendering to her parents. "This way," she said quietly, leading them toward the admissions desk.

Daisy had her eyes closed when McBride got back to their chairs. "I'm not asleep," she told him.

McBride sat on the arm of the chair, ready to leave.

"Fix everything?" she asked acidly; this was like her, to tell him to do something, then ridicule him for doing it.

"I should go," he said.

"You should," she agreed, starting to not-cry again.

"I'll come back."

"I'll be here."

*　　*　　*

At home that evening McBride's current girlfriend Martha sat on newspapers painting chairs. In her spare time she decorated second-hand furniture; her house was full of it, colorful as a toy store. Yellow snakes wound up the spindles of one chair, blue tulips drawn free-hand popped along the arms of another. Sad music came from a bedroom, the mournful wailing of loons. Martha's gray head was tilted and her tongue was lodged beneath her upper lip in concentration. There was the odor of hearty food beneath the paint fumes, that and the burnt herby smell of marijuana, which she'd smoked earlier. The ordinariness of the evening, the simple and somehow unbelievable normalness of it—the way McBride could accept a healthy woman in the house where he lived doing something so utterly charming as painting furniture and cooking food—should have made him happy. Instead, he was irritated by the tableau. He felt domesticated, as if it had happened against his will. Time with Daisy, however brief, had left something under his skin.

"How was she?" Martha asked.

"Drugged. Nuts. I ended up dragging some other woman out of the street in front of the hospital."

"Alive?"

"More or less." He told her about the morning while she worked her brush around in her patient, stoned method. The room grew dim and she quit, leaning back on her hands, legs splayed open lazily. She was the first woman McBride had ever known who was not at war with her body: she liked it, it liked her. She walked around in the world unself-conscious inside of it, completely casual with its short-comings as well as its gifts. Fond, as if of a beloved pet.

"Oh, Daisy," McBride said, trying to sound as if he could dismiss his old girlfriend, laboring to evoke that useful wince that meant he was over her, ashamed of former passion. "How was *your* day?"

Martha quoted some of her accident victims' depositions to cheer him up. She worked in the police court downtown taking statements from bad drivers. This was only one of her jobs. She also interviewed rape victims for a professor at the University of Arizona, having some talent at listening. She was thirty-six, six years older than McBride, prematurely gray, and had lived with a number of men so she knew how to do it. Calmly. With a great deal of forbearance and humor. Even her name: Martha. Not Muffy, not Marti, nothing cute or hip, an old-fashioned name designating a person with both feet on the ground. She said, "'Coming home I drove into the wrong house and collided with a tree I don't have.'"

McBride smiled. Martha smiled, too, and rose to extract whatever she had cooked from the oven, which had the bloody odor of red meat and mushrooms. Wine. He suspected she made up depositions but she swore they were authentic. Her favorite went: "I had been driving for forty years when I fell asleep at the wheel and hit a telephone pole." The rape victims she and McBride had agreed not to discuss.

They ate on the front porch in the breeze of an oscillating fan. Even in February, the birds went on and on, noisy as a coffee klatch. The next-door neighbor the transvestite came out, as he always did, as the sun fell, lips a red bow, bosom an emphatic bolster. His era was the fifties: floral, with forgiving hemlines.

"Imagine going through all the nonsense he must go through to look like that," McBride had once mistakenly said. The shaving, the plucking, the makeup, the heels: torture. Martha had thrown her head back to laugh. She could really laugh. "Just imagine," she'd said.

They waved, as usual. The pretense seemed to be that two people shared the little house next door, a man and a woman who were never seen together yet wore the same shoe size. "Whatever," McBride muttered, also as usual. Martha liked her funky neighborhood. She liked the tree full of umbrellas as well as the lawn art on the corner, toasters and blenders and microwave ovens set out as ornaments among the plastic flowers and spinning pinwheels. She liked the car with toys glued onto its chassis. She had told McBride, when he complained of the weirdness, that as he grew older he would treasure the odd, shun the ordinary, grow easy as she with eccentricity. It would not threaten him so.

Personally, McBride thought that Martha lived among the bizarre in order not to feel so bizarre herself, normal by comparison. Plus, her neighbors' obvious dilemmas distracted her from her own, which was that she wanted a baby. Women were on timetables, cycles, deadlines. That ticking clock, bomb or alarm, irked McBride. His gender had forever, plenitude, a wealth of progeny waiting in the wings. Babies, like the rape interviews, was a topic best avoided.

Predictably, he dreamed about Daisy that night. He was in his old house, the one he'd grown up in in Oklahoma City. In the dream Daisy lived around the corner from his parents. She rented a small sunny room. McBride visited her there and she kissed him on the cheek. He woke feeling tender toward her. It had been such a sweet kiss, so innocent and discrete, like the kiss of a child, free of history or future, and it had such melancholy force that McBride woke in a state of pure desire, which impelled his waking Martha to make love with her, his fantasy life blurred by dream. Perhaps when he came, it was into the memory of his sleeping vision of Daisy. The memory—combined, Martha and Daisy, sanity and sickness—carried him through the day, their faces next to his, his sexual past shoved against his sexual present, an interesting friction.

He visited Daisy again a week later. The tenderness of his dream had faded. Her depression made him impatient. This aspect of Daisy seemed to him an enormous weakness and he did not tolerate weakness well, trying to get a handle on his own. She wore the same sweatsuit, the same muzzy expression, the same drained pallor. Today it was cloudy but they sat in the same hopeful Adirondack chairs outside, staring at the front door as if the drama they'd witnessed last time might also replay itself, the middle-aged woman fleeing her parents, the need to run into traffic. McBride was annoyed to discover he had on the identical shirt he'd worn then, too.

Without apparent emotion, Daisy said, "I'm pregnant I think."

McBride looked hard at her, trying to figure where the sensible part of her went when the other part came out.

"Don't worry," she continued, "it's not yours."

"It *couldn't* be," he said.

"True." She said nothing for a while, then added, "I could have had your baby after you moved away. I could have left her in Salt Lake, given her up to the Mormons to raise. Don't men ever wonder what happens to their sperm? I'd worry, if I were a man, but men— it's all just hit and run."

What occurred to McBride was that all the nasty forces of nature had female pronouns, typhoons and tornadoes and those mythic creatures, the Furies and Sirens. They were powerful, and they sent you reeling, they trapped you.

"Daisy, what are you going to do?"

"I don't know." She shook her fluffy head. "I have to get off of these drugs if I'm pregnant, that's for sure. But what else? You got me." She picked at the chipped green paint on her chair arm for a few minutes in silence. Then added, "There were two men in Salt Lake. We all three lived together, very French movie. Either one could be the dad, though they'd both suck at it."

McBride said, "You know, your life is kind of crisis-oriented, have you noticed that?"

She lifted her face to the brightest cloud, the one that hid the sun, and said, sullenly, "No," and then wouldn't say another word.

Two men. The image of Daisy at the fulcrum of a threesome wouldn't leave McBride. Somehow this wrinkle intrigued him, against his will. What kind of sleeping arrangements had prevailed? Was there an alpha male, stud one, stud two? Some homosexual stuff? How did the three of them behave at breakfast, sitting together over coffee in their underwear and ruffled hair?

At home Martha attempted to cheer him. "To avoid hitting the bumper of the car in front, I struck the pedestrian."

McBride told her, "I'm starting to believe these reports of yours."

Martha feigned shock, sucking on a joint. "You mean you didn't before?"

"Not before Daisy."

"Daisy," Martha said, looking bemused, annoyed in the unthreatened way a strong woman does in the face of a puny one.

"She lived with two men at once, she says."

"She's done everything, that gal, all the things I always thought I would do. It's disappointing to realize how staid I've become." But she smiled. Her complacency didn't really trouble her—look at what surrounded her, arty furniture, queer neighbors, clacking birds.

The pregnancy part went unmentioned, but the next time he visited the hospital Martha wanted to come with him. She insisted. She drove. For someone who evaluated car accidents for a living she handled an automobile very badly, swerving arrogantly through traffic, refusing to do head checks, one palm ever ready on the horn. She had lapses but mostly Martha was reliable, grown up. Now that he'd become one it surprised McBride how few adults were grown-ups. It still seemed all seventh grade, and you had to keep on your toes.

Daisy had dressed for McBride's visit this week. Someone—some anal-retentive obsessive-compulsive with a lot of time on her hands—had lassoed Daisy's wild hair into tiny braids which crisscrossed her shapely skull in a flattering style. The sweatsuit had been traded for black jeans and a glossy button-down shirt, under which her breasts bobbed. She'd smeared makeup over the sores around her mouth and the dark circles beneath her eyes, and she looked like a country-western singer ready to make a comeback. Next to her, Martha seemed far too robust, big and indestructible, like a Hereford beside an impala. McBride saw that the visit was going to go wrong in a way he hadn't anticipated.

Women intimidated Daisy; even in the sanest of moments she didn't like them, though she pretended otherwise. Without the possibility of an encounter ending in sex, Daisy was a bit at sea. McBride sat on the grass before the willing Adirondack chairs where the women sat leaning back, faces to the sun. He thought of triangles, the two women here together only because of him; the two men in Salt Lake maybe waiting to hear from Daisy, wandering around the house wondering what they were doing together, stuck with each other and a legally binding lease. Because he could come up with nothing to say in front of Martha, McBride understood he was not innocent in his current relationship with Daisy, a fact that made him tired of himself.

Martha said, "So how are you feeling?"

Daisy took the finger she was chewing from her mouth and said, "Sad. I'm having an abortion tomorrow and that makes me *really* sad, even though I don't think I'm ready for a child."

McBride felt Martha appraising him, compiling all the data, his not telling her about the baby, his phony forgetfulness on the matter. Then she nodded at Daisy. "That's understandable. I'm just now feeling ready for a child."

"You have time. You're not old."

"I *am* old, but it's nice of you to say. I've had three abortions and every time I think, I just saved another kid from being fucked-up. It's one way not to feel bad."

"Well, tomorrow I'll save my second from being fucked-up."

McBride was grateful he hadn't fathered any of these fetuses. Both women looked down at him, their expressions identical: what good was he, there on the grass? He didn't want to donate his sperm to Martha's desire, and though he was in the position of footstool, they couldn't even put their feet up on him.

"Coffee," he said, hopping to. And once he'd left them together he did not want to return and so roamed the hospital halls.

The place was poorly funded, understaffed, cheaply built and maintained. It was not old enough to seem gothically romantic nor new enough to appear at least clean and modern. In all the popular spots, the carpet was worn through; the furniture was crooked, broken plastic from the seventies, and the windows were smudged with years' worth of fingerprints, people pressing against the glass, longing to escape the big box they seemed to find themselves trapped inside. Everywhere televisions, laugh tracks and commercials fading in and out of every open doorway as McBride passed. Was there anything more representative of illness and confinement than daytime TV, anything more definitively the killing of time? This first floor was public; the upper ones required speaking with a station manager. To avoid returning to Martha and Daisy—he could see them from the second floor window near the elevator, still talking together in the sun, Daisy tilted back with her eyes closed, Martha watching her—he gave himself the challenge of lying his way past a station manager. The fourth was Daisy's floor; the higher one went, the crazier the occupants.

But it was no challenge at all. He merely mentioned Daisy's name and was pointed in the direction of her room. The woman at the desk didn't even have him sign in. He opened her dresser drawers and looked in her closet. Nothing but the portable typewriter she'd been found with on the highway. Also some odd articles of clothing, obviously stuff that had been donated, discards. Plain white underpants, high-waisted and modest, nothing like what she'd worn before. A picture of Jesus over her headboard, eyes pitched upward, just as exasperated as anyone else who had to deal with Daisy.

"I didn't know you were a patient here."

McBride whirled, caught. At the doorway stood the woman from the street, arms crossed as if chilly. She resembled Audrey Hepburn, he thought, willowy, frail, and jittery as a stray. "I'm not," he said, recovering. "I'm waiting for Daisy."

"Daisy." She said it skeptically. "Well, I'm glad you're not a patient because I would feel bad about not struggling more if you were. Couldn't have let another inmate be my undoing."

McBride smiled because she seemed to be joking but she didn't return the smile. She simply walked away, as if he'd made the wrong answer, the bones of her ribs and hips visible beneath her gray dress. From the hallway, he looked back outside. The Adirondack chairs were abandoned, big yawning laps.

* * *

Somehow Daisy wound up at McBride's house. This was because it was officially, legally, Martha's house, and Martha had invited her. She didn't believe Daisy was crazy. Confused, yes. In trouble, yes. Maybe even more trouble than craziness but not crazy. The thing on the highway, with the typewriter? McBride whispered this in their bedroom after Daisy had fallen asleep on the study couch.

"She was pregnant," Martha said. "Overwrought."

"She still is pregnant."

"True. But that's only till tomorrow. Then we work on getting her off the heavy-duty meds."

"What makes you want to do this? You don't even know her."

"She's your friend," Martha said simply. She wore a large white nightgown with ruffles and lace, matronly on her though it would have seemed sexy and Victorian on someone else, someone skinny, anorexic, or strung out like a junkie, like the woman at the hospital, like Daisy.

"She might still be in love with me," McBride warned Martha in the dark.

Martha laughed and wouldn't stop. It was lusty, gutsy laughter, and McBride didn't like it.

"What's funny? She might be."

"Oh, you sound so serious, like you wouldn't be able to defend yourself." She held her hands above her head as if shielding herself from an oncoming train. "Stop, stop! Don't love me." She laughed again. "Gimme a break. You're a big strong man, capable of fending off a crazy woman's love."

"You said she wasn't crazy."

"She shows all the signs of molestation."

"Naturally. She's a tabloid story, waiting to happen."

"I'm pretty sure she's been sexually abused."

"Only with permission," McBride said. "Only because she wanted to be."

"You don't believe that." In fact he did believe it, but best to keep that to himself. Best to leave that can of worms in the cupboard. On this subject they could not have an agreeable conversation. Martha had interviewed over a hundred rape victims, her specific interest in their notions of dress and how they felt about their bodies, before and after. She and McBride lay with thoughts of rape between them, a few moments of respectful silence. She believed he was better than he was; often he did not feel like dispelling this.

Then she rolled on top of him and became heavy. She loved to start sex this way, covering him like a blanket, breathing into his neck, heat, comfort. Her bed she'd made herself, headboard a pilfered road sign from high school days. Her friends had wanted DIP or PROCEED WITH CAUTION or MEN AT WORK, but what had Martha stolen? SOFT SHOULDER.

"The act of rape and the act of love are the same gesture," she'd told him once, explaining the messiness, the warring, scarring horror.

"Insert tab A into slot B," McBride said, deflecting, going for the joke.

"No, I mean that something twisted and confusing like that is called a paradox."

"A pair of ducks?" He didn't want to be educated; he knew he'd fail the final exam. He'd had it with complexity.

"A pair of fucked ducks."

There was something between McBride's girlfriends and it began to grow, like a romance, as if they had secrets. Daisy had only to say a word and the two of them would be uncontrollably amused, laughing so hard they couldn't speak. McBride vaguely remembered this about her, how she pulled you into her private chamber, made you feel that only you and she lived there, in the heady and ticklish dark. Her bratty sense of humor was surfacing, now that she'd stepped down from her meds. As well as her readiness to lie. "My brother was sexually ambivalent," she said, when the transvestite next door walked out one evening.

"Before or after the heroin overdose?" McBride said flatly. "Or maybe that was your cousin? She's always got a relative or ex-boyfriend to one-up with," he explained to Martha, who blinked at him, unmoved as a lizard.

"You're just jealous of my radar," Daisy claimed.

"Gaydar," Martha amended. And there they were, hysterical again.

There'd been no abortion, a decision made without McBride's input. One of those roommates in Utah had sent some little seed out innocent in the world, trapped and growing now inside crazy Daisy.

Meanwhile McBride continued to visit the county hospital. He went to see Claire. Claire: tall, and faintly British.

"Why are you here?" she asked him.

He shook his head. She never smiled, never let loose of a somehow reassuring seriousness. She was very somber. You could say anything. She never evaded. "Why are *you* here?" he asked.

"I can't keep house," she said. "I forget to eat. I take walks and get lost. I leave the doors unlocked. My parents' television and video camera and every single CD they owned were stolen last time they left me alone." Her parents were on an extended vacation in Greece. When they traveled, Claire stayed at the hospital.

"You're not sick," McBride told her, "you're just forgetful. If forgetfulness were an illness, the whole city would be in a straitjacket."

"I'm pathologically forgetful," Claire said. "I forget so I can hurt my parents."

"But not consciously?"

"Of course not consciously. They're retired, so this vacation they're taking is from me. Do you understand? They are sitting on a beach, a million miles away from their troubles. Meaning me. I am their troubles."

Then it was summer and McBride began sleeping with Claire. She put on her shoes and they signed her out and drove to a motel on the highway not far from the hospital. Coincidentally, it was across the street from the Triple T truckstop where Daisy had been found. Twenty-five dollars, no questions asked. The cash exchange without receipt or bill, no evidence, no residue. What McBride liked about the Sands Motel was its air-conditioning—no swampy evaporative cooler here—which worked beautifully. Otherwise, the rooms were typically hideous and disturbing. They would not let you forget they'd accommodated hundreds of strangers before you, some sogginess in the carpet, lingering odor of cigarette, ripped sheet where someone else's toenail had pierced through. Claire in sex was the same as Claire in conversation: thoroughly confrontational, right there. "I've heard that this is the most sensitive spot on a man," she might say, pressing the pad of her thumb against his perineum.

"Yes," he would breathe, lifted as if upon a salty sea wave. "You heard right."

She had a thespian's voice, or a smoker's, and she hummed when she was up against McBride, melancholy and rousing as a distant train whistle. She alone called him by his first name, murmuring it. "Your name is like a kiss," she claimed, illustrating by placing it in the hollow of his throat; "Peter," she said, humming lungs, mouth releasing warm air. After sex she lay quietly on his chest and slept, a small smile on her lips. He nestled his palm against her scalp. She had a dainty head. Everywhere her bones were close to the surface, where her fair skin showed tiny blue veins, a network of hairline cracks, porcelain. When he pulled his hand away, her fine black hair shivered with static electricity. In sleep, she looked like what she must have looked like as a child, that smile like a dim memory, as if she were happy.

As he stroked her hair and the painfully knobby knuckles of her spinal column, he wondered why it was he had begun fucking older women. He thought he'd matured, but maybe younger women just didn't like him anymore. Was he more complicated, or more desperate? "We love each other's damage," Martha had once said, to explain their relationship. Apparently, Martha loved his, whatever it was. But only now did McBride actually follow her meaning. He couldn't have said that he loved Claire, but he felt ready to go to the mat for her. To protect this brief easy sleep. To defend her against her parents, for example, if need be, against her own self-loathing.

"You don't have to worry about suicide," she told him one day as he dropped her off after.

McBride had not, until that moment, given it a thought but from then on, of course, he thought of it frequently.

"She hates me," McBride told Martha, referring to Daisy. What he meant was that he hated her.

He and Martha had met for lunch downtown near the courthouse where McBride was laying brick. The summer had become so hot that the workday began at 5 A.M., ending by 1:00. Martha chewed her taco before answering. "She thinks you take me for granted."

"*I* take you for granted? The total stranger who's not even helping with bills, let alone *house*keeping, thinks *I'm* taking you for granted?" He was outraged; then he remembered his affair with Claire and calmed down. The checks and balances of intimacy.

Martha smiled. "I have a feeling she's got a kind of crush on me, frankly. I think she thinks I saved her. She's had enough of men, for a while."

He didn't say that he didn't believe Daisy *could* capture a man, these days, so changed was her body, skin, appeal. She had an aura of illness, contagion, that only a maternal impulse could love. "How do I take you for granted?"

"I didn't say you did; Daisy said it."

"But why does she think so?"

Martha leaned forward over the paper wrappings of their lunch, looked at him with her healthy hazel eyes. "She says you used to be much more physical with her than you are with me."

"You listen to this stuff?" His voice was louder than he intended;

the lawyers at the next table shifted. Daisy was right, and it made him want to go kill her.

Martha leaned back. "I'm not worried about us. I like you, I think you like me. We laugh enough, even though we don't fuck as often as we used to." She tilted her head, squinted; she could wait. "You asked me what Daisy thought and I told you, but it doesn't bother me. So don't fret."

McBride found Daisy in Martha's sewing room, asleep on the Hide-a-Bed. When he sat beside her she woke without alarm; nothing in human nature would surprise her.

She propped herself sleepily on an elbow, letting the sheet drop to reveal she wore a soiled spaghetti strap T-shirt, nipples large and brown through the sheer material, abdomen like a cantaloupe. "I was thinking you might come to me someday, Mac," she said, placing a warm hand on his thigh.

McBride stood abruptly. "I'm not seducing you," he told her. "I want you out of here, in fact. If you're well enough to think I'd sleep with you, you're well enough to get the fuck out."

"I know you're sleeping with someone else," Daisy said, her eyes leveraging the threat. She would tell. She would ruin his life. There was no correct response so he simply stared at her, hating her. Then she began crying, and it was all McBride could do to keep from throwing a tantrum himself. Her face before him—quivering chapped lips, fair eyebrows full of acne—seemed to want to be struck. What did she expect from him? It enraged him to see her sobbing; he felt like grabbing her by the shoulders and flinging her back against the couch. How dare she know his secret? She looked up from under her hair and suddenly smiled through her tears, as if she'd caught on to a trick. She was a slutty, easy girl, and McBride could not deny the appeal. He remembered her in bed: her pleasure came only in extremity, at the very moment that might mark pain. She liked to bite and be bitten, hair clutched and yanked. Now she reached a hand for his kneecap and spread her fingers slowly, as if she might insinuate herself just this way throughout his system.

Infuriated, McBride lurched away, stumbled onto the floor. She followed, into his lap, and they were wrestling, Daisy sinking her teeth first into his arm and next his neck, hard enough for his nerves to trill. He put a knee between her legs and forced her arms apart. Below him, crucified, she breathed deeply, a strand of saliva across her cheek. The fact that her T-shirt and underwear did not cover her made McBride aware of her odor, which was powerful, unwashed and sexual. Rank, with a need to be hurt, and him not so far from obliging.

"Go away," he told her desperately. "Please. Go. Away." He felt his swelling erection as a betrayal—but of whom? What?

She rolled out from under him and curled toward the dark cavern beneath the bed like an animal. From the back she looked just like she always had, sinuous, nocturnal.

In the bathroom McBride tilted his head and checked the spot she'd bitten on his neck in the mirror. There were tiny broken capillaries but they looked enough like razor burn to reassure him his struggle with Daisy would go undiscovered. His heart, he noted, was beating so hard he could see it in his chest, in his reflection, pulsing there like a mouse in his pocket.

"If you want to make love with me, you can't do it with anyone else," Claire told him the next day as she ran her fingers over the bite marks on his arm. Leave it to the woman he didn't live with to sniff out his deception. "I know you live with Martha, but that doesn't necessarily mean you make love with her."

"We have sex," McBride told her, wondering why he found it necessary to convince her of this fact while obscuring others.

"Sex with someone you live with is more like masturbation," she said. "Just some warm object to rub on until you come. Do-it-yourself sex."

"I'm a do-it-your-selfer from way back," McBride said, wanting the punch line, wanting to stay out of the deep well, out of the tricky web. Women were so prone to abstraction, to pitching you into outer space. They were not afraid of the dark, the absence of gravity.

"Fucking her isn't necessarily making love," Claire said. "*We* make love." Then she fell into her postcoital nap, a little gift her body gave her, exhausted childish sleep.

He took home Claire's theory and tried it on the next time he and Martha had sex. In the living room, Daisy watched television, a habit she'd adopted at the psychiatric hospital and had not given up. She sat around the house indulging an adolescent appetite, Chee·tos and Skittles, Count Chocula.

"Where are you?" Martha whispered in his face, holding it in her plump fingers, peering inside him, nose to nose. She was stoned, a state that made her want orgasm and honesty. McBride thought of Claire's words and Daisy's pregnant breasts while he worked his penis inside Martha. Where was he, indeed?

"You can go," she breathed into his ear, his mature girlfriend with her solid legs around his hips, feet locked behind him, "but you have to come back."

The next time he visited the hospital, Claire had been moved to a new ward. They were doing what an aide called a suicide watch. Claire had been caught sawing at her wrists, using a plastic knife, but still. "Those things have serrated edges, man," the aide said. "Ser-*rated*," he repeated.

McBride found her tranquilized, staring apathetically at a *New York Review of Books* tabloid. "I can't read this," she said. "The words are floating around like boats." Her wrists were wrapped with gauze, bright clean bracelets. "I feel poisoned," she declared, sailing the book review across the room like a Frisbee. "They're trying to kill me." Considering her behavior, McBride couldn't hold it against the hospital.

"Why?" he asked, hoping simplicity would be his strong suit.

"Why not, you big asshole? That's the real question." She drew a soppy breath, her fine features blue, as if she weren't getting enough oxygen. She cried in the slow, drugged way of hopeless sedation. *Asshole* was not really part of her vocabulary. That was the drugs talking.

"Baby," he said, embracing her, careful of her bandages.

"That's what I need," she said, "a term of endearment. *Muffin. Kitten.*"

"Maybe you should eat? You look kind of . . ."

"I hate fat," Claire said flatly. "I work hard to be thin. I *don't* eat, in order to be thin."

"That's kind of sick."

She simply stared at him, waiting for something she didn't know to emerge from his mouth. "Your girlfriend is fat," she added. It wasn't a good moment. McBride liked her better when she wasn't catty. Also, he was too tempted to respond in kind, to be catty with her. They could get nasty together, it turned out, eat each other's spleen. "She's got a big *tush,* that girlfriend of yours."

"Where are mom and dad?"

"Flying home, wringing their . . ." She held out her own hands, illustrating by twisting her palms, wrists stiff in their wrapping. "They don't have a notion what to do."

"What should *I* do?" he asked.

"Save me," she said, collapsing against him. She wanted to take him with her, he thought. She was drowning, and if he did not escape this clutch, he would wind up washed ashore somewhere, bloated and cold.

"You can't save her," he told Martha that very night, referring to Daisy, hoping he was right. Daisy, seven months pregnant, had disappeared into south Tucson. The three of them had been eating Mexican food across from the greyhound track; they'd made money betting on those strange creatures, then celebrated with burritos and beer, Daisy on her best behavior, sipping a soda, consuming protein and calcium, like a good mother. But after the bathroom run, she was gone.

Their waiter gave an elaborate shrug, his mustache a wriggling caterpillar on his upper lip.

"Fucking Daisy," McBride said, vindicated. She could not be saved, see? "I guess we have to call the police." He got ahead of himself, saw himself standing around with a cop describing his lunatic ex-girlfriend, driving through dangerous south Tucson looking for a fuzzy-headed pregnant woman . . . but Martha was giving him such a glance full of disappointment and impatience that he returned to the present moment, Corona bottles, coagulated quesadilla.

"It scares me how much you hate her. You used to love her."

"Come on, Martha, she's manipulative and dishonest and so totally fucked-up . . ." Wasn't the evidence capable of speaking for itself? Furthermore, he refused to believe he'd ever loved Daisy. No one could prove it.

"We have to find her," Martha said, rising from their booth. "You pay, I'll be out on Fourth Ave., walking."

"You can't walk on Fourth—" But she was through the door, and the waiter was handing McBride the ticket, shrugging again, apologetic.

They fought while they searched for Daisy. McBride considered how efficient the situation was—usually a fight required so much energy, such a commitment of time, the yelling part, the pulling-the-phone-out-of-the-wall part, the walk-around-the-block part, the silent thoughtful part, the making up part, the crying and fucking, headache and hangover, raked-over-the-coals, run-through-the-wringer, launched-into-space, deep-in-the-hole part. Hours could go by; a person could lose a day. So it was good, in his opinion, to be occupied with the quest for Daisy while they had their squabble. The problem was that Martha had more experience fighting, a more logical mind-set, and made points like a lawyer. Like a public defender, the type doing pro bono business, the righteous path of the Good Samaritan. She took the moral high road—Daisy in trouble, loyalty, humanity—which left McBride with the inevitable role of bastard. Add to this the affair with suicidal Claire, and you had the picture of a man in a futile argument, perhaps about to be dumped by a nice woman in whose nice house he was living, driving badly in a bad neighborhood, to boot.

He found himself hoping they would see Daisy out there in the dark.

But Daisy was gone for five days, and the fight with Martha wasn't resolved even after all that time. Somehow the stages had gotten messed up; they couldn't progress past sullen silence with each other. Martha was *disappointed* in him. He couldn't make himself fix it. She had every right to be *disappointed* in him. As much as he'd once lusted after Daisy, he now reviled her; that was what troubled Martha, the degree to which love could flip to hate. "Paradox," he wanted to tell her savagely. "That old saw."

He avoided Claire. He abandoned her by telling himself he was being true to Martha.

Daisy managed to phone them up from Phoenix, where a truck driver had left her after buying her a new wardrobe and giving her a stack of *Watchtowers* to contemplate. His name was Buck, and Daisy entered the house referring to his kindness constantly.

Martha hugged her wayward stray, patting Daisy's back maternally; McBride resisted the urge to punch her in the face.

"You're not a burden," Martha insisted when Daisy tried to explain her running away. "I want you to stay with me, even after the baby. I love babies." Embracing, the two women looked decidedly freakish, in McBride's opinion. "You're just bored," Martha insisted. "You need some meaningful activity during these last weeks. Maybe I could teach you how to drive?"

They settled on shopping. Neither of them was a mall type, which made the trip that much more thrilling. Daisy came home wearing her old perfume again, an expensive scent, describable in the way of fine wine: the amber plushness of pears, velvet, oak, wealth. McBride remembered it with equal parts revulsion and nostalgia.

"*Host*algia," he thought: sick desire.

That night, when he couldn't get into the spirit of a fashion show featuring maternity clothes and hair clips, Martha accused him of impersonating an adult. Abruptly she threw him a curve, direct from her stoned keenness. "Are you in love with someone else?"

"What?"

She waited.

"No," he croaked, wanting to ask if Daisy had told her something, knowing that would backfire. "No," he repeated, unconvincingly. Just a week ago it would have been a lie, but how could he explain now? The timing made him want to laugh like a madman.

"I'm sleeping in the sewing room tonight," Martha said, taking her pillow.

"Maybe you should fuck Daisy!" he blurted.

"Maybe I should," she agreed, calmly, leveling an unashamed glance in his direction.

Where did women get it, that composure, that open-minded fluid sense that not only might anything happen, but that it might be amazing? McBride could all too easily envision Daisy and Martha naked together, tongue to nape of neck, breast to breast, quivering haunch to ropy one, the homecoming embrace pushed to a climax. It was pretty, candlelit, its sound track full of saxophone.

Men with men: who could look upon it with anything but perplexity? Erections bobbing between them like those annoying trick snakes, coiled in a peanut can, unsealed and sent sproinging in your face. Ha ha. Meanwhile in the background, sound track a circus organ grinder, perhaps a kazoo.

He lay awake alone beneath the SOFT SHOULDER sign thinking of Martha. Was she trying to make him her little boy? Punish him? Improve him? "You know what your problem is?" she'd once told him, laughing yet serious. "You have gag reflex."

"Meaning?"

"Meaning, you can't deal." She did not suffer from this impediment. Why had she attached herself to *him*? Only lately had he wondered—was he a project, not unlike flaky Daisy, someone shell-shocked and deemed for whatever reason worthy of Martha's concern? He didn't want to be her project. He preferred to think of himself as her willing plaything, the party boy, the one who could choose to leave the party. He paid rent, he stocked beer and toilet paper, he had volition.

"You're a coward," Martha told him in the morning. Overnight, she seemed to have chosen against him. She didn't even seem concerned enough to be hurt. Just that disappointed. "You won't commit to anything. The hard parts embarrass you. You feel like everything's a scene instead of just another opportunity to get close to someone. That's what is unforgivable. You're terrible in a crisis. You just want the easy parts, none of the work."

He could not not think of Claire, but what he said was, "Is this about having a baby?"

"This is about *you*," Martha said. "A topic with which you should be fairly familiar. This is about a woman you not only left behind like some dog on the highway, but about whom you won't say one kind word." McBride had to marvel: even angry she wouldn't leave her prepositions dangling. "Not one," said Martha. "I can't get over what a jerk you seem to be. Actually, what I can't get over is that I'm in love with a jerk. I should know better."

"I love you, too," he said quickly.

Martha sighed. "That is *so* not the point."

Meanwhile, Claire's parents sprang her from the psych hospital, which meant that McBride had to sit in their living room drinking iced tea making small talk with them before taking Claire to the motel across from the Triple T. He was conducting an experiment, testing his maturity, trying to recapture what seemed to have scurried off. Were his intentions honorable? her parents' faces asked, forlorn, unsure how to behave if the answer were no. The scars on Claire's wrists were disconcerting, raised welts with tiny suture holes on either side.

"Will those go away?" he asked at the motel, putting his lips on her scars, working at not being disgusted.

"How should I know?" Claire was naked now, but what she'd removed were seafoam green scrubs, as if qualified to dress like a doctor, having hung around them for a while.

"Why so testy?" McBride asked, checking his watch. The iced tea and chat had seriously cut into their time. When Claire smacked him, he didn't know if it was for the question or the looking at the watch. She was one unpredictable girl. They made love then, and following, went through the requisite small sleep.

Leaving McBride to think. Who did he love? Could he ask his women to put in bids for him, sell himself to the one who turned in the most impressive vita? Was he looking for a particular kind of woman and had to have these three to provide one whole? He considered the virtues of each—Martha's good humor and stability, Claire's startling honesty and tragic openness, Daisy's wild sexuality and obsessiveness—and understood their individual appeal as well as their limitations. But perhaps it was having three of them that really excited him. His affection was maybe like a dropped watermelon, three rocking wet seedy parts. Or like a trident. He pictured his penis, three-pronged instead of one.

Or maybe he needed the compounded guilt each relationship made him feel, especially as it related to the other two. High drama had its own charm, like living on a fault plane.

Claire's parents sat right where they'd been left, on plush Barcaloungers before the television. Their iced tea glasses still full of tea, diluted, sweating puddles. The strange stasis that had apparently prevailed here while McBride had been off in a rutting fever, ravishing their middle-aged daughter in a cheesy motel gave him pause. *This* gave him pause—her father looking sad, her mother looking sadder—not the preceding insanity.

He would not be back. His last look at Claire was like his first: she with her parents, sullen, struggling.

He arrived home to find Daisy entertaining the transvestite. They sat in the chairs that McBride and Martha had used to sit in, in the breeze from the oscillating fan. The transvestite had left lipstick prints on a hand-thrown coffee mug. In his large palms, the cup was dwarfed, silly. His nails, unpainted, were smooth, on the verge of being long, and his knuckles, McBride took a moment to notice, were shaved. Unbelievable. The man stayed seated as he extended one of these hands for a shake, like a lady.

"Alberta," he announced. "Your neighbor."

"We've seen you around," McBride said, gripping a little too firmly, a little too masculinely.

"I love the furniture! Your wife is amazing with a paintbrush!"

"Not his wife," Daisy was quick to say. "How was *your* day, Mackle?" she asked coquettishly, grinning up at him, employing a long-ago pet name, reminding him of others: *Prozac,* because he'd pulled her out of a depression, way back when. *Moon Pie,* he'd called her. And meant it.

"I gotta pee," McBride said, exiting. Entering. Well, here was his house but where was his confidence about belonging in it? On the porch sat the man, the woman, the soon-to-be baby, a fundamental threesome unrelated and weird. "You're not strong enough to accept the limitations of others," insightful Martha had informed him. He wished she would quit knowing him so well, stop being so smart. Why *did* she love a jerk like him? Was that the weakness he would have to object to? He felt like a rung bell, jangling in a lonesome tower, village idiot down below yanking his chain.

"Did you know it was going to be black?" McBride asked Martha.

"I knew it was a fifty-fifty chance." Martha was flushed, wearing a set of green scrubs like the ones Claire owned. Six women had attended Daisy's labor and delivery, Daisy screaming like a tortured crow, the rest of them murmuring and assuring, room of pigeons. The baby, a perfectly healthy girl, was purple as a Nigerian. McBride could only gawk. No one else was fazed; their role was to adore, congratulate, rally. Martha cradled the baby in such a manner that McBride finally understood he would have to leave her. Already that baby meant more to her than he did, or could. Never had a decision been clearer. It made him feel oddly selfless, to see his responsibility.

"Isn't she amazing?" Martha positively glowed, face ruddy with effort, good work, the species' only real priority. She could have been the mother herself, with her wide hips and open heart.

"Unbelievable," McBride said. He looked at the tiny bundle in her arms, dark and constricted. Hard to believe she'd grow up to wear cheap jewelry and eat junk food. Let boys put their hands between her thighs. "Reminds me of an eggplant," he told Martha.

She looked at him as if through the retracting lens of a spyglass: good-bye. "You're so cold," she said, turning back to the room of women.

The deal is, it always goes from bad to worse. The living trajectory, birth to death, going up means coming down. Like that.

McBride told himself these things as he drove to the hospital emergency room a week after Donatella's birth. Claire had jumped from one of Tucson's few overpasses into the traffic below. Everything was broken, head to toe; she would die. She lay now unconscious while a team of experts tried to put her back together. McBride was not innocent in this, as he had not seen her for more than a month, pretending he was tired, pretending he felt guilty about deceiving Martha, pretending he had problems as profound as hers. How was it that affection turned, tiny tender gears no longer meshing, gone suddenly, overnight, eroded with pity? Sour with scorn? When her mother called, three in the morning, Martha had handed him the phone with a single scathing word, that one that had been like a kiss: *Peter.* They'd just failed to have sex, McBride pumping furiously, stiff as a stick of dynamite, unable to explode.

Now he screamed into the ER parking lot, horrified. One more portion of his life, another member in his tribe of female troubles, gone haywire. You build complication like a house of cards, geometrical, tricky, fragile. And like a child, you then like to step aside and stamp your feet, watch as it folds up on itself, flat one-dimensional deck. Dead.

Oh, those parents. Once again, sitting unmoving, identical drinks before them, same condensation. On the television: television. His intentions hadn't been honorable, apparently, after all. Had she wanted to die for love, or its lack? She lay in the highly technical, highly temporary ICU, wrapped, strapped, tracheotomy tube in her neck, metal bolt in her skull, suction hose in her mouth, monitors around her like a recording studio, flashing numbers, graphs. Crust of rusty blood here and there, and her beautiful eyelashes, like folded fragile spider legs, wilted on those pale cheeks. Did this sleep replicate the one she fell into after sex? McBride swooned. Fainting wasn't what he had imagined. He was aware of himself crashing, vital fluids rushing from head, hands, feet to pool and churn in his stomach. His thought was that he would vomit, and be left empty as a pocket. And there was the nurse, the woman who, like a mother, materialized beside him at just the proper moment to smooth his brow, bring him 'round.

He held Claire's letter to him, unopened, missive from the grave, given over by the parents. Her heart, in his hands. On his porch sat four females, lover, ex-girlfriend, her black infant, and the neighbor who counted himself among the girls. Where did McBride fit? He could not be what they required. Nothing to do but squeeze out, he had already been squeezed out.

And he was glad, he told himself. Glad for his simple body, its fixtures out in the open, the expression on his face projecting exactly what was behind it in his head. What was it with women and all this hidden equipment? They dressed up, made up, faked orgasms, cried when happy, laughed when bitter, stirred up protoplasmic stews of life and then pulled aces from sleeves, wreaked havoc all the wide world over, forever refusing to come clean.

That was how he wanted to feel, driving his car with his worldly possessions: clean. Free. Was that the same as being cold? Cowardly? He'd left Salt Lake City and he could leave Tucson; the West was full of cities where his slate would be blank, his plate would be empty. There was a girl out there, he could almost see her, radiant, blonde, a healthy hiker a few years younger than he, straight teeth, muscular calves, sentimental taste in music. He would find *her* . . . but how did that accident claim go, the one that had amused him not so long ago? "I saw a slow moving, sad-faced old gentleman as he bounded off the roof of my car . . . " Nothing to do but plunge on. Set the cruise control, lower the windows, raise the radio, stay between the broken yellow lines, and don't look back. No no no.

About the Author

Antonya Nelson was born in Wichita, Kansas, in 1961. She attended the University of Kansas and the University of Arizona, where she received an MFA in 1986. She is the author of three short-story collections (*The Expendables, In the Land of Men,* and *Family Terrorists*) and three previous novels (*Talking in Bed, Nobody's Girl,* and *Living to Tell*). She lives in Las Cruces, New Mexico, and Telluride, Colorado, and teaches creative writing in the Warren Wilson MFA Program, as well as at New Mexico State University. She is married to the writer Robert Boswell, with whom she has two children.